Glyph

Max Ellendale

Cover Artist: Mina Carter
Editor: Deadra Krieger
Contributor: J.L. James

Max Ellendale
www.maxellendale.com

ISBN-13: 9781520131856

"Out of suffering have emerged the strongest of souls; the most massive characters are seared with scars."

~ Kahlil Gibran

CHAPTER ONE

Sometimes the voices in my head reminded me of a swarm of bees stuck in the wall of an empty house. A chronic buzz that no one could ever seem to turn off. Especially me. So there I sat, hiding out in a closet surrounded by syringes and sterile medical supplies, squeezing my head and hoping that I would get a grip before the next emergency. At least this time I'd kept the lights on, and it was a good thing too because Staci flung the door open.

"Doctor Twofeathers, the transfer is here." Her gentle, cerulean eyes lingered on me for a moment. I could tell she was trying to keep the worry from her face. Poor Staci. She always caught me in the strangest of circumstances. One day she'll start asking questions.

"Thanks. I'll be right out."

I tossed my stethoscope around my neck and took a deep breath. As I braced myself against a tower of bandages, I took a moment to prepare for my next encounter. Transfers were common in the emergency room, but lately, I'd seen some pretty bad cases. The last thing I needed was another dead baby or burn victim.

Ruckus filled the ER by the time I arrived. Nurses ran,

1

EMTs shouted, and Staci stood by the exam room with her mouth hanging open. I had to push my way through the crowd just to get to my patient.

"What've we got?"

No one answered. Everything appeared suddenly still, as if the room held its breath. I knew it was something bad, very bad, for my trained staff to have such a silent reaction. The energy in the room seemed to vibrate, though not a soul moved.

Please not another smashed-up teenaged drunk driver.

Moving in perceived slow motion, I lifted the corner of the blood-soaked sheet covering the gurney and peeled it back. The fabric clung to the sopping mess beneath it. My grip tightened as I pulled. The sound of slurping blood and sticky tissue set off a wave of response from behind me. The sound of someone retching followed a gasp. On my table lay a skinless little girl. Nothing remained of her except striated muscles and oozing tissue. I was sure that she was dead until the slightest turn of her head had her looking at me. Crystal blue eyes reached out to me, screaming for help. My breath caught in my throat and my stomach churned.

Where to start? Where do I even begin to start? She was going to die, and I knew I couldn't do a thing to help her. My hands hovered over her as if trying to find something to do, somewhere to press or pause. Then came the rattle. The gasping rattle that only death brings. Primal and desperate. It made me ache just to hear it. My knees trembled. With blue eyes staring at me, she took her last breath.

The heart monitor wailed to a flat line.

***

Dawn approached by the time I left the hospital. Bitter night air filled my lungs, causing the delicate tissue to seize in an icy grip. No matter how hard I tried, I couldn't stop seeing the image of those blue eyes burned into the back of my eyelids. *What the hell happened to her skin?*

2

I nearly met my death when I slid across a patch of ice, only to slam into a solid something that giggled without so much as a jostle.

"Well, hi to you too," she said, flinging her silky black ponytail off her shoulder. Her bouncing body and bright smile reminded me of a giddy teenager who had just returned home after sneaking out.

"Sorry, lost my footing." I ambled up the steps to my apartment building, choosing my path across the hazardous concrete with far more care than before.

"S'okay, I locked myself out, as usual..." She rocked on her heels, staring at me with a hopeful, impish smile.

"I'll let you in." I pulled my keys from the pocket of my lab coat, taking comfort in the sensation of the metal in my hands. I couldn't wait to get home and put the day behind me. My couch was the best place in the world sometimes.

"I've never seen you here." The woman hopped up the steps behind me, arms out, as if playing hopscotch and each step was a square.

"I've been here." I unlocked the door and held it open for her before stepping inside.

"I'm Xany."

"You're zany? Should I be worried?" The door clicked shut behind us. Xany couldn't be her real name. Who would name their kid something as crazy as *Xany*? Maybe her parents were hippies, or part of one of those strange religious sects that worshipped leaders with bizarre names.

Or maybe they were just sadists, like your father.

I shook off the echo and barely managed to catch the woman's reply.

"Only on the weekends." Her words rolled through a giggle.

"Well...then I'm glad it's Friday."

"Friday is considered the weekend," she retorted as we climbed the inner stairwell of the building.

"Wonderful..."

"What's your name?" Xany giggled again, an annoying,

3

nagging, constant kind of giggle that was pretty much the giddiest laugh I'd ever heard. With all that was on my mind, the last thing I wanted to do was engage in some useless conversation with the girl who had a crazy name. I had to get myself out of it somehow.

"Vanessa." I winced at the sound of my own voice, flat and tired. That wouldn't do the trick.

"That's not your name." She stared at me with a risen eyebrow. A smirk played across her lips.

"How do you know?" I frowned, annoyed by the fact she didn't let the lie go.

"You don't *look* like a Vanessa." Her gaze swept over me, studying me until my skin prickled under the weight of it.

"What do I look like then?" I asked, trying to ignore how uneasy she made me. Maybe her name was more accurate than I thought.

"Not Vanessa." Xany cocked her head to the side with a knowing smile.

"All right, then I'm Not Vanessa."

"Smart ass." Her smile turned into a full-blown grin.

"Only on the weekends," I replied.

"Ha..."

Xany seemed sort of immature, though I couldn't put my finger on just how young she was. She had lighter skin than me, but by the looks of her, she was most likely Native American. But not pure blood, that much I could tell. I had never met anyone quite like this girl before. Her dark green, almost hazel, eyes made her appear a bit untamed. Not to mention that she wore the absolute minimal amount of clothing required to walk around in public, let alone in the middle of winter. I'd never be caught dead wearing anything like that. A tube top and cutoff jeans in February? *Get real.* This girl was confident, silly, attractive, and had the strangest name I think I'd ever heard. She intrigued me. Something most people don't do.

We walked up three flights of stairs together. I longed

for the moment that we would part ways, but it didn't happen. By the time we got to the fifth floor corridor, we stepped into the hallway together. Xany's sneakered feet scuffed along the carpet when I approached my apartment door, second on the left. Xany paused at the fourth door on the right.

"You've lived here all this time? How come I've never seen you before?" She removed a hidden key from above her door.

"I don't know... That's not very safe." I nodded toward the key.

"Were you hiding?" Xany shrugged off the key comment, lifting both eyebrows at me while she unlocked her door. For some reason I had the impulse to shove her inside.

"No..." Not from anything I could tell her about anyway. Or tell anyone for that matter.

"Sureee..." She wagged her brows and stepped into her apartment, only to peek back out. "It was nice meeting you, *Not Vanessa.*"

"You too." She was at least a little bit nutty, yet I found myself amused by her—in an irritated kind of way.

"Maybe I'll catch you on a day when you're not hiding."

"Maybe," I agreed. *Don't bet on it.*

"Well, nighty-night."

"Good night." I opened my door and flicked on the light switch before entering. As I turned to lock up, I noticed Xany still watching me from the hall. "My name is Shawnee," I admitted in a sudden moment of boldness.

She gave me a catlike grin before slipping into her apartment. Xany's door shut with a faint snap. I shook my head and locked up all three chains before making my way to the kitchen.

Did you really think she cared what your name was?

I rolled my shoulders when an insurgence of haunting voices blared loud and clear into my brain. My feet grew heavy and my shoulders slumped under the weight of the phantom racket. I was tired of it, and there was only one way to get some peace. I grabbed a beer from the fridge and stalked over to the sofa.

You're so stupid.

My whole body relaxed when I cracked open the can and sunk into the cushions. The slurp-snap sound had been in my life for as long as I could remember, except now I was the one making the noise. I had control.

No, you don't.

The slurp-snap was mine.

Nothing is yours.

The cooling burn of the first sip set my mouth at ease.

No one cares about you.

I gulped down the beer, desperate for relief.

You'll always be alone.

Please. Stop.

Always.

One can...two cans...three cans...four.

Alone.

Five cans...six cans...thoughts no more.

CHAPTER TWO

Black. Green. Blue. Flash. Crash. Scream. Fur. Eyes. Fangs! I awoke from the nightmare gasping and sweating. The clock perched on top of the television told me it was 3:33A.M. *Great.*

I stood, shaking off the drunken sleep that tried to dig its claws in and drag me back down into the nightmares that awaited me. My lungs burned like they'd spent the last few minutes struggling to breathe. I needed air. Fresh, clean air to clear my head.

I grabbed my keys from the desk, slipped the house key into my sock, and headed out of my apartment. Unable to resist, I glanced at Xany's door before taking the stairs down toward the rear exit. Meddlesome thoughts plagued my descent. Screams from my nightmare echoed in my ears as images of the bloodied body of the blue-eyed girl flashed across my field of vision.

It's your fault.

Shaking my head, I wrapped my arms around myself and ducked out into the night. The faint scent of decayed foliage met my nose as my boots scrapped against the frozen ground.

Should have taken a jacket, idiot.

Luna, as my mother called the full moon, greeted me at the edge of the woods. "Give thanks to Luna," she'd say. "She is our guiding light." Sadness bubbled up in my chest, but I pushed it away.

A snow-coated branched tugged my hair when I approached the thicket. Streetlights faded, and shadows from the trees wrapped around me as I strolled through the little niche of nature tucked away from the hustle and bustle of the small city. For a moment, my heart beat with contentment.

I passed a maple tree, wishing I could become part of it. Maybe then I'd be able to stand tall and proud, like my mother. A sharp inhale washed off the uncomfortable thoughts. I half expecting to hear the echoes that normally bothered me. Instead, from somewhere in the distance, a snapping twig shattered the silence.

My body tensed as I strained to listen over the pounding of my heart. It was stupid of me to think that I was alone in the woods. After a moment of pause, I continued on.

You're just hearing things as usual.

I know. I know.

When I turned back toward the apartment building, a whiff of something that resembled a mix of dirt, leaves, and wet dog snared my nostrils. The snap of another branch echoed in the darkness. I stood as still as possible and gazed into the void. Something definitely moved in front of me. I wanted to run, but my legs wouldn't budge. Darkness closed in on me, consuming me and narrowing my vision. Soft thuds on the soggy earth drew closer. Pungent odor seared the back of my throat. My lungs seized and recognition melted over my psyche. The familiar stink haunted my nightmares and shadowed my dreams. I squeezed my eyes shut, pleading with myself to wake up.

A shudder ran down my spine when a deep rumbling pierced the hush. I opened my eyes to find myself staring at a furry wall of muscle. The bated breath of the beast bore down on me. My heart beat like a drum in my ears— a deafening decibel that I was sure the beast could hear. Every part of me wanted to run, scream, cry, kick. But I couldn't. My body trembled in horror. *This is it, I'm dead.* All I had to do now was wait for my head to be bitten off or my skin filleted. The monster's golden eyes met mine. I couldn't force myself to look away. I stared so hard that its gaze tore through me. His whiskered muzzle dripped with saliva.

Here it comes. Time to roll over and die.

Finally, my body unlocked. Muscles released and I took a step back. The monster heaved a deep breath as if ready to roar in rage and stood to its full towering height. I swung myself around and tore ass out of the woods.

I slammed into the back door of the building and my jittery hands fumbled with the keys. The expectation of searing pain overwhelmed me as I imagined the beast ripping into me. A strangled cry of relief left my throat as the key finally caught and the lock turned. I rushed inside and yanked the door shut behind me. My sleeve caught in the doorjamb but I tore it away and raced up the stairs. *Not a dream... I'm awake...*

"Wow. That must've been the date from hell." Xany's giggling voice interrupted my panic. It took me a second to recognize her as I hurried to unlock my door. I shook so severely that everything around me seemed blurry.

"Hey... Hey, Shawnee, are you okay?"

Xany followed me inside. I stumbled to the sofa and sat, hugging my knees to my chest.

"Forget, forget, forget," I said, rocking back and forth. I couldn't get the smell of the monster out of my nose. Xany sat down in front of me, her eyes wide with worry. Urges to run, cry, and scream all at once tightened my chest.

Never show your pain.

My gaze remained focused on the stain in the carpet by

her feet. I hated that Xany saw me upset and, in my opinion, letting anyone see even the tiniest bit of emotion was a mortal sin. Especially a stranger like Xany. She watched me in silence for a moment, toying with a beaded leather armband that she wore on her left forearm like a gauntlet.

"What happened?" She placed her hand on my shoulder, but I jerked away. Xany seemed to tolerate the rejection and returned her hand to her lap. Eventually, my freak out subsided.

"There was a...a bear in the woods or something."

"Bear? There aren't any bears here." She snickered before asking, "Are you sure it wasn't just a little bobcat or coyote? They can be pretty scary."

"Yeah...probably. It was probably nothing."

"Probably nothing," she repeated. Xany stood, patting me on the head before disappearing into the kitchen. She returned with some water a moment later. "You're so pale. Drink." She held out the glass to me, maintaining a firm grip on it until I cupped it with both hands.

"I'm fine, you can go now." I obeyed and sipped the water, my hands tremoring as I held the glass. I needed to deal with this on my own. It wasn't a dream this time. Xany's presence proved it.

"You sure don't look fine to me. Well, I mean, not lookin' all scared like a rabbit anyway. What happened to your shirt?"

"I'm not a rabbit." I glared shot her a glare.

"You're acting like one. Running like the big bad wolf is after you, little red." She tugged at my torn sleeve. Her expression changed when she saw the birthmark on my arm, just below my right shoulder. It was a few shades darker than my skin and looked more like a sunken scar than a birthmark. It had the distinct shape of four wiggly lines resembling a claw scratch.

"What did you just say?" I yanked my sleeve back down.

Xany turned from me to saunter around my living room. Her own bit of scrutinizing, I imagined. It wasn't much to look at. Relatively small with only essentials and a few empty beer cans lying around. Suddenly I was self-conscious about my living space. She glanced back at me as if she had been distracted. "What? Oh, I was just saying that you're skittish like a rabbit being chased by a wolf."

"I'm *not* a rabbit! Why would you even say that?" Talking about wolves and anything related to the subject made me uneasy. I stood to face her, crossing my arms over my chest, ready to defend myself should the need arise. I wasn't about to let Xany, or anyone, into my world. "What would you even know about wolves anyway?"

Xany ignored my standoffishness. "Have you seen those men down at the Double D Pub? All paws, I tell ya!" She sniggered.

"You work at that place?"

"Mhmm, all the old coots hang out there, and I'll be damned if they still don't paw at you every chance they get." A grin tugged the corners of her mouth. "So you see? I do know a thing or two about wolves." She nodded in a matter-of-fact kind of way.

"Uh-huh..."

"Trust me, the coots at the bar are much safer than the wolves out in the woods." Xany made her way over to sit on the windowsill and gazed outside.

"You...you've seen wolves out there?" I tried to hide the quiver in my voice.

"I've seen wolves. Nothing out there though. I hear them howling at night, sometimes. Average folk can't usually tell the difference between a howling wolf and a coyote." She blew hot breath on the cold window then drew hearts in the fog.

"And I take it you're not *average* folk, if you can tell the difference." I didn't like Xany. Her ego was larger than her breasts and usually that's a bad sign.

"I'm as average as you are. You don't get out much do

you?" Her eyes wandered down my body, then back up to meet my gaze.

"What's *that* supposed to mean?"

"Let your hair down." She hopped off the windowsill to stalk over to me and yank the bauble out my ponytail. "Maybe a little makeup, not that you need it, just to bring out your eyes. It's not every day you see amber eyes on a Cherokee girl, but maybe that's just 'cause you're a little scared." She ended with a giggle.

My jaw hung open at the violation of my personal space. Without thinking, I shoved her. "Get away from me! What do you think you're doing? My hair is fine." I huffed. "You've got to be the strangest person I've ever met. And besides, I'm only part Cherokee so you don't know as much as you think you do."

"You're right, but all I had to do was guess and you filled in the answers for me." She lifted an eyebrow at me.

"Please leave." I sighed, weary of the conversation, and exhausted from my ordeal in the woods.

Xany smiled victoriously. I got the sense that she liked winning. "Okay, okay. Just don't go crying wolf so loudly or else someone might think you've got a one way ticket to the loony bin." She skipped jovially toward the door.

"It's a psychiatric hospital, not a loony bin," I shot back, narrowing my eyes at her.

"G'night, Shawnee. Sweet dreams." She grinned in a way that didn't sit right with me. I followed behind her and secured all three chains.

I put my hair back in a ponytail and stomped over to the window. Xany was annoying, and she invaded my privacy. I snatched a dirty shirt off the floor and irritably wiped her drawings off the window before opening it to let in some air. The moon hung high in the sky tonight. A sigh escaped me as I watched it.

In the distance, I thought I could hear the faint yipping howl of a coyote. I nodded to myself as my gaze dropped down to scan the woods. Xany's pink shorts disappeared into the shadow of the trees.

"That's enough hallucinations for one night," I grumbled.

I locked the window and went to bed. If I was lucky, I would forget about tonight just as I had forgotten about so many others.

CHAPTER THREE

The following morning I returned to work and tried to keep myself busy so that I didn't think about the events of the night prior. While signing off on a few charts that had piled up on my desk, one of the residents interrupted me.

"Doctor T?"

"Hmm?" I continued looking over a chart as I waited for him to continue.

"Reynolds wants you in the lab."

I glanced up at the fair-haired twenty-something-year-old and nodded. He stared at me as if trying to read my expression. I stood up, carelessly dropping the chart that I had been reading on the desk.

"Had to send a messenger of course." I smirked at him.

"Don't *shoot* the messenger." He held his hands up in a gesture of surrender.

"Noted. Thanks, Kurt."

"No problem." He continued to watch me.

I ditched my stethoscope on the way to the door and paused beside him. "What is it?"

"You're smart," he stated.

"So are you. Is that abnormal?" I furrowed a brow and crossed my arms over my chest.

"Thanks. It's not abnormal." He held open the door for me.

"Then what's with the weirdness?" I met his gaze for a moment.

He seemed shaken. His eyes zipped back and forth over my face as if searching for some response on my part. "No reason I guess." He looked away, which made me even more suspicious.

I stalked past him and decided to drop it. Thankfully, he didn't follow me. I took the long way around the second floor of the hospital in case anyone decided to tail me. I'd been working here for nearly four years, since my second residency. When I first met the hospital administrators, they said that I was the "youngest resident in nearly thirty years." I was barely twenty-one when I graduated medical school. The hospital was happy to take me on and keep me.

I used the private elevator to get to the lab. Kurt was one of only two residents who were allowed to work in this particular part of the hospital. It wasn't your ordinary lab. Or hospital. It required special security authorizations. I guess working with genetics, DNA, and microbiology is a Homeland Security issue. Everything is these days. There was no such thing as access cards for this part of the hospital. Retinal scans only. I placed my chin on the display so the little blue lasers could scan my eyes. It beeped after a few seconds, and the electronic doors swung open. With doors like these, you had to move fast or risk your ass getting pinched off. The timer was set that way so no one else could jump in on your retinal ticket.

Dark corridors stretched out in front of me as I exited the lift. Overhead lights remained off unless they detected movement in the hallway, which not only alerted people at the other end of the hall that you were coming, it also prevented you from stumbling upon anything that was privy. Even if you happened to overhear a conversation, there was no face to put with the voice. It was creepy, but

I was pretty used to blocking things out. After a second retinal scan, I entered the lab to see a middle-aged, balding man standing over one of the incubators with his hands on his hips. Shiny metal cabinets lined the walls around pristine tile. Everything in the lab had its place. Beakers and test tubes filled a glass cabinet to my right as sneakered-feet followed their usual path toward the workstation in the back.

"I've got an assignment for you." Doctor Reynolds spoke without looking at me. I remained silent while watching him. He moved from the incubator toward the glaring lights of the analysis area where he had several rows of Petri dishes set about and a color-coded collection of viewing slides. With a grunt, he sat on a stool, a huge microscope in front of him. "Up for a challenge?" He lifted his gaze to meet mine, accompanied by a wry smile that made me uneasy.

"Always. What've you got?" I asked, slipping my hands into the pockets of my lab coat. The gesture was a mild attempt to hide my interest in his alleged *challenge*.

Dr. Reynolds took in a slow breath. "Doctor Twofeathers, what you're about to witness is classified information. My sharing this information with you can alter your position here at the hospital and in the future."

"Your point?" I lifted a brow at him. I'd heard this lecture nearly a dozen times this year alone. Doctor Reynolds was the kind of person that made a big deal out of the littlest things. Good thing I could pretend to be patient.

"Shawnee, do you understand what I'm saying to you?" he asked in a serious tone that accompanied any bullshit experiment that he failed to complete himself.

"Yes. I understand. What's the assignment?"

Doubt wrinkled his brow. I might've been able to take him more seriously if his experiments held up through replication. Anonymous donors funded his "breakthrough" sciences through grants to Mercy General.

They expected him to produce results or risk losing the money. I wasn't sure how he still had it to begin with.

"Right. Well...it appears I've stumbled upon something. Something *irregular* to say the least." Frustration laced his tone. "Come, come. Look into the scope." I glanced at him suspiciously before doing so. "What do you see?"

"Grapefruit. What do you think I see?" I leaned back from the scope to scowl at him.

"Live, normal human cells." He exhaled as if his patience wore thin.

"Yes..."

"Adolescent cells," he said, drawing this out painfully.

"And?" I glanced at him.

"Observe." He used small eyedropper to suction out some fluid from a beaker. I returned my attention to the scope as he added a bit of whatever it was to the Petri dish. Nothing happened.

"What am I supposed to be seeing?"

"Those cells are temperature controlled by the substance in the dish to mimic the average core temperature of the human body, ninety-eight point six degrees Fahrenheit, thirty-seven degrees Celsius. I will add heat to the sample." He spoke through clenched teeth.

And so he did. Reynolds placed a heating coil beneath the sample under the microscope. I watched carefully. At first nothing happened. Frustration pressed in on me and I fought the urge to smash a beaker.

"I'm elevating the temperature to exactly one-hundred and four degrees Fahrenheit, forty degrees Celsius," his voice seemed to growl in response to my agitation. "You will know when I have reached optimal temperature."

I had to admire him for the details at least. Reynolds didn't have the best track record when it came to recreating matters of the *irregular*. But this time, something *did* happen.

As the temperature neared 104 degrees, the cell structure began to change. A rapid succession of multiplication, growth, expansion—you name it followed. The entire sample in the dish changed, and my jaw dropped. The cells became unrecognizable as human cells, and I looked from the microscope to Dr. Reynolds, my mouth still hanging open. He spoke again in monotone, as if he was trying to hide his excitement.

"Your assignment is to prevent this reaction from occurring. You are to create a substance to stop the mutation of these cells when the chemical reaction occurs."

I looked back into the microscope for a moment. "What was the reactant?" My poker face faded away as I allowed the shock to seep through.

"The cells went through puberty. I added the proper combination of growth hormone, calcitonin, et cetera, to age the cells. Then I induced a high fever." Sometimes he sounded so arrogant. Which, quite frankly, he had nothing to be arrogant about. With all the failed experiments, wasted money, and lack of anything better to do with his time, Reynolds was not the vindicated scientist everyone thought him to be. I wondered how much people actually knew about his lack of success, or if Kurt and I were the only two to bear the burden of this knowledge.

"You're telling me that you've been able to create a non-spontaneous chemical reaction using a normal human developmental process with the addition of heat to make the entire cell structure change and mutate into something else?" I asked, narrowing my eyes. "Clearly this doesn't happen in all human beings." A nagging sensation inside me insisted that this should sound familiar—like I was missing something so obvious—but I couldn't seem to place it.

"You're right. However, that's not your problem. Your assignment is to use the samples I have provided with the formula to induce this reaction and then create a serum to stop it." He tossed his latex gloves in the biohazard bin and put his stethoscope back around his neck.

"You weren't able to create this *serum* yourself, I take it." His lack of information pissed me off, but I was determined.

"No. But I believe you can. What do you think?" He cleared his throat.

"Of course I can."

"Shawnee...if you're able to develop the serum, your life will be changed forever. You'll be rolling in riches one can only dream of." A maniacal expression widened his eyes, curving his mouth into a creepy tooth-laden smile.

"I'm not interested in riches. Leave me to it then. This is going to take a while." I turned back to the microscope and watched the reaction continue as the heat remained under the sample. The door to the lab hissed shut after Reynolds' exit. There was something eerie about his behavior, but I didn't care. *Crazy old man.* I could do this. It was a piece of cake.

CHAPTER FOUR

"Shawnee! What are you doing home so early?" Xany shouted from the door of her apartment.

I tried to hide my exasperation and glanced over my shoulder at her as I opened my door. "It's 1:30A.M. That's hardly early." I stepped inside and dropped my bag on the floor. Xany skipped in behind me. *So intrusive.*

"Then it's a good thing I'm awake." She giggled. "C'mon. There's someone I want you to meet."

Before I could protest, she grabbed my arm and tugged me out of my apartment and into hers. I stumbled along with her, jerking my arm away just as we entered her living room.

"Obnoxious, seriously."

Xany offered me a sweet smile and rocked on her heels, attempting to put on her best innocent act. I glared at her, then suddenly realized we weren't alone in the room. Two hulky Native men stood by the sofa. My heart sank and my trust in Xany suddenly faltered even further. What was she dragging me into? She noticed my discomfort for once and slipped her hand into mine to squeeze it. Intrusive thoughts about the identity of the men and their intentions weighed heavily on me. My pulse raced and I fought the urge to bolt away from the situation. Xany's hand offered only a tiny bit of solace to my overwhelmed state.

"Shawnee, this is my brother Michael, but we call him Mal, and his friend Caden." Xany pulled me closer to the men.

Mal stood a good six-two, lean, and well-muscled. He wore his long, black hair in twin braids with a beaded leather headband, worn jeans, hiking boots, and a red flannel shirt. He spoke to me first, extending his hand in greeting.

"*O'siyo*, Ms. Twofeathers."

I shook his hand, my own grip loose and weak like a floppy old fish. Hearing someone speak in my native tongue scared the crap out of me. His eyes, hazel and earthen, seemed born out of the wilderness. I couldn't understand why I would even allow myself to look into them. I flinched when I heard the sudden screech of an eagle echo in my head and dropped his hand. I rubbed my clammy palm against my jeans as I tried to work out the tingling reminder he left on my skin.

Caden broke our gaze when he stepped toward us. My stomach knotting up and I stepped back. *Caden was huge.* Clad in a casual T-shirt, cargo pants, and work boots, his calm demeanor unnerved me more than it should. He stopped a few paces away from us as if he sensed my concern. He stood a bit taller than Xany's brother did. Unlike Mal, he had pulled his hair back into a loose ponytail. With a thick, muscular build, soft chocolate eyes, and skin to match, there was no mistaking his heritage. His posture loosened when he extended his hand.

"Hello, Shawnee," he said, accompanied by a warm smile. "It's a pleasure to meet you."

I didn't dare meet his gaze as I shook his hand, awkwardly swift, before letting go. Xany whispered, "Caden is so sexy," in my ear and I shot her a glare. She released her grip on me and I wrapped my arms around myself.

When I glanced back at the men, Caden drew his gaze away from Mal and caught Xany's eye. A faint nod in her direction followed. Squeals burst from her lips and she tossed her arms around me in a bone-crushing hug. I shoved away as confusion and fear warred inside me. A frown met my lips and I narrowed my eyes at the suspicious brood.

"I'm leaving," I said, and stalked away from the group. I was *not* about to let these people interfere with what I had built for myself.

Weak little walls. Watch them crumble...crumble.

"No! You can't. Not yet! There's so much to talk about." Xany bounced up and down with excitement. Her breasts followed her body oppositely.

"No, there isn't. Whatever sick games you three are playing, I'm not into it." Terror-fueled movement had me gripping the doorknob and I turned it in a sharp jerk.

"Shawn—" Xany's voice stopped abruptly, and I glanced back to see that Mal had his arm around her waist.

In a quiet voice he said, "You're scaring her."

Caden stepped forward. The endless stoicism plastered on his face worried me further. I'd seen expressions like that before. In places I'd rather not recall. "Dude, so are you," he said. "Everyone *relax.*"

Defeat hung heavy in my chest when my shoulders relaxed at his command. I sighed as I watched Mal let go of the wiggling Xany. Half in and half out of the threshold of the door, a scene from my nightmares played out before me. This was the reunion tour I never wanted.

"Shawnee, why don't you have a seat and join us for a while." Caden gestured toward the sofa just as he sat down on one of Xany's oversized armchairs. I made sure to stare at his hairline rather than meet his gaze. Mal perched on the sofa first while Xany plopped down on the carpet. She squirmed around like a kid waiting to open Christmas presents. Her wild, excited eyes never left me. Mal's calmness now mirrored Caden's. I didn't want to be anywhere near them.

"C'mon, Shawnee. They won't bite. Well, not unless you want them to," Xany's words tangled in with her usual giggles.

Rage continued to burn inside me. And, after careful consideration, I returned to the apartment and closed the door behind me. On some level, I knew what they wanted from me. There was no way I would concede. Not this time. I cautiously made my way into the living room and stood with my arms crossed beside the sofa. Mal shot Xany a chastising glare at which she turned up her nose.

"Just get to the point. What's the purpose of this not-so-random powwow?" I nearly spat and worked to keep the quiver from my voice.

Caden smirked as if he appreciated my humor. *God he's enormous...*

Mal watched me as I spoke. His serious expression hinted at underpinnings of sorrow. I pulled my arms tighter around myself and rolled my shoulders. Even though I was used to looks like that, it didn't mean I had to like it. I focused on Xany because her ridiculous bouncing was much easier to tolerate.

"It's real!" she burst forth. "Now you don't have to be afraid anymore. And you're one of us," she announced with pride as if I had just popped out of my mother's womb.

Caden leaned forward, moving swifter than I would have expected someone of his girth to do. A gesture clearly meant to silence Xany, because it did. Mal's narrowed eyes and broadened shoulders made him seem like he was going to leap over the coffee table and strangle her. She glanced between the two men and batted her eyelashes.

"I can't help it." She huffed.

"You're many things, if not precious, Xany," Caden said, then turned to me with a steady gaze that seemed to penetrate my soul. I tore my gaze away from him and stared at the carpet beneath his feet.

"Shawnee." He rested his hands on his knees and leaned forward slightly. I'd never met anyone as *still* as Caden. At times, he barely seemed to breathe. My anger turned to fear, and my tongue began to tingle. The tell-tale swirling bubble of anxiety in my stomach rose to my chest.

"What?" The timid sounding question in my voice betrayed me.

"Do you have dreams?"

"Everyone dreams," I shot back.

"True, but I think you know what I'm asking." Caden leaned back again, returning to his formerly relaxed position.

"Yes. Fine. I have dreams." I clenched my teeth and balled my hands into fists. *I wish someone would turn off the damn drumming in my ears.*

"Any monsters make guest appearances over the past few years?" He posed the question almost nonchalantly. *Hello, Shawnee. How's the weather? And the monsters? What are they up to?*

"Fuck you," I spat. My pulse continued to wreak havoc in my ears and my legs twitched as my body prepared its favorite defense.

Mal perched on the edge of his seat, eyeing Caden while Xany's nerves seemed to be keeping her quiet. Caden, however, was calm and unmoving as if every word he spoke was deliberately articulated.

"I know you're scared, Shawnee." He paused. "Though...I think you know more than you've let on..." He trailed off and glanced to Mal.

They must have shared some sort of silent communication because Mal nodded to him. I clutched the edge of my shirt as my breathing caught up to my heart rate. The room grew hazy around me, clouding my vision and squeezing away my peripheral vision. I blinked a few times to try to focus. More words left Caden's mouth though the underwater, garbled sound of them prevented me from understanding.

I couldn't take it anymore. My chest heaved and perspiration beaded across my forward. My body shot into action and I bolted for the door. I raced through the hall, down the stairs and out of the building. Running was the only time my body never betrayed me. I ran and I kept running, down one street and up another. By the time I stopped, I found myself outside the hospital. I knew they hadn't followed me, but that didn't soothe my panic. I didn't want to deal with this. I did *not* want to acknowledge what Caden wanted me to face. *It's my life.*

Crumble. Crumble.

I snuck in the back entrance to my empty office to avoid as many of the night staff as possible and crawled under the desk. Hugging my knees to my chest and shaking with dread, my consciousness slipped away...

CHAPTER FIVE

"E-he-na, Dodi. There is no need to hide," I hear my mother say. Her strong, safe hands pluck me from my hiding space. "Waya means you no harm, he wishes to play. He is young like you, my sweet."

I reach my hand out and see my fingers slide into a tuft of brown and black fur. I look up at my mother, and she smiles. "Baby waya," I say.

She nods and kisses my forehead. "Baby wolf, yes."

The little wolf cub looks to me with his sweet hazel eyes and licks my hand. I giggle in delight and move from my mother's lap to sit in the grass with the wolf cub. It nibbles my fingers, and I laugh harder before I stand and shout, "Catch me!" I run and the little wolf pup chases after me, finding me difficult to catch.

My mother's voice echoes from somewhere inside me. "She is my Runs-Like-Wolf."

"Doctor T?" A familiar voice interrupted my dream. "Hey, Doc," Kurt's voice cleared me from my slumber.

I sat up quickly, forgetting where I was, and slammed my head into the desk. Little flashes of light sparkle in front of my eyes. "Ow..."

"Not as painful as it's going to be after sleeping on the

floor all night. What are you doing here?" He didn't help me up. Like many of my coworkers, he knew better. They knew never to touch me. I didn't like to be touched.

"I forgot something and must have fallen asleep," I lied, standing up to dust off my jeans.

"Oh...okay then," his tone suggested that he didn't quite believe me.

"Did you need something?"

"Oh, um no, I'm okay." He edged toward the door. I watched his retreat, puzzled by his odd behavior, but didn't force the issue.

"I'll see you later then, Kurt." He left, and I dropped down into a chair.

My dream was more than that. A memory, though it was easier to tell myself otherwise. I stretched to crack my back and, as soon as the haze of the uncomfortable sleep began to lift, my thoughts drifted to the events of last night and my meeting with Caden and Mal.

There was nothing about Caden that stuck out to me other than the fact that he was super huge and scary. Mal, on the other hand, invaded my thoughts. The way his eyes never seemed to leave me, and who could forget the way his shirt melted to his body? I never really noticed those things about people I'd just met, but for some reason, Mal stood out to me. I shook my head with clenched teeth and grabbed my lab coat. *There will be no thinking, only working.*

I worked for three days straight. Any time my thoughts drifted anywhere near Xany, Caden, or Mal, I distracted myself with another task. The assignment Doctor Reynolds gave me was finished yesterday. He asked me to "prevent the reaction from happening," and so I did.

I think the reason he failed in doing it himself was the way he went about it. He kept trying to *stop* the reaction after it already began. I *prevented* it by creating a vaccine. Not the lifelong kind like polio or hepatitis—it wore off after a while—but it still worked. Eventually he and I would work on stabilizing the compound so that it was longer acting. The funniest thing about it was that the final product turned this interestingly bright orange color. *Strange. So where are those riches Dr. Reynolds promised?* I rolled my eyes at the thought.

After I completed Dr. Reynolds' task, I spent the last portion of my three-day work streak in the emergency room. Dr. Snyder, a tiny waif of a man, tended to a patient who had been stabbed by his wife during a domestic dispute. The handle of the knife protruded from the top of his thigh while the man uttered curses at the ER staff while they stabilized his injury and removed the knife. Two police officers stood beside him, taking his statement. I stood near the nurses' station watching the scene.

"Another failed *Bobbit* attempt," one of the nurses said to me in passing.

"What do you mean?" I asked.

"She caught him in bed with her aunt."

I shook my head.

"At least he kept it in the family," another nurse said as she dropped a chart on the counter. Both women laughed. I was about to lecture them on their lack of compassion when the sudden sound of sirens pulling up to the entrance cut me off. The EMTs raced in with a patient and began rattling off vitals, saying something about loss of blood, which immediately drew my attention.

"We found her in the alley by the bar," one of the men said.

"What happened?" Doctor Snyder chased the rolling gurney into the exam room. Naturally, I followed the rush of ER staff. Snyder was used to my random appearances.

"Unexplained trauma to the neck. We heard screams and there was a man holding her down when we arrived at the scene. He must've stabbed her with something," the EMT explained.

I butted my way in to examine the unconscious woman. Blood spurted from her ravaged throat. Snyder placed gauze on her neck to apply pressure to the wound. Twin puncture marks appeared above the torn out portion like whatever bit her had missed the first time.

"This is the third one this week." Snyder worked to stabilize the woman. His glove-covered hands moved expertly from one piece of equipment to the next.

"She's lost too much blood," one of the nurses said.

As if on cue, the monitor flat-lined. Snyder attempted a round of CPR but after a few minutes, he removed his hands and sighed. "Call it."

"Time of death?" My eyes lingered on the devastated flesh when Snyder removed the gauze.

"1:07 A.M.," he said and pulled the sheet over the woman's face.

***

Thoroughly exhausted, I finally went home. With soft footfalls, I snuck into my apartment as quietly as possible to avoid any interaction with Xany. The only way I was going to be able to fall asleep after my *irregular* encounter in the ER was downing a few beers and passing out in front of the television while watching *Golden Girls* reruns. I grabbed a twelve pack of beer from the fridge and parked myself on the sofa. Chugging the first four helped expedite my numbness, and the tingle of satisfaction spread throughout my body. While Blanche, Dorothy, Sophia, and Rose took a trip to Saint Olaf, I downed another three. With the next episode, Dorothy told bad "Yo Mama" jokes as I drank two more.

A knock on the door interrupted my binge. At first, I thought somebody was knocking on the window so I answered that. While I looked out the window, another knock sounded. I spun around a little too quickly, stumbled, and clocked my head on a shelf, sending several books crashing to the floor. I rubbed my head and answered the door.

"I knew you'd be he—Shawnee, you look *awful.*" Xany invited herself inside. Her voice was even more irritating than usual.

"What do you want?" I slurred.

"Are you...*drunk*?" Xany waved a hand in front of her nose when I breathed near her.

"No. Go away."

She ignored me, frowning when she saw the beer cans scattered around my living room and the unopened ones on the sofa. "You *are* drunk."

"S'none of your business." I slammed the door, stomping, or stumbling, my way over to her. Xany's figure whirled around my field of vision along with the rest of the room.

"It *is* my business." She picked up one of the beer cans. "Do you really think this is helping you?"

"What do you want from me?" I stumbled and caught myself on the sofa. *Stupid sofa, doesn't it know it isn't supposed to be in my way when I'm walking?* I kicked it.

"Easy there. I came to tell you that Caden still wants to talk to you, but not when you're like this. We need to get you sober."

"I'm fine." I grabbed another beer, craving the bravado it offered me. As I popped the top, Xany snatched it from my hands, spilling it on me and the floor.

"Enough, Shawnee. Why are you doing this to yourself?" She stomped off to the bathroom with the can. I stormed after her.

"Give me that, you nosy, big-breasted bitch!" I grabbed at Xany's arm, causing more liquid to spill.

"Quit being rude." She shoved me and emptied the can down the drain. I stumbled backward and fell on my ass, grabbing at Xany in a feeble attempt to pull her down with me.

"Fuck you!"

"Nothing can be so bad that you have to drown yourself in this." She fought against me, turning on the faucet to fill the tub.

"You don't know shit about me," I yelled at her.

"I might if you'd stop being so *rude*," she shot back,

grabbing me by my shirt and dragging me toward the tub.

I struggled against her, muttering something about her being a jerk when she tossed me into the water. I gasped and splashed, trying to surface above the glacier that Xany let loose over my skin. My clothes weighed me down, but my rage toward Xany was all-consuming. "You bitch! I hate you!"

"Now you stay in there until you sober up." She turned on the shower, letting the cold water beat down on me. I sputtered and coughed, pulling myself up from drowning. Xany stalked out, leaving me in the bathroom with the door open, blubbering something about coffee.

Suddenly, I heard her shriek and say, "Who the *hell* are you?"

I turned off the water and let the tub drain. When I stood, I slipped and caught the shower curtain, tearing it down with me. Sprawled in the tub, huffing and puffing, my teeth chattered as I watched a redheaded blur bolt into the room with Xany rushing behind her.

"Hey!" Xany shouted. "Get away from her."

The woman turned toward Xany, stopping her in her tracks before crouching down and untangling me from the curtain. I swatted at her as she helped me stand.

"I found her drunk and was trying to sober her up," Xany explained. The woman glanced at her again before lifting me out of the tub.

"Put me down, Vanessa, I can walk." My fist pounded her shoulder in a feeble attempt to break free.

"Shawnee..."

"I'm not drunk. Get away from me." I jerked away from her and snatched up a towel from the floor to wrap around myself.

"She is *so*," Xany said with a huff.

"Who are you?" Vanessa's brow narrowed as she rounded on Xany.

"I'm Xany. I live down the hall," she said, gesturing toward the living room with her thumb.

"What happened, Shawnee? Did you have a dream?" Vanessa tried to take my hands in hers. I pulled away from her again, then suddenly lunged at her in a failed attempt to shove her backward.

"Get the fuck away from me. You're always in my way," I spat though Vanessa kept blocking my attempts to leave the bathroom.

"Is she always like this?" Xany asked. Vanessa glanced at Xany speculatively and nodded.

"Shawnee, calm down." Vanessa backed up to allow me to enter the bedroom.

"You're just as bad as that nosy bitch." I tossed the towel to the floor, anger made my motions jerky and quick. Vanessa ignored my insults.

"Hey." Xany shot me an offended look.

"What happened?" Vanessa remained in front of me as I moved about.

"Nothing! Get away from me before I rip out your fucking throat!" I screamed and charged at her again, desperate for an outlet for my rage and pain. This time Vanessa caught me, and we dropped to the ground. She wrapped her arms around my torso, restraining me as I thrashed and struggled against her. Xany looked on with eyes widened by horror.

"Stop it, Shawnee," Vanessa whispered in my ear. "No one's going to hurt you."

"I hate you! Let me go!" I tried to scratch at Vanessa, but she caught my wrists and held me until I began to cry. Xany knelt beside us when she saw my tears.

"No, I won't let you go. Tell me what happened," Vanessa implored.

"No!" I cried. My struggling grew weaker as I did. "Don't make me."

"Tell me," Vanessa whispered again, letting go of my wrists to wrap her arms around me, no longer restraining me but hugging me instead. I screamed but stopped fighting her. Tears streamed down my cheeks, and I turned so that I was lying against her chest. She rested her chin on my head.

"Don't make me," I begged, fatigue washing over me and pulling me down toward the blackness.

"I won't make you," she whispered though her gaze remained on Xany.

The last thing I saw before passing out was Vanessa and Xany sharing a silent stare.

CHAPTER SIX

A headache pounded at my temples when I woke up around noon. Hangovers will do that. I had little memory of the night prior, but I did remember insulting Xany and Vanessa. Not only had I embarrassed myself in front of Vanessa, which was pretty common these days, but I also embarrassed myself in front of Xany. A neighbor who I was sure would run off and tell her big ol' Indian brother about the crazy next door. I stomped into the kitchen, fixed myself a measly bowl of cereal, and sat in silence while eating. The sound of my crunching was like a jackhammer inside my head.

It's your own fault.

The jackhammer turned into an earthquake when I heard someone banging on my door. I dropped my spoon with a clatter that made me cringe. Blinded by the pain, I opened the door without thinking. There stood Xany.

"Hey... How do you feel?" Her voice was soft, her demeanor almost submissive.

"Fine, why?" I raised an eyebrow.

"Well, after last night, your head should be pounding."

"I'm fine." My head *was* pounding though. "What do you want?"

"Caden still wants to talk to you." She shifted uncomfortably, as if she knew the news wasn't going to sit well with me.

It was strange seeing her subdued and a little put off. I knew I had been rude to her lately. She didn't deserve the way I had treated her, and now seeing her appear so overcome, guilt settled in the pit of my gut. Maybe it was the hangover, but still.

"I'm sorry for being rude to you."

Her eyes grew wide at my words. "You don't have to apologize, just talk to him."

"I do have to apologize. You meant well..." I hesitated before adding, "I'll talk to him."

I hated when other people were hurting, particularly if I was the source. I was a doctor. I was supposed to fix the hurts, not cause them. A surge of life sprung to Xany's features, and she smiled at me.

"Come over in about half an hour okay? I need to wake him up." She giggled, and the bounce returned to her step as she hopped out the door. I smirked and closed it behind her.

The bathroom curtain was on the floor when I entered to take a shower. I frowned at it and carefully put it back in place before slipping out of my clothes. I didn't really want to talk to Caden, but I figured owning up to the truth was the only way to get them off my back. In a way, it might be easier. After twenty minutes of enjoying the hot water running down my body, I brushed my fingertips over my stomach where the heat of the trickling water had started to irritate my sensitive scar. It was my father who had given me that scar— a zigzag below my navel that happened when I was about eight—along with many others. It was hard to hold back the tears that came when I remembered the rusty old ski pole that caused the scar. I hated ski poles. I hated garbage too. And trailers.

That's right. Don't you dare cry.

I shrugged off the uncomfortable memory when it

snuck up on me, then finished my shower. Wrapping a towel around myself, I combed my hair, before making the fatal mistake of glancing in the mirror. A sudden sickness swirled in the pit of my stomach.

"I think you know more than you've let on." I heard Caden's voice echo in my head. In the mirror, a flash of piercing yellow eyes surrounded by tawny fur replaced mine.

I shrieked and stumbled out of the bathroom, slamming the door behind me. I held the towel tight, trying to calm my trembling. Would my haunting ever go away? Lately it seemed to be getting worse...

I dressed quickly in my usual jeans and oversized T-shirt. While I was getting ready, I kept thinking about how I had been acting toward Xany. Usually, people left after I was cold to them. I expected Xany to go away as well, but she took all the crap I dished out and kept coming back for more.

Just like Vanessa.

Yeah...just like Vanessa. I rolled my shoulders as I thought about her—the only person I think I ever called a real friend in my entire life. I probably owe her a few apologies too.

A few hundred, you ungrateful little bitch.

***

Half an hour later, I found myself knocking on Xany's door. I smirked at the irony. In a way, I knew what Caden wanted to talk to me about. If he was what I suspected he was at least.

Xany opened the door with an excited smile as she tugged me inside. "See, Caden? I told you she was coming. Never doubt me!" She giggled and let me go.

Caden sat at the kitchen table eating a sandwich, and Mal lounged on the sofa with a bunch of leather strands in his lap. Both men greeted me with a nod, and Caden gestured for me to sit with him. His mouth was too full with sandwich to speak.

I walked over to him warily, my arms in their usual

position around my stomach. When I sat like this, it made me feel less likely to fall to pieces in front of people. Caden glanced over my shoulder to Xany and gave her a sideways nod that kindly told her to leave us alone to talk. Xany's shoulders slumped, and she looked disappointed, but she went over to join Mal on the sofa, within eavesdropping distance, of course. I joined Caden though avoided his eyes while waiting for him to initiate the conversation. He pushed his plate aside and surveyed me. Thankfully, he cut right to the chase.

"How much do you know, Shawnee?" He set his soda down on the table.

"I know enough." I leaned away from him. *So huge, scary.*

"Do you know what you are?" The question wasn't exactly the most abnormal one I'd ever been asked, but a cold chill still shuddered down my spine at his words.

"A doctor." My stubbornness made him laugh.

"Was it your mom or dad?"

"My mom..." *I hate you for making me do this.* The truth was that I was really scared to death of him, but I answered anyway. "She's dead."

"Did she teach you?" He watched me closely, probably trying to see how far he could push me.

Mal sat quietly behind us pretending he couldn't hear. Xany made no effort to pretend. She continued to stare at us mercilessly.

"Yes. Where's your pack?" I asked.

"On the sofa," he said blandly.

"Ha. Where's your *real* pack?"

"My father's pack is farther west. He's the lead Alpha of the Tall Oaks Sept in Northern California. I left to get away from the politics and corruption. The pack is large, and I'm not a conforming kind of dude."

"A real rebel," I joked.

"What can I say?" He pretended to dust off his shoulders.

I began to relax a bit. Caden seemed all right, even

though he was big and intimidating. Defeat pressed in on me, slumping my shoulders as I slouched in the chair. I hated what I knew. I hated that I knew he was a dominant werewolf, Alpha material really, and that I couldn't fully trust my reactions to him. He could make me feel at ease even if I was terrified. That's what Alphas do. They control. I was tired of being controlled.

"You thought I was a Lost One because Xany saw my glyph." I rubbed my arm where the birthmark hid below my shirt.

"We did," he affirmed. "Xany is a Breeder herself. Part of the reason Mal and I left Tall Oaks was to find Lost Ones before anyone else did. We want to help educate them so that they don't fall prey to Those Who Collect." Caden's chest seemed to broaden at the disclosure like he tried to smother an actual emotion.

"Those Who Collect? What are you talking about?" I was annoyed at his cryptic responses and sayings. Caden shook his head at my tone. My attitude problem was my favorite defense.

"There has been an uprising over the past several years of packs and rogues who round up Breeders, both Knowing and Lost Ones. The Lost Ones being the most vulnerable and the easier targets. They round them up and use them as...well, Breeders. They hold them captive and impregnate them to continue their bloodlines. Changers are a dying species," he mocked, knowing full well that Changers were not at all a dying species.

The events he spoke of weren't foreign to me. I pulled my arms tighter around myself. I'd heard of Breeders being captured and raped repeatedly by rogue Changers, but I didn't expect that whole packs would be doing it. Werewolves were the biggest offenders of this type of behavior, and yet they had the largest numbers of all were-species. Or maybe it was because of it.

I let my thoughts go, and the telltale pounding returned in my ears. I gripped my shirt and closed my eyes, trying to block out the panic so that I could stay focused on the conversation.

You're losing it, crazy bitch.

The last thing I saw was Caden's confused expression before memories overcame me—blinded by the flashes. My father's hand crashing against my skin. I heard myself screaming. Hands were on me, pain inside me—his snarling face pressing closer to mine—and just when my experience reached unbearable terribleness, I snapped out of it.

I found myself on the floor of Xany's kitchen, huddled in a corner with three sets of eyes staring at me. My pulse raced. Xany crouched beside me with her hand on my shoulder. Mal knelt down beside her. Caden stood behind them, with a stunned expression on his face. I nearly jumped out of my skin, cowering away from them with tears rolling down my cheeks. Mal was steady and unmoving, with one hand on the floor, looking ready to leap. Shame washed over me as I realized that I'd had a panic attack in front of these people. I was too afraid to move. The memories continued to assault my body. They were all looking at me and the pathetic mess that I was.

Before I could begin my self-hatred parade, Xany whispered, "It's okay, Shawnee. We won't hurt you," and dropped her hands from my shoulder.

"Just leave me be." I twisted away from her and stood up slowly.

My legs wobbled, and I held my breath, expecting pain. When none came, I rushed past them to the door, sobbing once as I tried to pull it open without releasing the chain. Caden let me go, but Xany and Mal both followed. Mal approached me in silence. He met my gaze for a moment, and a bit of the panic washed away. With slow, careful motions, he reached across me and unlatched the door.

You look like a sorry and disgusting excuse for a human being.

My gaze lingered on his as he dropped his hand, his chest rising and falling in masked calmness. I broke away from him, though part of me didn't want to. Part of me wanted to stay in the shadow of the overwhelming heat radiating from his body. By the time I got to my apartment door, I sobbed into my hands. Xany attempted to follow me, but Mal stopped her.

"Leave her be," he said softly. Xany whimpered at him as I disappeared inside.

I crawled into bed and didn't get out. I think I slept on and off for nearly twenty-four hours. It was Vanessa who pulled me from my pseudo-death.

"Shawnee, wake up." Her voice was soft. Vanessa knew I was awake without having to look at me. I guessed that she could tell by my breathing. When I opened my eyes, I saw her silently moving around the room as if she were searching for something. There was no sound emanating from her like there usually was.

"Why do you smell like wet dog?" She spoke as she sat down on the bed beside me.

I rolled onto my back with a grunt but didn't answer her. She released a heavy sigh and brushed my bangs off my face while trying to read my expression. I looked up at her flatly, giving her my "doctor face." Her eyes were like emeralds even in the dim lighting.

"What happened?" she queried, her characteristic purrs returned to her chest when she caressed my cheek, tucking a strand of hair behind my ear.

"How long have you known I was a Breeder?"

"For about as long as you've been ignoring my purring." She watched me. For once, Vanessa appeared worn out. I couldn't remember her really ever looking that way before. "What happened?" She lay down on her stomach beside me, resting her chin on her hand. Her constant purring, which made the bed vibrate, was soothing.

"I freaked out," I replied. Her gaze darted around my face again, as if trying to tell if I was being serious or sarcastic. She glanced away when she couldn't figure it out.

Vanessa was uncomfortable with ambiguity. "They thought I was a Lost One."

She met my gaze again when I affirmed my seriousness. "Who did?" She ran her fingers through my hair.

Vanessa was the only person allowed to touch me. Concern spread across her porcelain features cradled within the red hair that draped over her shoulders. She crawled closer to me with the grace of the majestic feline that she was, her movement nearly undetectable. I watched her lithe body settle beside me and wondered what it was like to touch her.

"Xany, and her brother, and his Alpha friend."

"The girl down the hall? What is an Alpha doing here?" She sat up a bit. It didn't take a genius to sense her sudden aggression when the muscles in her torso tightened.

"Xany probably called them. They thought I was a Lost One and came to rescue me, or something. Caden figured out that I wasn't lost and that I knew exactly who I was, and he started asking about things..."

"And then you freaked out." Vanessa's emerald gaze bore into me as they had many times before.

I held my breath to fight back the uprising of emotions. I was ashamed by having a panic attack in front of the strangers. And by the fact that I didn't remember what happened when I have them. I put my arm over my face to hide and tried to curl into a fetal position. Vanessa was familiar with my hiding and didn't let me get away with it that easily. She rolled with me and joined me on the pillow. Vanessa nudged my arm away from my face. I swallowed back my tears and avoided looking at her.

"It's okay, Shawnee." She paused. "I know that bad things happened to you on the reservation with your mother's pack, I get it. No one can make you relive that. You have control over what you want to share. But you're avoiding everything and it's making it worse and worse. I think you're starting to see that..." Her voice was tender but pressured, like she'd been holding it in for a long time.

I sobbed and clenched my teeth again, as the panic rose in my chest in an all-too-familiar way. Vanessa's hand found its way to my stomach, rubbing in slow circles. It calmed me much in the same way that Mal did when he let me out the door. I didn't understand any of it. Why Vanessa's touch and the heat of Mal's presence soothed me, or why I found myself wanting it.

"You're dying, Shawnee, and I'm enabling you by coddling you in bed, letting you get away with not talking, and using alcohol and bad sex to numb away your pain and hurt yourself. You put on a good act as a doctor and hide behind your genius, but someday, Shawnee, that's all going to fail, and you'll find yourself alone in a strange place, missing months of time because you let your panic and *forgetfulness* go unchecked. It's happened enough already..." She glanced away, looking thoroughly exhausted from the effort it took to say that. Of course she was right; I knew she was. I sniffled and examined her.

She doesn't really care about you; she's just sick of cleaning up your messes.

I closed my eyes tight to fight away the voices. Vanessa put her hand on my face and purred loudly. *I know she cares about me...*

You wish!

"She does so!" I said aloud, without meaning to.

"Yes, I do," Vanessa responded, acting as though she could hear my inner battle. Normally this would upset me, but tonight the timing was perfect. I leaned my head against her chest. She accepted and wrapped me in her arms.

"What should I do?" I sniffled again, as I tilted my head to survey her. Maybe she'd have some bit of wisdom, some great insight that would make everything better.

"Eat something." She wiped my tears away.

"Eat something?"

"When was the last time you ate?" She lifted a brow. I shrugged, not remembering and not caring to admit that I didn't remember. "Mashed potatoes?" She got up from the bed, holding her hand out for me to join her.

I nodded and got up, taking her hand warily. "My favorite," I croaked.

She squeezed my hand and led me to the kitchen. "Then after that we'll talk about Caden and Mal. Particularly about what their plans were if you were a Lost One."

"They didn't say anything about plans. Just that they inform Lost Ones so that they're less vulnerable to being hoarded."

"Do you think that informing them, then leaving them to their own devices is a good plan?" She glanced back at me expectantly and then worked her way toward the refrigerator to take out the potatoes.

"Well...no. Not really." I sat down at the kitchen table, watching her move with the grace that only a feline could conjure.

"Exactly. I'll go with you in the morning when you talk to them." She took out a knife and placed it on the table in front of me.

"Wait, who said I was going to talk to them?" I reached for the knife and gripped it tighter than I intended when I heard her statement.

"You said the way they were going about it was a bad plan. So naturally it's up to you to tell them that." She took the knife from me and began to peel the potatoes.

"Vanessa! You suggested that it was, not me." I huffed.

"I merely asked a question, you're the one who answered."

I sighed, realizing I had been tricked. Vanessa attempted to hide her mischievous smile from me as she sliced the potatoes. She often had secret agendas, and I assumed this one was about getting face to face with a semi-packless dominant werewolf. Like many werecats, Vanessa was a troublemaker.

CHAPTER SEVEN

We took our time, eating in silence as I allowed my thoughts to wander. Vanessa went home for the night after our meal of mashed potatoes and fish sticks. I made my way back to bed, contemplating what we spoke about. She tricked me into assuming Caden and Mal had a weak plan for helping Breeders, but my guess was that she felt there was something of importance in their story. Something she believed I should explore.

The following morning, Vanessa invaded my shower just as I was rinsing the conditioner out of my hair.

"Hurry up already."

I gripped the curtain and nearly tore it down again. "Dammit, Vanessa, use the door!"

"Bending is easier." She snickered and peeked into the shower.

I splashed her with a bit of water in retaliation for her intrusion. She hissed at me before letting go of the curtain.

"Why do you always bend into the most obscure places to find me?" I asked.

"You always seem to be around water, windows, or mirrors." She snickered. "And doorways are just a given."

"Yeah well, one day maybe I'll learn to bend and appear

in your room while you're entertaining one of your gentleman callers." I smirked.

"Very funny. Breeders can't bend." She pulled the shower curtain back again, and I shrieked, splashing water at her like crazy.

I finished my shower and dressed quickly for fear of annoying the ever-impatient redhead in my kitchen. I didn't need her intruding on my shower a third time. When I emerged, Vanessa perched on the counter, eating cheesy puffs out of a giant bag and wiping her hands on her favorite green velvet dress.

"You're going to ruin your dress if you keep it up." I tied my worn pair of Chuck Taylors.

"It washes out. You smell nice." She grinned.

"Not like wet dog?" I smirked.

"No, but you will after we talk to them." She scrunched up her nose and hopped off the counter, then washed her cheesy fingers in the sink. I smiled while watching her. For some reason, I always felt more...normal when Vanessa was around and less trapped in my head.

"You're looking at me funny," she observed.

"Am not. C'mon, let's go before I chicken out."

Vanessa followed me to the door, and we walked down the hall to Xany's apartment. I glanced up at Vanessa, who was taller than me, waiting for her to knock. She lifted an expectant eyebrow at me, and I gulped before doing it myself. I wasn't looking forward to entering Xany's apartment in general, let alone with a werecat at my side. Wolves and cats didn't get along at the best of times, and I worried about inciting some sort of werecreature riot.

Xany came to the door a few seconds later. She wore a pair of black spandex shorts with a tiny apron and top to match that had the letters D D right on her breasts. She apparently just got home from work. Vanessa's eyes went right to the double Ds. I smirked, avoiding looking in the same direction.

"Nice shirt," I said, swallowing the lump in my throat.

"Thanks, just got home." She smiled at me before directing her gaze at Vanessa. "You brought the redhead?"

Vanessa's hands slid to her hips as she quirked an eyebrow at Xany. Xany seemed unfazed by the gesture. I smirked at the interaction between the two of them.

"This is my friend, Vanessa. At least she is for the moment, until she does something unbecoming. We came to talk a bit about umm...some stuff."

I put my hand on the small of Vanessa's back to urge her to remain calm. She was about to enter an apartment where two werewolves currently resided, and the last thing I needed was for her to charge in demanding things.

"We've met." Xany grinned before waving us inside. "Caden is here, but Mal ran to the store because they eat too much, and I have no food left. It's a good thing you showed up today, they were planning to leave soon."

Vanessa silently scanned the apartment while we followed Xany to the living room. I was about to ask how they met when Caden interrupted.

"Yes, Caden is here." He emerged from the kitchen, and his gaze went immediately to Vanessa, then to me. "You know a *hell* of a lot more than you let on, don't you?" He smiled before extending his hand to me in greeting.

This time I shook it with less hesitation. There was a tense moment of silence when Caden and Vanessa made eye contact. Werewolves and werecats, by history, have joined forces when faced with a common foe despite their differences. Vanessa was a weretiger, which were the fiercest of the werecat species. They were known for their intense fighting style and for being way too aggressive. Many werecats chose a more solitary lifestyle and didn't really get along well with others, though some live in groups called Prides. Werecats didn't blend in as easily as werewolves, due to their risky behaviors and quirky natures. And their indiscriminant sexuality.

"What does he mean you know a lot more?" Xany interrupted the awkward silence. At the same time, I pulled my gaze away from them, and Vanessa put her arm around me.

"Vanessa is—"

"A cat," Caden said as he cut me off.

He broke the gaze and allowed Vanessa to win the standoff. It wasn't claiming territory. Her gesture clearly indicated to him that she possessed *me*. When Caden looked away, it meant that he acknowledged her assertion and would allow me to be *hers*. She was satisfied, and her body relaxed against me.

"That explains it." Xany crossed her arms.

"She's protecting, nothing more," Caden said.

Vanessa remained silent, as she often did in mixed company. Xany nodded in understanding. Caden seemed comfortable like usual and sat down on the sofa. He was probably one of the calmest dominants I'd ever met. Maybe I was wrong about his position. Xany sat on the adjacent loveseat, keeping her eyes on Vanessa. I joined her, and Vanessa perched herself beside me on the arm.

"Caden, you might have to tell Mal before he..." Xany hesitated.

"I'll tell him when he gets closer; he's somewhat out of range. I wouldn't let him walk in to meeting a cat unknowingly." Caden grinned at Xany. "Though it might be entertaining."

"Caden!" Xany giggled at the idea. "It would, wouldn't it?"

"Shawnee, you said you wanted to talk about 'some stuff.'" Caden slouched in his chair.

Vanessa slid to the floor, settling beside me with her chin resting on my knee, quietly purring as the tension in the room began to lift. Xany watched her while listening to the conversation.

"Oh...yeah, I did." I forgot that, like Vanessa, Caden's hearing would be superior. I reminded myself not to trust my reactions around him yet. "I was just...curious, I guess. You know how you all thought I was a Lost One?" I hesitated. I was about to tell a dominant wolf that his plan could suck. *Good thing I have a bodyguard with me.* Caden nodded for me to continue. "Well...what if I was a Lost One? What would you have done? I mean other than tell me what I was. What if I couldn't handle it or was too afraid to exist?"

"You mean other than informing you of what you were and the dangers out there?" he asked. Relief filled me over the fact his voice remained steady.

"Yeah, I mean, what if the Lost One didn't feel safe anymore and didn't want to be alone in the world of monsters she suddenly learned about?" I avoided his gaze and stared at his nose instead.

"Good question." He looked at Xany. "What exactly was our plan? Did we have one?"

"That I would keep her safe," she declared with a nod.

"Keep me safe?"

"Uh-huh. You live right by me anyway. You would know that I was a Breeder, too, and we could keep each other safe." Xany smiled brightly. I returned her smile, allowing a tad of affection to seep through.

"But what about the other Lost Ones that don't have Xany right down the hall and are all alone?" I dropped the bomb.

"I didn't think that far ahead. You would've been our first Lost One." Caden scratched his chin.

"I thought you said it was your job to inform the Lost Ones!" I frowned. Vanessa leaned up when she heard me raise my voice.

"That's still true, of course. It is my job. I just hired myself recently so give me a break, will ya?" He grinned, then addressed me with seriousness. "Regardless, you raise a valid point."

"You can't just leave them to their own devices, Caden. It might do more harm than good." I glanced down at Vanessa for reassurance. She lifted her chin to me and purred louder. I guessed that was the equivalent to a pat on the back.

"She's right, Caden. That was a really stupid plan to just walk into their lives and say 'hey, guess what—you can make werewolf babies and, oh yeah, everything in the movies is real and there is a potential you could be raped or killed because of it. Well! Nice talking to you.' That's not very well thought out." Xany tried to suppress her giggle but ended up snickering regardless.

"Well, unlike the pope, I am fallible. I'm up for suggestions."

"My daddy would say if you found a Lost Cub, that cub was yours to raise and teach the ways. Why shouldn't it be the same for Breeders?" Xany suggested.

The same was true in my Pack-family tradition. Lost Cubs were Changers that were either abandoned by their parents, born to unknowing Breeders, or human parents who carried some Breeder genes, or whose parents were killed in battle. If they were found by the pack, they became the responsibility of the pack and were adopted into willing homes. Lost Breeders were more difficult to come by. Lost Cubs were often exposed when they had their First Change or what was often referred to as a *Firsting*.

"I agree with Xany," I spoke up.

"That would require a pack," Caden said.

"Then make one," Vanessa interjected. "Lone dogs are annoying."

I swatted her for the insult and cringed. Werewolves hated to be called *dogs*. Caden handled it better than me though. He seemed to let the rudeness roll right over him while I prepared to duck.

"Yeah, Caden! Why not make your own pack? That way you and Mal don't have to listen to the stupid rules of other packs and neither do I." Xany grinned at him, her expression hopeful.

"Despite the slur, Vanessa, thank you for the suggestion. That's a lot to take on, don't you think?" Caden glanced at me as if he were asking what I thought about it.

I faltered. Was I really about to suggest to a dominant wolf, who's habits I knew nothing about, that he create a pack of his own? "I um...if your intentions are as chivalrous as they seem, why not? You would have a safe place to take the Lost Ones and protect them from harm at the same time. Eventually, they would know enough to decide whether they wanted to stay in a pack or live independently," I said, adding the ending clause so that Caden knew I was pro-free will. No one should be forced to do anything against their will.

Caden watched me as he raised his eyes thoughtfully. "I'll see what Mal thinks. By the way, he's nearly here."

Right on cue, Mal walked through the front door carrying at least a dozen grocery bags effortlessly on one arm with car keys hanging out of his mouth. He gave the entire room a nod of acknowledgement before he put the bags down and spit out the keys. "Sorry. Not enough hands," he said and walked over to us. He paused beside the sofa when he saw Vanessa lazily sitting on the floor next to me. After a moment, Mal glanced at Caden and made a gesture with his hands that said "what the hell?" I guess Caden prepped him for some sort of encounter. Caden laughed and shook his head. Vanessa lifted her gaze and frowned at him, narrowing her eyes in a "try me" manner. She hissed and put her hand on my stomach.

"Yours, I get it. She's yours." Mal sat down beside Caden and his gaze left Vanessa's as he looked to me.

Very cautiously I met his gaze, flinching when I heard the echo of a screeching eagle in my head again. I blinked a few times and took a deep breath. Even with all the other scents in the room, I could smell Mal the strongest. He smelled like the woods.

"It's good to see you again, Shawnee," he said softly.

I nodded to him, then looked down at Vanessa's hair and decided to play with it to distract myself. *Please don't freak out*, I begged myself.

"A weretiger, you say?" Mal asked Caden.

"She almost bit my head off before, dude, seriously," Caden joked.

Mal looked confused and glanced between Xany and Caden. Xany nodded matter-of-factly, trying not to giggle.

"You should have seen it, Mal. It was nearly a blood bath."

Vanessa snickered, hearing them tease him. I couldn't help but smile as well.

"You're all shitting me. See what I get for being the brave hunter and killing all those poor helpless potatoes to make your chips." Mal sighed in mock defeat.

Everyone laughed together at that, and the climate in the room seemed to shift.

"You got chips." Xany hopped up and rushed to the table. She grabbed a few bags and passed them out on her way back.

"So what's with the 'not-so-random powwow' this time?" Mal stole my phraseology with a smirk.

"Shawnee and I think you and Caden should form a pack to take in the Lost Ones that you find instead of letting them run around scared of everything," Xany summed up, crunching on a chip right after.

Vanessa reached over and snatched a chip from Xany's bag without making a sound until she bit down on it. I whispered "thief" in her ear.

Mal leaned back against the sofa, glancing at Caden. The two of them sat in silence; however, they gestured as if they spoke aloud and made facial expressions to match.

"Excuse me!" Xany shouted, and of course everyone looked at her. "Would you two wolves refrain from the mind talking when in the presence of the rest of us? Thank you very much. Have a nice day."

The guys laughed.

"Mind talking?" I asked.

Vanessa perked up.

"Mhmm. They do it all the time. My darling brother has

a gift that can make him talk in your head when he wants to. And to leave me out!" Xany threw a chip at Mal who caught it and ate it.

Vanessa snickered and eyed Mal with sudden curiosity. Werecreatures often had various gifts that allowed them to have certain abilities. It's all about the magics. The same magics that help them shift. Breeders can have certain gifts as well, but their gifts are different. Changer gifts are there to support them in battle, and Breeder gifts are in place to support the Changers. It's Earth Mother's way of keeping the balance and affirming that we should cherish Breeders and Changers in the same light because one is reliant on the other.

Caden grinned at Xany and finally spoke out loud, "Mal and I will consider what you've suggested. I have a friend in Utah that leads his own small sept. We will visit him tomorrow to discuss the situation and see if it's suitable for us to form a pack."

I nodded as I listened to him. Regardless of the result, I was glad that he at least considered the suggestion of protecting the Breeders rather than dropping a bomb on them and leaving them alone to dig out of the rubble.

"Isn't he cute when he speaks formally?" Xany seemed smitten with Caden.

"Yes, he's just darling." Mal rolled his eyes at Xany.

I smiled, enjoying the antics of the brother and sister before speaking. "We better get going then. I have work tonight. I'm glad you heard what we had to say, Caden. Thank you." I stood with Vanessa, moving toward the door.

Caden joined us and shook my hand again. He met Vanessa's gaze for a moment before extending his hand to her as well. She looked from Caden's hand to his eyes, then back to his hand again, then back to his eyes, and finally lifted a brow at him. I nudged her. She hissed at me and shook Caden's hand quickly, then wiped her hand on her dress in the same spot she wiped the cheesy puff crumbs. Mal seemed a bit surprised when Vanessa accepted the gesture and smirked when she wiped her hand. Caden chuckled as I urged Vanessa out of the apartment.

"Bye, Xany."

Xany laughed hard while she waved, entertained by the awkward interactions between the "cats and dogs."

On the way back to my apartment, Vanessa huffed. "Now I smell like wet dog."

"Correction... You now smell like a cheesy, wet dog." I grinned and hurried inside, just out of reach of the swat Vanessa attempted at me.

CHAPTER EIGHT

I spent another night alone in the lab. Doctor Reynolds had left me a note to tell me he would be out of the office for the next few days while he attended a conference in Cheyenne. For the first time in a while, I found it hard to concentrate on work. My mind kept wandering to the conversation I had with Caden. My Breeder side was something I'd managed to keep under wraps for years. Vanessa was right when she said terrible things had happened to me on the reservation, and when I left, I'd vowed to never look back at the pack lifestyle.

There were plenty of people in the world who went around unaware of the mystical, magical, and dangerous creatures around them. So what if I carried the werewolf gene? That didn't mean I had to live among them. I made the choice to live in the human world and deny anything and everything that I once was, even if my closest friend in the world was a weretiger. I could easily pretend that her chronic purring was a random breathing condition like sleep apnea. Humans had those things. *Normal* things. I wanted to be normal. A normal doctor living a normal, ordinary life. The blinders I wore helped me get through school and work.

And be alone.

I shrugged off the annoying thoughts and decided to change tasks.

I had about an hour left to my shift so I decided to head up to the ER to see if there was anything interesting going on. When I arrived, the attending physician greeted me.

"I'm surprised to see you in here, Dr. T," said the forty-something-year-old Doctor Snyder who walked toward the nurses' station where I flipped through charts.

"Hmm...boring night in the lab. Anything interesting here?"

"Nothing as interesting as your skinless kid. We had a woman who snuck out from the Behavioral Health Unit wearing a nightgown and white lipstick. She stood at the front door with her arms spread out saying she was waiting for the *Second Coming*. But other than that, nothing too exciting."

I shook my head at him. "Did you ask if you could wait with her?"

"Huh? Why would I do that?" he asked, trying to hide the distaste in his voice.

"Because she's sick and maybe would have appreciated the company. Eloise may not be able to communicate in the same way as you and I, but she still has a lot to say if you make the effort to listen." I glanced at him and dropped the charts back in the bin.

Dr. Snyder remained silent as he watched me.

"Her son was planning to visit her this weekend and stood her up. Eloise's waiting for the *Second Coming* was her way of telling you that."

"Well...sounds like you pay attention." I could tell that he didn't appreciate my mild lecture on empathy.

"It doesn't take much to sense when another human being is sad, regardless if they are in a state of psychosis. Good night, Doctor Snyder," I said dismissively. I felt his gaze follow me down the hall as I walked away.

I thought about Eloise on my way home. I'd visited with her on the many occasions she'd come in through the emergency room. Schizophrenia isn't a gentle disease. Sometimes the patients in the psychiatric unit reminded me of myself. Especially the ones that came in having panic attacks that they thought were heart attacks. I couldn't dwell on those thoughts though, because Breeders didn't have mental health issues, the same way they didn't have physical ailments.

There wasn't as much frost on the ground tonight; spring was just around the corner. I began the ascent up the hill toward my apartment building just as a black SUV with its blinding headlights drove down. There was a sudden break in the beams of light when a shadowed figure bolted across the road. I gasped when the driver slammed on the horn and the brakes at the same time. There was no impact. The driver got out of his car and looked around. When he found nothing he got back in and drove away. I wrapped my arms around myself, trying to contain the unease that crept across my skin and prickled the hairs on the back of my neck. The street, eerily silent, had an ominous vibe as I continued walking up it. I hated when eerie and nighttime were paired together. Why couldn't it be an eerily quiet *day* instead?

With the entry to my building a mere fifty feet ahead, I thought I was home free—until I heard a loud crash in the alley next to the building.

"Damn cats," I muttered, before pausing.

Instead of the telltale yowling of battling alley cats, I heard the murmur of voices. My stomach did a terrified lurching thing, like when an elevator drops down to the next floor too fast. There was no way I was going to make it past the alley undetected. I moved closer to the building, pressing my back against the bricks, and stepped nearer to the alley. The murmuring voices became audible when I was only about a foot away from the entrance.

"Trust me, you'll love it," I heard a raspy male voice

say.

"I told you to get lost already," a familiar female voice replied.

"C'mon, sweetness, just one little nibble," the male voice spoke again, dropping an octave.

"I told you to beat..." The female voice paused midsentence, then suddenly giggled. "Just a nibble?"

My eyes widened when I recognized Xany's distinct laugh, and I held my breath, listening again.

"That's a girl...just a little nibble. It won't hurt a bit." The male voice seemed to hiss.

With a sickening awareness, I realized what was about to happen. I'd heard a hiss like that before, and it did *not* belong to a cat. Turning to gaze down the alley, I saw Xany with her back against the wall and a dark figure in front of her. He had his hand on her head, tilting it to the side while Xany stood frozen in place with her hand braced on his chest.

"No!" I shouted, surprising both myself and the vampire.

Xany remained still until he turned and glared at me, baring his fangs and emitting a guttural hiss. Xany awoke from the thrall, her body tensing, and she looked to the creature in front of her. When the vampire sensed Xany's lucidity, he turned back to her and bore his fangs, grabbing her hair, and tossing his head back ready to strike.

Before I could think about what I was doing, my legs carried my body forward. I closed my eyes and ran right at the vampire, throwing my entire body weight against him. The impact knocked him away from Xany and into a stack of aluminum garbage cans. The tremendous sound of the crashing cans caused several neighborhood dogs to bark as the vampire thrashed about to regain his footing. I got up as fast as I could and ran back toward Xany.

"Go, go! Run!" I shouted and shoved at her.

Xany glared at the vampire whose leg had gone right through the aluminum, which he was trying to pry free. I shoved her again, and this time she ran with me out of the alley. When we were back under the glare of the streetlights, I could hear the pounding footsteps of the vamp running toward us, and then suddenly it was silent again. I had a hold of Xany's arm, nearly dragging her until she stopped running and looked back.

"He's gone," she said, scanning the area while panting.

"He's hiding. We need to get inside, hurry." I pulled at her again, and she jogged with me, constantly glancing over her shoulder.

"We can take him!" she shouted and thrust her chest out as if she were ready for a street brawl. I stopped dragging her for a moment to stare at her.

"What?" she asked with an innocent shrug.

"So now you're Buffy? You really think you and I could take on a leech? Get real. Now let's go." I grabbed her again and pulled her inside the apartment building, knowing full well that a glass door would not protect us should the vampire come back for more.

"Hell yeah!" she added, huffing at me as the door locked behind us.

"That *thing* nearly had you for dinner. Didn't your brother ever tell you not to look into the eyes of a leech? You were *thralled*." I frowned.

"So! I... We could still take him." She nodded matter-of-factly.

I shook my head. "And here I thought you were the one who was supposed to keep *me* safe," I said and cocked an eyebrow at her, in a poor mimicking of Vanessa's favorite gesture.

Xany giggled. "I said we'd keep each other safe!"

"You're so strange."

Xany beamed with pride. "And damn proud of it. Who taught you to tackle vampires anyway?"

"My mom always told me, 'close your eyes and move fast.'"

"Did she say 'close your eyes and move fast, directly

into the line of fire'?"

"Well no, I guess I added that part." I couldn't help but smile. "The leech is probably pissed off now though. We should tell Caden or Mal in case it comes back looking for you."

"They left to go talk to his sept-y friend in Utah," Xany said as we started walking up stairs to our apartments.

"I'll call Vanessa then. She'll enjoy a decent hunt, I'm sure." I unlocked my apartment door.

"Your great protector cat," Xany said with a smirk.

"Yeah...she does that sometimes. Not fond of cats?"

"She's my first." I walked into my apartment, and Xany followed as usual.

"Well, Vanessa's quirkier than most," I said.

Xany changed the subject. "I'm hungry. Want to order a pizza?"

"Um...all right, I guess."

"And then we can have a sleepover!" she shouted as she grabbed the phone from the table and began to dial.

I took a deep breath. Save someone's neck by accident and get a sleepover in return. I hoped Xany didn't talk as much in her sleep as she did while awake.

CHAPTER NINE

"So Brutus scared you the other night, huh?" Xany asked, trying to stifle a giggle by taking an extra-large bite of pizza.

"You said pizza and a sleepover, that's it. No questions," I replied. I didn't want to talk about my encounter in the woods with the alleged werewolf called Brutus. It was bad enough he had the gall to scare me, but what if I were a human? His behavior was irresponsible and his Alpha should be notified.

Regardless of the events that had happened over the last few days, I still wasn't into talking like I was a part of the pack paradigm again. I worked too hard to live harmoniously in the human world without preternatural influences to just abandon all of my efforts and return.

"That's not fair." Xany turned to me with her bottom lip sticking out in a pout. "Talking is a part of sleepovers."

"Sleeping is a part of sleepovers. That's why it's called a *sleepover* and not a *talkover*," I grumbled.

"You're always rude to me when I try to talk to you and get to know you...meanie." Xany pouted harder, shoving her hands on her hips.

"And what does that tell you?" I cocked a brow in

response.

"That you're hiding something."

"You already know what I'm hiding. You figured it out ages ago." I rolled my eyes.

"Yeah, but *why* are you hiding it? That's what you haven't told me yet... So tell me." She giggled and attempted to bat her lashes at me like I saw her do to Mal and Caden.

"That's none of your business," I said with a frown.

"So?"

I shook my head at her. "Enough. Let's just move on, okay?"

"Does the redheaded cat know?" she pressed.

"Yes." I sighed.

"Good. I'll ask her then."

"Xany! What is wrong with you? What part of 'it's not your business' don't you understand?" I shouted. In anger, I tossed the slice of pizza that I wasn't eating back into the box and stood up.

Xany seemed to settle after my reaction. "Fine, sheesh... I was just trying to help."

"I don't need your help, or anyone's for that matter," I said. Frustrated, I stalked off to the kitchen to grab a beer from the refrigerator.

"No one but the cat's, huh," she said, crossing her arms over her chest.

"No."

"Drinking is bad for you," she jousted.

"So is being nosy." I popped the can open right in front of her and took a swig.

"You can't die from being nosy." She turned her nose in the air like an arrogant kindergartener.

"Yes, you can. Especially if someone gets tired of it and kills you," I retorted with a smirk.

"Cool." Xany giggled, brushing off my fake threat.

I couldn't help but laugh at her a little. "You're a bit off, aren't you?"

"Mhmm. Just like you." She arched an eyebrow at me.

"Noted," I said in my usual doctor voice, which made Xany smile.

"One day you'll tell me." Xany sounded smug as she voiced her belief.

"If you say so." I rolled my eyes again.

"Want to watch a movie?" she asked, changing the topic.

"Do you talk as much during movies as you do during sleepovers?" I couldn't help but smirk.

"Of course not."

"Fine, then let's watch a movie," I said as she hopped up and began looking through my DVD collection.

"It's after the movie you have to worry about," she added, shuffling through a few disks.

"Fabulous." A sigh escaped me.

"Yes, I know I am. Thank you. Let's watch this one," she said and popped in *Nosferatu*. How very suiting...

During the movie, Xany was mostly quiet. She only spoke to point out her favorite parts or elaborate on what it would be like if vampires really looked like Nosferatu. I reminded her that some of them do. While the movie played, I couldn't help thinking about how suddenly everything seemed to be out in the open. Not just with Xany and the wolves, but with myself. A few days ago I'd never admit that vampires existed or that I was friends with a weretiger. And now look where I was at. At least I had beer to dull my thinking.

When the movie ended, Xany yawned and stretched. "I'm beat."

"You can take the bed. I'm fine with the sofa." I stood and began to collect the dishes and trash from the coffee table.

"That's silly. We can both take the bed," she said with finality.

I sighed on my way to the kitchen, depositing the dishes and trash in their respective places, not having the energy to argue.

Xany stripped down to a camisole and boyshorts, while I changed into a pair of sweats. I glanced at her as she pulled back the covers and climbed into my queen-sized bed. As I got in, I positioned pillows between us. Xany giggled at my fort building and lay on her side facing me. I shrugged at her as I tried to cover the fact that I was afraid of having one of my usual dreams with a near stranger in my bed.

"Good night," I said to Xany and rolled onto my side with my back to her.

"G'night. Don't let the bed bugs bite."

I remained awake for quite a while. Xany's soft breathing pulsed beside me as I watched the shadows circle in the room. I thought about the events of the night and shuddered, remembering the vampire's fangs as they nearly bit into Xany's neck.

How did I go so long without having any encounters with these creatures and then suddenly, all in the same week, three werewolves and a vampire make appearances? Not to mention the weretiger I had been friends with for the past twelve years. It's not that I *ignored* the fact that Vanessa was a werecat. I recognized it; I just...chose not to acknowledge it. I guess that *is* ignoring it. I was so used to blocking things out that I supposed when I began to take notice, not by my own choice, it all hit me in the face at once. *Great.*

My thoughts continued along this route until I slowly drifted to sleep. I dreamed of the skinless little girl with blue eyes, and of the woman who gave birth to a clawed child covered in hair. *Hypertrichosis*—excessive hair growth throughout the body—was the diagnosis. *What a lie.* I was a liar because I was in denial. What had happened to those kids? It was my fault. I could have prevented it. I could have...

Ravaged necks, dog attacks, spontaneous electrocution. My fault! My fault...

Tell the truth, Shawnee.

I tossed and turned in bed, tormented by the thoughts until my dream suddenly changed.

I hear a voice say, "This is our secret. If you tell your mother, I will kill her, and then I will kill you." The light in my room turns off, and I can't see my dolls on the shelf. I feel hands on my chest that press me into the bed. The blankets pull back. A hot voice against my cheek says, "I'll kill you."

I can't breathe. I push at the darkness above me, but it does little to help. I feel cold. Then hurt. So much hurt. I cry for e-tsi.

The hand on my chest raises, then hits my face. "She's dead."

I cry harder.

I want to die with her.

I woke up clutching my chest and gasping for breath. I heard Xany's voice but couldn't make out what she was saying. The weight of the bed changed as she left it, and my eyes burned as light filled the room. The panic in my chest tightened at the invasion of my senses.

"Shawnee," she said and reached for me.

I pushed at her and screamed. I wanted to run, but there was nowhere to go so I just kept screaming. Xany tried desperately to soothe me. She stroked my hair and rubbed my arms. It didn't work. I cried and pushed at her again when she tried to get closer to me. My body trembled uncontrollably as I thrashed at the sheets. Then suddenly she was there with arms around me, squeezing me tight.

I fought against her embrace. I fought hard but she didn't let up. I clawed at her arms, leaving scratches that rose to vivid, red welts. Xany's hands were suddenly on top of mine, and our fingers laced. She held me there with her warm body engulfing me until I was able to calm down. When my head cleared, I realized where I was and that she was holding me. Nauseated and dizzy, I tried to wiggle away. She didn't let me. Instead, she squeezed me tighter.

Eventually, I relaxed, and my breathing slowed as the

pressure of her arms around me calmed me down. My steady crying turned into sobs that wracked my very core. A cold sensation enveloped me, causing my muscles to go lax. Chills and weakness filled my body. Xany lifted my chin so I would meet her gaze. She had tears of confusion in her eyes. Xany's eyes reminded me of Mal's.

Then everything went dark..

CHAPTER TEN

"She will be okay," Vanessa's voice said. A soft purring accompanied her words.

"Are you sure?" Xany asked, her voice softer than usual.

"It's happened before," Vanessa responded.

I woke up to the conversation. When I rolled over in bed, I saw Xany seated by my legs and Vanessa by my side with her hand on my stomach. Without addressing them, I scooted closer to Vanessa and put my head in her lap. She purred louder and ran her fingers through my hair.

"You scared your friend," she whispered, leaning down and brushing her lips against my cheek.

Xany looked at me tentatively, biting her lip before speaking. "Are you okay, NeeNee?" she asked, leaning forward and rubbing my arm affectionately. "You passed out."

I nodded and curled up tighter. My stomach churned with nauseated embarrassment. Though I noticed what she called me, I decided to ignore the new nickname I had just been assigned. Vanessa perked an eyebrow at Xany.

"No more hiding," Vanessa said after a moment of quiet, then lifted me to sit upright.

I was used to her doing this to me. Werecats, like most werecreatures, have exacerbated strength. Vanessa, despite her tall and slender frame, could carry me with as much ease as a bodybuilder. She sat me up, leaning against her to face Xany. Xany seemed to enjoy watching her toss me around like a rag doll.

"It's funny when you move her so easily," she said. Her words broke some of the tension.

Vanessa snickered and purred against my neck. I leaned into her and shivered a bit, enjoying the gentle sensation that ran down my spine.

"Shawnee, remember how I said I wasn't going to let you get away with not talking? Well, this is part of it. It's your responsibility to explain to Xany about your nightmares," she said with a firm tone.

I wasn't happy about it. It was moments like this where I usually turned to Vanessa to help bail me out. I frowned at her words, uncertain of how to even start. In effort to escape her decision, and possibly persuade her to change her mind, I allowed my lip to tremble in a pout.

Xany giggled as she scooted closer. "Pouting only works for me."

"I umm..." I hesitated when I heard my voice, raspy from screaming. I cleared it and continued. *Damn you, Vanessa, for making me do this.* "I...have dreams sometimes, about bad things that happened. I should have told you before you slept over. Sorry you got scared."

"I called Vanessa from your phone after you passed out. I thought you *died*," she said with a huff. "Dying is not allowed." She smiled before reaching out and touching my face.

I flinched but couldn't pull away because Vanessa sat too close for me to back up.

"Vanessa popped through the window pane. It was the craziest thing I have ever seen," Xany added with a giddy grin.

Vanessa snickered and slipped her hand under my shirt

to rub my bare stomach. I slouched back against her. Xany's eyes narrowed as she watched the gesture, but Vanessa didn't seem notice.

"Vanessa can bend," I explained. "I'm guessing Mal and Caden can't."

"Umm... Mal can't. Caden can a bit." She shrugged, distracted for a moment before she perked up. "Speaking of which, Caden called this morning and said that they were heading back today to tell us what their new plans would be."

"I'm going to have a quick shower," I said, purposely avoiding discussing the return of Mal and Caden.

I wriggled away from Vanessa and slid off the bed. Vanessa lay on her back after I moved and squirmed around a few times which made Xany giggle. Vanessa's purrs emanated from her like an overly contented housecat. She lifted her chin at Xany and gave her ponytail a swat. I smiled at the playful, attention-seeking cat and disappeared into the bathroom, closing the door behind me.

The nosy women in my bed seemed to truly care, but I needed some time away to digest what had happened. A shower was the perfect escape from their presence and it allowed me time to scrub the memories from my skin. I always felt so disgustingly dirty after dreams like that.

With a flick of my wrist, I turned on the water and allowed it to run for a minute, giving it time to get extra hot. As I got undressed, I let my thoughts wander.

I should have fought harder to sleep on the sofa. Then Xany would never have seen me freak out.

Yes, she would.

In an attempt to ignore the voices, I rolled my shoulders and forced myself to relax. This was the second time Xany had seen me freak out over nothing. I hated it. I stepped into the shower and allowed the water to run over my shoulders. The most troubling part of the dream was not the memory of my father abusing me. Rather, it was the memories of all those kids that never saw justice. How could I have ignored what had happened to them? I was denying who I was and thus denying any and all supernatural explanations for things that had happened.

That baby boy did *not* have hypertrichosis, and whatever happened to the skinless girl was not an accident. They were victims of something terrible. But acknowledging what they were victims of would mean I'd have to acknowledge myself and what I was too. I let the water beat against my face as I mulled over the possible ramifications.

Injustice. I forced my mind into silence and brushed my fingertips over the scar on my stomach, remembering again how I got it.

Injustice.

Those children were victims. Like me.

It was the Andrus's fault. They were the ones to blame for those deaths. Andrus Synnax International was an organization that researched unexplained phenomenon and performed experiments on preternatural creatures all under the guise of a not-for-profit ecological organization. They had branches worldwide that worked to infest other companies with their agenda, particularly for funding. Recently, they had infested the hospital where I worked. I knew this because of the sudden uprising in bizarre cases appearing in the emergency room. They were logged as *accidents* and I did nothing about it. My heart sank into my stomach.

I was in the shower for nearly an hour before Vanessa knocked on the door. The water grew cold, but I was too lost in my thoughts to realize it until I heard her speak.

"All right, Shawnee?" she asked then pulled the curtain back to peak in at me. Fear dilated her pupils though she tried to hide it.

"I'm okay." My teeth chattered, and I shielded my chest from her view.

Vanessa turned off the water and grabbed a towel from

the cabinet. She wrapped it around me then lifted me from the tub. I leaned into her warmth and sighed. "Stop taking care of me."

Light purrs rumbled from the core of Vanessa's chest. She remained silent as she wrapped a second towel around my dripping hair. Her face held no expression; a sign that she was trying to hide her concern. "Then take care of yourself so I won't have to."

Pursing my lips, I glanced at her. "I'm sorry."

"For what?" Vanessa asked as she dried my hair gently with the towel.

"Being awful to you for so long." I paused. "I was rude to Xany, too, and she was only trying to help. Just like you."

"Thank me by getting better," she said when I sat down on the stool that faced the vanity mirror in the bathroom. She moved behind me and draped her arms around me, resting her chin on my head. I saw our reflection in the mirror. My eyes welled with tears, so naturally I glanced away. I hated to see myself cry almost as much as I hated crying.

"Where's Xany?"

"She went home to get dressed. Caden and Mal should be back soon," she responded, picking up a hairbrush, then began smoothing out my tangled hair. I watched her in the mirror.

"I can do it." I turned and looked up at her, holding my hand out for the brush.

Vanessa hesitated before handing it to me. I brushed out my hair like I normally do when she isn't around. She smiled at me when she understood the gesture and nuzzled my cheek gently. Her purring calmed as she exited the bathroom and allowed me to finish dressing on my own which, on mornings like this, took a tremendous amount of effort.

When I emerged from my room, dressed in my usual jeans and sweatshirt combination, Vanessa had made eggs and toast for breakfast. A soft ruby-lipped smile lit up her pretty face when she saw me. She was in the middle of setting two plates on the table and, once finished, began slathering heaps of butter on a slice of toast. I smirked when she licked the butter first and served myself a few scoops of scrambled eggs.

"There's about twenty beer cans under the sofa," she said as she bit into her crunchy toast.

"That many?" I tried to sound surprised.

"Clean them before you get werebugs."

"There's no such thing as werebugs!" I huffed at her threat.

"Sure you believe that?" she asked with a perked brow, then snickered.

I couldn't help but laugh. "Shut up."

Xany knocked on the door just as we finished breakfast to tell us that Caden and Mal had arrived and wanted Vanessa and me to join them.

"Right now?" I asked, swallowing the anxiety bubble that rose into my throat.

"Mhmm," Xany said, giving me a soft smile. "You look better than this morning, NeeNee."

"I umm... Thanks." I glanced away from her. Sometimes it was hard to take compliments, even if they were only the slightest acknowledgments of my improved appearance.

Vanessa joined us, and we walked over to Xany's apartment. As soon as I entered, I could smell Mal and Caden's distinct scents. It was a mixture of fresh air, shampoo, and woodlands. Caden greeted us with a sandwich hanging out of his mouth. Vanessa gave him a mischievous grin as her fingers twitched. I knew she was fighting the urge to torment the wolf by grabbing his food and running. Caden seemed to catch on to her shenanigans and quickly took a bite before putting his lunch back on the plate. *As if that would save it.* Xany giggled and bounced on her tiptoes next to him.

It was the shadow rising from the floor beside the sofa that drew my attention away from the others. The ebony creature stretched its front paws in a gesture of laziness, with hindquarters thrust into the air. It shook out its fur and trotted toward us, lifting its gaze to meet mine. I recognized the hazel eyes immediately as belonging to Mal, and that recognition locked me in place. Werewolves that kept their eye color in all forms were closer to their beast and considered more feral. But I already knew that about Mal; it didn't take his eye color to tell me so. I could smell the wilderness on him—and hear it too. I dropped my gaze immediately as Mal approached me. Vanessa stepped aside in distaste of the wolf that brushed past her. He paid her no mind and stopped in front of me to sniff my hands and jeans. My heart raced and my breathing quickened. I closed my eyes as I begged for the panic, set off by the wolven reminder, to cease. Then, unexpectedly, it did. It washed away and left me with a sense of peace— something I hadn't experienced in a very long time.

Vanessa, Caden, and Xany watched us. Vanessa's posture screamed of tension. Her fingers twitched with readiness, and I knew she was prepared to jump in and save me should I need it. Xany smiled while Caden returned to eating, a clear gesture of his confidence in Mal's control. I looked down at Mal, who now sat on his haunches while watching me expectantly. I smiled and slowly sat down on the floor before him, tucking my chin to my chest in a submissive bow.

"Waya *means you no harm.*"

Mal's tail swayed in acceptance, and he made a soft chuffing noise in greeting. I met his gaze only after he accepted my submission and slipped my fingers into his fur, parting his coal-colored pelt enough to see the tawny undercoat. When I reached out to him, he moved closer, pressing his wet nose against my neck to sniff. I laughed softly at the little puffs of air that tickled my neck and gave me goosebumps.

In lupine form, werewolves are nearly indistinguishable from regular wolves, depending on their ancestry of course. Most Native American werewolves resembled timber wolves or gray wolves respectively. Mal nuzzled my cheek before he stepped back and placed his paw on my leg. He chuffed, then whined to tell me what he wanted. I grew up around wolves, and that allowed me to understand their language. In a way, they were easier to relate to. Wolves communicate in a series of yips, yaps, chuffs, whines, whimpers, facial, and body cues that made up an entire language. It was easy to forget that werewolves were people when in this form.

Vanessa watched us closely. She seemed surprised by my calm interactions with this wolf. Xany appeared entertained and kept bouncing on her tiptoes while Caden had a subtle sureness about him that kept him relaxed as he observed. Mal whined at me again and plopped his paw back in my lap. This time I responded and put both of my hands into his fur, rubbing vigorously. He thumped his rear leg on the ground, imitating a dog to communicate that he got what he wanted.

Vanessa grinned and cocked a brow at Caden as if saying, "See? I told you wolves were dogs." I smiled at Mal who licked my cheek. For the first time, I was content to be in the room with all three newfound strangers.

CHAPTER ELEVEN

Following my playful interaction with Mal, Caden brought everyone together in the living room to discuss the plan he had promised to make. When we were all seated, Xany interjected before he even got a chance to speak.

"Well? What did Hank say?" Xany pressed.

Caden tried to hide a grin. I got the feeling he was the type of wolf that enjoyed a challenge like Xany. Mal trotted between us then crouched beside the sofa. The fur along his back began to fade, smoothing into the soft copper of his human skin. He rose from the floor as if ending a graceful bow, and seated himself on the sofa beside Caden. He wore nothing more than a pair of worn out jeans. Smooth muscular curves covered his chest and abdomen. Vanessa nudged me when my gaze lingered a moment too long.

"Well...he said that a small pack for orienting Lost Ones was not a bad idea. He also said that he had a large amount of land that he'd be willing to hand over to us in order to do so. Sort of his way of pitching in to help the Lost Ones. Mal and I scoped it out. It's several acres in the middle of the woods in northern Utah. There's a river that runs through the nearby mountains, separating the property from the more populated part of the territory. It would be perfect for teaching not only Lost Breeders but Lost Cubs, too, without much influence from others," he said.

"And did you decide to do it or not?" Xany pushed for more.

Caden chuckled at her impatience. "Yes. We did decide to do it. We'll need time to build suitable housing. The best part about the land is that it is relatively pure and untouched as it once was a part of tribal territory that now belongs to Hank. It's very much untainted."

Taint, or pollution, was a huge priority for werewolves in particular. They believed that they were put on this planet to protect Mother Earth or Gaia, as she is often referred. This concept is strongly rooted in many tribal traditions.

"Yay!" Xany cheered. "Are you going to build a really big house?"

"There is a moderate-sized log cabin on the land now. Caden and I are going to work on updating it and building a smaller cabin close by as well," Mal chimed in.

"We'll have several bedrooms, and the smaller cabin will have a bunk room, just in case we suddenly have more on our hands than expected. There's plenty of room to expand if our numbers grow," Caden added.

I looked between Mal and Caden, nodding once. I liked the idea of a somewhat secluded place for Lost Ones and Lost Cubs to learn and grow.

"That's awesome!" Xany bounced excitedly, then ran over and hugged Caden, who chuckled in surprise. "You'll make a great Alpha."

"Why thank you," he said with a smile while returning Xany's hug.

Mal grinned goofily at Caden and Xany, which made them laugh. "You're all welcome to come with us if you like." Mal glanced at me in particular. I looked away from him to Vanessa, who was snickering mischievously when he extended the invitation.

"Sure, I'd love to join your pack," she replied with a bright grin.

"A lying puss is what you are." Caden laughed.

Vanessa laughed as she looked up at me. Her eyes searched mine, waiting for me to refuse Caden—which of course I did.

"Thanks for the offer but I've got a job and stuff here. I'll keep it in mind if I ever find any Lost Ones though," I said.

"Aw, Nee. You have to come. I'm definitely going." Xany giggled and grinned at Mal.

He shook his head at his sister, the way any older brother would. "Of course you are."

"Woohoo!" Xany shouted and launched herself at Mal. A grin plastered on her face. He caught her and smirked, glancing over Xany's shoulder toward me. I continued to try and find something else to look at besides him.

"Well...it's good to know you're going to be handling things now. I think the Lost Ones will be in good hands," I said dismissively and stood up. "I've got work tonight so I better get going."

Vanessa stood with me and took my hand. Caden raised an eyebrow at me. There wasn't any doubt in my mind that he sensed my lie. Vanessa led me to the door as Xany waved, and Mal offered me a genial nod. We walked back to my apartment in silence and were safely inside before Vanessa spoke. "They can tell you're lying, you know." She let go of my hand and crossed the room to sprawl out on the couch.

"Well...then they got the message. I'm not going to run off and join a pack just because I've suddenly come to terms with my identity. I've lived in the human world for twelve years, and I'm not about to spoil that by acting like a foolish Breeder following orders from a dominant Changer." I stalked around the apartment, deciding now would be the perfect time to clean up the mess that I had created over the past few weeks.

"No one is telling you to abandon everything and run off and join a pack, Shawnee. Calm down." The rattling purr returned to her chest. Part of me wanted to snuggle close to the comforting sound. Vanessa seemed to purr more often as a way of soothing herself or calming down. At times like this, I thought she did it just to soothe me.

"And besides, you couldn't come with me even if I did go. You would end up killing the wolves eventually, or trying to at least." I huffed, looking away from her when my frustration grew.

"It doesn't matter where you go, Shawnee, I can visit anywhere I want in less than a minute. How do you think I go back and forth from Ireland so quickly?" A smirk tugged the corners of her pinkish lips.

"Yeah, well...that's different." I tossed a few beer cans into the recycling bin and piled the dirty laundry into a basket.

"All I'm saying is that you have choices," she said and turned on the TV.

"No, I don't." I frowned and stood in front of the TV with my hands on my hips.

"Everyone has choices. Maybe you should stop and think about that sometime. Now quit being rude before I pounce you." She hissed at me, then stuck out her tongue.

Naturally the most appropriate response was to sit on her. So I did. Vanessa snickered and purred, before yanking me down to lay on the sofa with her. I tucked myself up against her as we both lay on our sides facing the television.

"I'm sorry for being rude," I mumbled.

"S'okay. You're only rude to the people you care about most or see as the biggest threats."

I opened my mouth to speak, but paused to think about the truth in her statement. Vanessa knew me well, and that was something I often took for granted. I hugged the arm that she had around me as she nuzzled her chin into my hair. Silently we stared at the TV, though I doubt either of us truly watched it.

Did I really have choices? I didn't like that word. *Choices.* It annoying me. I preferred paths. It was easier to say that I had taken a path and I followed it rather than saying, "I have choices." *I'm following a path. I'm a doctor, and I want to help people.*

That is my path...

CHAPTER TWELVE

Doctor Reynolds stood me up again today. This time by e-mail.

Dr. Twofeathers,

Business has kept me longer than expected. I will return shortly. Your beta serum is a success. Please chart the formula for replication.

Regards,
Reynolds

"Of course it is," I murmured and closed the message.

It had been over a week since Dr. Reynolds left for the conference in Cheyenne. There must've been something rather interesting going on there for him to be away this long.

I found working in the lab not as distracting as I wanted it to be. Instead, I decided to wander further and visit the morgue.

"You have choices."

I shook my head at the echo. Choosing to visit the morgue over the ER did not change my path.

Empty this late at night, the morgue at Mercy General was as ordinary as any other with increased security in a small portion of it. The "quarantine" area was for corpses that had been exposed to biohazards, infectious diseases, or faulty Andrus experiments. *Finally some honesty from me...*

A retinal scan allowed me to access this portion as it had for many other layers of the hospital. Lights flicked on as I entered. Instead of the usual twenty holding tombs like the larger morgue, this secure one had only six compartments—half of which were empty. The occupied tombs had a piece of yellow warning tape over the door hinge that would break when opened so that the pathologist could tell whether the contents had been disturbed after sealing. Tonight, three doors had tape. I put on the usual protective garb over my scrubs, including gloves and a mask. I normally only visited down here after I lost a patient. It had become habit to make sure that their remains were taken care of properly or claimed by family. I knew that the blue-eyed girl would still be here. No one would claim her. She was an experiment gone wrong.

Damn it, Shawnee, you could have prevented this, my thoughts hauntingly reminded me.

"I didn't know they were experimenting on kids. I swear I didn't. I thought the deformities were accidental side-effects of experiments on adults," I whispered to no one in particular.

That's no excuse.

"I know..."

My eyes welled up with tears. I reached for the handle to open the door to the first occupied compartment. I blinked them away when I heard the suction release and the hinges squeal. The first tray contained the remains of a young man in his early twenties. He had pox marks and necrotic flesh that spread across his torso with his ribs and spleen exposed. Cause of death: flesh eating bacteria, advanced stage, untreatable and beyond amputation. My guess was his vital organs had been consumed as well. I placed my gloved hand on his forehead. His last days were not very pleasant. He'd suffered.

I closed the man back inside his frozen tomb and moved to the next. This was where my girl was being kept. The affirmative energy ran up my arm when I broke the second seal and slid out the tray. I gasped and took a step back. The bones of the girl sat in a molten puddle of flesh, muscle, and dangling tendons. Her hair acted as a pillow while her eyes remained in their sockets, glazed over with death.

It broke my heart, and I cried for the little girl whose toe-tag read "Female Subject 519." My guilt turned to rage. I screamed and lunged for the gurney in the center of the room, overturning it along with several trays of medical instruments. I smashed jars, slides, and Petri dishes. Anger flowed through me, helping me to destroy everything that I was physically able to lift. I hated myself so much. I could have stopped this. I raged not only for the blue-eyed girl but for all of the children, animals, and werecreatures who were subjected to this desecration and torture.

I stormed back over to the tombs and began pulling open the remaining doors, slamming open every single tray. The last one was heavier than the rest. I gripped it hard and yanked. Slowly the wheels gained momentum, and the large tray slid out, stopping with a disgruntled thud. What I saw before me was sobering enough to replace my rage with abrupt sorrow. There lay a full-grown werewolf in beast form. His fur was dark brown except for the white tip on his once fluffy tail that matched a white stripe down the bridge of his long snout. His body scrawny and sunken. Attached to his pointed ear was the equivalent of a toe-tag that read "Feral Subject 520."

Tears rolled down my cheeks as my fingers found their way into the wolf's fur. Glancing between the little girl and the wolf, I spoke to them. "You are Gaia's warriors. Go together into her arms. Little one, you are to be called Born of the Sea, your eyes are the ocean and you, Beast, are called Liberation, you will lead other lost souls to freedom in Gaia. May your souls be at peace." I continued to cry and closed the bodies back into the tombs carefully. Reassembling the room helped piece myself back together.

The hospital was quiet by the time I emerged from its frozen depths. Only a few nurses scattered here and there, gossiping about their latest flings with doctors or other nurses. When I was safely inside my office, I sat down and pulled out an empty notebook. I began to write down some *interesting* cases I had seen over the last few months in an attempt to trace back the uprising of bizarre incidents. This would give me a time frame of when this hospital became infested by the Andrus and a distraction from the horror I had just witnessed. For tasks like this, my memory was keen.

2/13 Blue-eyed girl, dead beast
1/2 College woman covered in pus, oozing sores,
yellow eyes
12/9 Old man with no pulse walks out of ER
12/3 Woman mauled by "bear"
11/17 Zombie man (kept trying to bite faces)
10/31 Woman gives birth to puppies (how did I miss
that?)
10/30 Anxious man with chain-link burns
9/1 Meth addict screams of hexes, witches, genital torture
(maybe?)
8/8 Woman with puncture wounds to common
carotid artery
7/23 Baby with hypertrichosis
6/18 Mute woman with alopecia (maybe)

Eleven incidents in nine months. All of these patients were brought into the ER and, since I only frequent the ER randomly, that number should probably be multiplied by at least five. Andrus infestations are best tracked with ER statistics. When experiments go wrong and the subject is due to die, they are transported to emergency services from the containment cells—often found in the same hospital—so the ER staff will deal with the John and Jane Doe's, either with urgent care or disposal of unclaimed corpses. My hospital was officially infected.

And so was I.

CHAPTER THIRTEEN

Few doctors and staff had all-access passes to the hospital. I did. Doctor Reynolds did. So did Kurt. By process of elimination, it was safe to deduce that I had unknowingly been working for the Andrus. My heart was already broken, so it couldn't break again with this new knowledge.

I left work early, something I never did, and walked home with a cloud of despair dangling above me. My blindness, my blocking out, had gotten me into quite a rut. *You put on a good act as a doctor and hide behind your genius but someday, Shawnee, that's all going to fail, and you'll find yourself alone in a strange place, missing months of time because you let your panic and forgetfulness go unchecked,* Vanessa's voice echoed in my head.

She was right, in a way. My forced cluelessness had left me in a metaphorically strange place, missing months of time and feeling like a failure as a doctor. I was supposed to *help* people. That was the vow I made to myself many moons ago when I ran away from the reservation. I promised that I would break the cycle to protect and help as many people as I could. Because I chose not to help myself, I ended up hurting more people than I helped. What if I had been clear-minded? What if I was able to identify the threat and reach out to a large pack for help to reclaim the territory? What if I recognized sooner that the Andrus had infested Mercy General?

I took the long way home in an attempt to clear my head. I had to do *something*. The Andrus and Dr. Reynolds used me. They used my intelligence and my gifts to benefit these experiments and studies, or whatever it was they were doing. All those assignments that Dr. Reynolds gave me, what had they done? What was their purpose? What was that *serum*? What had it been so successful at doing?

My heart sank. I took a deep breath, puffing out my chest when I held it briefly. I never told him how I made the serum. *I never will.* I stomped up the steps to my apartment building and threw open the door. My anger took hold again as I stalked through the hall toward my apartment. I glanced over to Xany's door, noticing there were several collapsed boxes stacked near it, and remembered that she would be leaving soon to live with Caden and Mal in their newfound pack in Utah...

"Everyone has choices."

Mindlessly I fixed myself a bowl of cereal and sat down at the kitchen table, my thoughts haunted with visions of the deaths I witnessed and the list I had made of several others.

How stupid can you be, Shawnee? How stupid can you be to ignore the fact that a perfectly human woman gave birth to puppies on your table? What the fuck is wrong with you?

The thought left me nauseas and despairing. How could I have blocked that out? How could I be such a terrible person? I abandoned my cereal, ambled to the fridge, and grabbed the last beer. I nearly jumped out of my skin when a sharp knock interrupted my pity party. I slammed the door of the refrigerator and stalked over to the front door, jerking it open. Aggravation caused my movements to be rigid and tinged with anger. The moment she saw me, Xany's jubilant expression sunk.

"You look awful, Nee," she said without hesitation.

"Gee, thanks," I replied and made to crack open the

beer can. Xany snatched it out of my hand before I had a chance to get my fingernail under the metal ring.

"Drinking is bad for you." She invited herself into the kitchen, opened the beer, and poured it down the sink.

"Xany! That was my last one. What the hell?" I rushed over and grabbed her arm in attempt to save at least some of it. She pulled away from me and emptied the can. "Oh well, now you'll just have to deal with me instead." She tossed the can into the trash.

I wanted to smack her across the face so badly that my hand twitched with desire. The thought scared me and I felt the blood drain from my face. When did I become such a horrible person that I would consider smacking someone for taking away a beer? Emotions overwhelmed me as my vision swirled, darkening my periphery. Xany reached out to catch me on my way down to the floor.

"Whoa. Okay, let's go sit down, you're not passing out on me tonight." She tossed my arm around her neck, supporting me over to the sofa. Her warm body pressed against mine as tears welled up in my eyes.

Don't say a word.

Xany sat me down on the couch, cupping my face in her hands and forced me to look at her. "What is it? What happened?" she asked.

"I can't tell you," I whispered. My body trembled when the realization that I couldn't tell her or Vanessa anything without endangering them.

"Yes, you can, NeeNee. You can tell me anything." She brushed my hair away from my face.

"I'm a bad person," I leaked and tears began rolling down my cheeks.

"You're not a bad person, Shawnee," she argued, her voice still soft.

I watched her wrestle with the confusion of what was happening. Her brows furrowed as greenish eyes bore into me. She had no idea what she consoled me about, though she was trying her hardest to make me feel better. I didn't believe what she said. I *was* a bad person. I had done bad things.

"I need to shower." I sniffled and wobbled to my feet.

"How about a bath instead, that way you won't have to stand," she suggested when I reached the bathroom. I nodded and nearly tumbled into the bathtub when turning on the faucet. Xany caught me and turned the water on herself.

"Careful, NeeNee."

It was easier to listen to her when I felt like this. Out of control, desperate, and scared.

This is our secret. If you tell your mother, I will kill her then I will kill you.

My father's voice echoed in my head. The similarities in the situations had me sobbing. I was trapped, and I couldn't ask for help without hurting someone else.

Xany turned to me when she heard me cry and helped me remove my scrubs. Normally, I would never let anyone do this. I would never let anyone touch me, remove my clothes, or see me naked—except for Vanessa. As soon as the hot water surrounded me, my breathing slowed down. I grabbed the bar of soap and began scrubbing my arms and hands. My hands had caused the hurt by creating things. I couldn't scrub my brain for thinking it up so my hands had to suffer the wrath. Xany watched me then offered me a washcloth. Her gaze lingered on the scar on my lower abdomen.

"That's a big scar." Her normally boisterous voice now barely a whisper.

Hearing her pulled me further away from my panic and my brain started to work again. I nodded to her.

"My daddy told me that scars aren't always bad things," she added, her expression lifting when she noticed she had my attention.

"How are scars not bad?" I asked, pulling my knees up to my chest while watching her. She distracted me, and I liked it. She distracted me like Vanessa did.

"My dad said that scars serve purposes. A scar means we survived a battle because, if we didn't have a scar, we might be dead instead. And he said that scars are naturally more sensitive because they're new skin. If you touch a scar gently it can feel nice, or tickle a little." She giggled as if being tickled herself. Her juvenile nature soothed me, making her appear less threatening.

"Battle scars. Like that story," I said, resting my chin on my knee.

"Uh-huh. It's a story about the Trail of Tears, how some people died and others had battle scars that made them more in tune with Gaia or something like that. I don't remember much of it," she added.

I nodded because I recognized what she referred to even though the whole story had been lost to me as well. "My mom used to tell me stories like that."

"My dad too," she said and then used her cupped hands to rinse the soap off my arms and back. "Feel better?"

"A bit," I admitted. "Just tired."

"C'mon." Xany lifted a towel from the hook beside the shower and held it open for me. "Before you get pruney." Xany's giggle echoed against the bathroom walls.

I surveyed her a bit before pulling the plug and covering my breasts with my arms. She let go to allow me to wrap the towel around myself once I stepped into it.

"I'll wait outside while you finish up." She stepped out of the bathroom, glancing over her shoulder as she closed the door behind her.

The only clothes I had in the bathroom were my usual worn-out T-shirts and sweatpants. I slipped into them and tied my hair back into a messy ponytail before entering my bedroom to see Xany sitting on the bed patiently. Patience looked different on her, like a tomboy wearing a dress for the first time. It suited Xany best to be buzzing and bouncing around intrusively. When she saw me, she patted the bed for me to join her. I stacked a few pillows by the headboard and lay down next to her in a slightly upright position, my hand naturally resting on my stomach. My thoughts lingered on my scar.

Xany continued on the same train of thought. "How did you get it?"

"My father." Part of me wanted to tell her the truth. The more I harbored my memories, the more my hatred for them grew. And hatred for my father. Vanessa always encouraged me to talk, to open my mouth, rather than to relive it on my own, but I just couldn't. I knew that holding back contributed to my panic attacks, but what else was I supposed to do? Talking isn't as easy as it sounds.

"Was he the reason you left the reservation?" She frowned.

I nodded, glancing at her. The urge to talk burned inside me, pressing unspoken words against my lips. I couldn't tell her about the Andrus because that would put her in danger, but I could tell her about...about the things I'd told Vanessa. My father was long gone and couldn't hurt anyone anymore.

Xany paused before asking the next question. Her hesitation made it obvious she was deliberately cautious to not press too far. "How did it happen?"

"I ran from him and fell... There was...um...a broken skiing pole near the trailer, and he grabbed it and hit me with it. Caught me in the stomach. I had fifty-eight stitches, I think," I answered, glancing up at her. The anxiety began to rise in my chest again. "Talking about it makes me scared." I bit my lip, freaking myself out with not only the bit of story but with the honesty following it.

"He can't hurt you now. Watch this." She moved closer to me, lifting up my shirt and tugging down the waist of my sweats to expose the scar. I gasped when a fresh round of fear flooded me.

"Don't, don't..." I gripped the bedding tightly, clenching my teeth.

"Trust me?" she pleaded, putting one hand on my

cheek and laying down beside me. When she was no longer above me, I calmed down.

Did I trust her? Not really. But I nodded anyway. I think she knew I lied, but that didn't stop her. Xany placed the tip of her finger on my scar and dragged it upward toward my navel. I braced myself, expecting to feel pain, or fright, or something negative. Instead, it just made my stomach twitch, and I startled. Xany giggled.

"Pay attention," she said.

I guess my expression looked distracted, and she did it again. This time I squirmed and smacked her hand automatically. She snickered and grinned at me.

"See? It tickles, right?"

Again, she touched my scar, and this time I smiled but pushed her away impishly.

"Not fair." Her playfulness lifted my mood a bit. Sometimes I forgot what *fun* felt like. My friendship with Vanessa always seemed so serious. Xany was different. I was beginning to appreciate her immaturity.

Xany giggled continuously and bopped me with a pillow. "No more hurt, just tickles."

She was right; tickles didn't hurt. I turned on my side to face her and pulled a blanket over me. Fatigue crippled me, which was often the product when my anxiety lifted. She watched me with a light smile.

"Want me to stay with you while you sleep?"

I thought about it before responding. "No talking."

"Yes, ma'am, no talking during *sleepovers*." Xany giggled.

I smiled, and Xany turned out the light. It was weird to feel safe with someone who wasn't Vanessa. That night, sleep washed over me with ease.

CHAPTER FOURTEEN

I woke up alone the next morning. The morning sun set a warm, soft glow across the linens. The pillow beside mine held Xany's imprint. I glanced out the window and guessed it was around 9:00 A.M. Rolling out of bed, I ran my fingers through my hair and looked around. I paused a moment because I didn't remember dreaming, which was strange because I dreamed almost every night. It was different. There was no explanation for it other than just *different*, and quiet... Much quieter than usual.

I found Xany in the kitchen, cooking something that made my mouth water when the odor hit my nose. Bacon and toast mixed with something else.

"Morning, sleepyhead. I made breakfast. You had no food in your house. So I ran home to get whatever I had." She grinned and waved me over to her.

It amused me that both Vanessa and Xany had officially used my kitchen more than I had. Cereal was my food of choice for all meals and didn't require any sort of appliance to make. I gazed over her shoulder as she cooked a ham and cheese omelet in cookware that wasn't mine either.

"You brought your own pans?" I asked.

"All you had was a small sauce pan. And cereal." Xany

giggled, patting me on the shoulder as if saying, "there, there."

I smirked, amused by Xany's critique of my cooking supplies. "Can I help?"

"Sure, the bacon is done. You can take it to the table." She nodded toward the plate perched on the counter beside the stove. The red cookware stood out against my murky gray cabinets.

Xany's eyes remained on me as I reached over for the dish and brought it to the table. "What?" I asked.

"Hmm?"

"You're looking at me funny." I crossed my arms over my stomach protectively.

"Only for a second." Xany grinned as she slid the omelet onto a big dish and carried it to the table.

"That doesn't make me feel any better. You know that, right?" Orange juice sloshed into the glasses as I poured out two. The glasses didn't belong to me either. Silently, I wondered if Xany had snuck off to go shopping, otherwise her house was pretty well stocked with food and dishes. Xany's everlasting giggle continued while she sliced the omelet into triangles, serving me first.

"Just being honest."

"Noted." I stared at the food on my plate. Admitting that I was still suspicious of Xany might come across as rude, so I remained quiet. I didn't exactly have the best track record of keeping trustworthy people in my life.

"What's wrong? Think I'm going to poison you?" She took a bite of bacon. Xany never missed a trick. She seemed alert to nearly every gesture, slight change in expression, or shift in mood that I had.

"Nothing, *nothing*," I answered too quickly, keeping my gaze averted.

"Eesh," she said and took a bite of her own food, then switched her dish with mine. She gazed at me from under a risen brow. I held my breath for about five seconds before blurting out,

"You're an empath."

"That would be cool." She ate some of the omelet on the new plate, shrugging as she sprinkled some crunched up bacon on top of the filled fork.

"You *are* an empath, aren't you?" I accused, leaning forward a bit. Xany merely smiled and kept on eating. "That's why...that's why you've been following me around and being so pushy and everything isn't it?"

"I'm *always* pushy." She put a few pieces of bacon onto my plate.

"That's not fair. You can tell how I feel and what I think."

"It's not like I do it on purpose, Nee, and you know it," she defended. "Just eat and don't be rude. And empaths aren't mind readers you know."

"No, I'm not going to eat. You've been following me around because I'm some sort of empath magnet with a shit history and scars to go along with it." I thumped my hand down on the table.

Xany frowned. "And what if I *wasn't* an empath? What would you say then?"

"I... I don't know." I was so intent on being angry with her for hiding her empathy that the idea she might not be an empath had me feeling guilty for my upsurge of anger.

"I'm not an empath, Nee, at least not officially. Is it so hard to believe that someone can actually care without having to have some sort of gift or hidden agenda?" she asked, tilting her head to the side.

"I'm sorry, I didn't mean to accuse you. Yes, it's hard to believe."

"Well, shame on you. I can just tell. It doesn't take an empath to notice when someone is scared," she said.

I took a small bite of bacon and smiled when the salty crispness melted in my mouth. "Can't remember the last time I had bacon."

"You probably had it yesterday." She giggled, shoving my shoulder playfully.

"Xany!" I laughed and tossed a piece at her. "Probably right though."

She grinned at me and dodged it. "Mhmm. See. I learn quickly."

A surge of affection for Xany hit me like a brick wall, followed by a sudden glumness. "When are you leaving?" Of course, someone I grew interested in becoming friends with would leave after sharing barely a few hours together.

"On Friday. Caden bought a truck, and they're driving out to pick up some of my stuff."

"Friday?" I tried to hide my frown by taking a sip of juice. Was I really upset that Xany was going to be leaving? A few weeks ago, I wished she would disappear and leave me alone, and now I wished she wouldn't.

"Mhmm." She paused and served herself a bit more omelet. "You can still come you know."

"I... I can't... With work," I stammered. "And Vanessa won't be able to live close being surrounded by wolves." I knew I was making up excuses before the words even left my lips.

"Vanessa can bend. She can go anywhere she wants. And they have hospitals in Utah, probably bigger ones too." She watched me over her juice glass.

I tried to keep my expression as blank as possible. "I just can't."

"Okay. Just offering you a choice. Mal and Caden aren't like typical dominants. Caden's really laid back and protective, and Mal just likes being in the woods. Other than me, he doesn't boss people around. That's part of the reason why they both left Caden's dad's pack in California. That pack is so bossy and strict."

There was that word again: *choice.* "Why did you leave the pack?" I asked. I'd finished my breakfast and made the effort to turn the conversation back to Xany's life instead of mine.

"I never joined." She shrugged, tapping her fork against her lip. "My parents were part of a small pack around

Cheyenne when I was growing up, and then they moved to Florida when I turned fourteen. My mom didn't want me to end up a baby-making machine at such a young age. Mal got to stay with Caden since they went to high school together while I had to move to blue-hair-ville. I think they even had their Firsting together," she said, rolling her shoulders after. I noticed that whenever Xany dismissed something that could be a big deal she shrugged. "Once I turned eighteen, I made my way back to Wyoming." She grinned at me, then continued. "When Caden's dad moved the pack to California, Caden and Mal came up with the idea of helping the Lost Ones," she ended and downed the rest of her juice.

"Why are you joining one now?" Breeders didn't usually separate from the protection of a pack. I couldn't help my curiosity.

She shrugged again. "Why not? And plus Caden's cute and Mal won't boss me around too much anymore. Utah has better work than here. I could probably make more money there."

"What if Caden bosses you around?"

"He's not like that. He doesn't give orders. He makes suggestions and waits for feedback. He always has." She grinned proudly.

"Caden is a strange dominant. He'll make an interesting Alpha. Mal seems..."

"Feral? He is. He's closer to his beast than most. Caden has really good control of his own beast and helps Mal with his. They're kind of a pair like that."

"Like an Alpha and Beta."

"Uh-huh." A smile curved her plumps lips. "Mal has always been closer to his beast. He's closer to Gaia too. My dad said it's because he was born under a full moon. It makes him more in tune with things."

"That makes sense," I said, thoughtfully, as I pondered Mal's predicament. Something about him kept me interested. Maybe it was his feralness. Or maybe something else. "Did he ever get into trouble because of his beast?"

"No, not really. He's just a really strong fighter and likes to go for the kill all the time. Caden is more for umm... What's that word? Subjuctatering, or something."

"Subjugation," I corrected.

"Yeah, that. Caden has strong will, and he would rather have his enemies fear him than kill them, especially other wolves or people who have the power to change. Caden says killing isn't the way to solve the world's problems."

"That's pretty honorable. But don't you think he would use his will to make his pack submissive too?"

"No, because he knows what it feels like to be overpowered like that. He says that a pack is there to be a team, and each member supports the next. Breeders should be cherished because without Breeders there would be no werecreatures to begin with. He really believes that." A dream expression veiled her features, widening her pupils and smoothing her brow.

"It's a little bit hard to believe. I mean, I can see he is different just by the fact he allowed a weretiger into a room full of wolves and Breeders, and that he listened to our suggestions." I bit my lip. I didn't necessarily want to believe that Caden was a good guy. I hadn't met many good guys.

"He *is* very different." She smiled at me and gave me the last piece of bacon before taking a few dishes to the kitchen.

"Do you think you'll be happy there in a pack?" I asked, gathering soiled utensils and following her into the kitchen.

"I think so. I can always come back if I want to. But I won't know until I try." She shrugged as we cleaned the kitchen together.

"Guess you're right." I focused on drying the dishes while Xany washed. Friday was only two days away. In two days, she would be gone, and I would probably never see her, Caden, or Mal again. "I better get ready for work. I've got to be there in an hour."

"Awww, I was having fun." Xany pouted while I stacked the dry dishes on the counter. "I quit working at the Double D a few days ago. No loss there."

"The old men will miss grabbing *your* double Ds." I smirked.

She giggled, shimmying her breasts side to side. "They'll find something new to get their rocks off with."

I laughed at her as I wiped off the table. "You're ridiculous. And thanks for breakfast."

"Any time." She grinned. "Don't ask me to make any other meal though. I'm not the greatest chef. Breakfast is easiest."

"Maybe I'll see you when I get home."

"Hope so." She bounced forward and gave me a hug.

I cringed at first before patting her on the back awkwardly. She sniggered at my return gesture before breaking the hug and prancing toward the door.

"Don't stare at any leeches while I'm gone," I called after her, and I heard her crack up as she skipped down the hall.

CHAPTER FIFTEEN

I rushed to work after Xany left hoping that Doctor Reynolds would still be away at the conference. The desire to find the root of the Andrus infestation burned inside me. I had to do something before it got any worse.

Just before I arrived at the hospital, I pulled out my mobile phone and called Vanessa.

"Hi, Shawnee," she said when she picked up.

"Hi," I replied stiffly, chickening out on what I had planned to say to begin with.

"Are you okay?" she asked. I could hear music in the background, which meant that she was probably at work. The music faded away when I assumed that she moved to a different room.

"I'm okay. I, umm...will probably be working late tonight so I wanted to tell you that," I said awkwardly.

"You...work late every night." She sounded confused.

"I feel bad about being rude to you. I'm sorry I always push you away. I don't mean to do that," I blurted out, closing my eyes to stop tears from falling.

"I know you don't mean it, Shawnee. *Are* you okay? You sound different. I'm coming over in a minute, all right?" Concern flooded her voice.

"No, no... I'm fine. I'm about to go into work. I just wanted to say that. I wanted you to know it, okay?" I gulped back the lump that rose in throat. Being honest with Vanessa wasn't something I was accustomed to.

"Okay..." She paused. "I'll come over tonight after work, all right? You can tell me what you need to tell me then."

"Okay." I hesitated, then added, "Thanks."

"For what?"

I knew I needed to get off the phone quickly before she had a chance to ask any more questions. "I dunno, just thanks. See you tonight."

"Bye, Shawnee."

"Bye."

I held my breath as I put the phone back into my pocket.

You can't tell her. You can't tell anyone.

"I know... I know I can't."

Early afternoon at Mercy General meant shift change. Some of the staff waved to me on their way past. With as much politeness as I could muster, I nodded and joined in small talk, if nothing else than for the illusion of normalcy. The minute I found an opening to escape, I made a beeline for my office to check e-mail. No news from Doctor Reynolds. I hadn't seen Kurt in several days either. To be sure, I checked the lab and the logbooks to see if he had signed in. The last time he signed in for a shift was several days earlier. So now all I had to do was bide my time until midnight.

For the first few hours, I spent time down in the lab reviewing some of the assignments that Dr. Reynolds and I had worked on. The most frustrating thing was the lack of details he provided me. He would present me with a task, and I completed it. Stop this reaction, create this one, destroy this hair follicle, create a new one, map this genetic sequence, match this DNA strand, etc. There was a reason for his ambiguity, and now I knew what it was.

I sifted through a few of the file folders where Dr. Reynolds kept failed experiments—he didn't have a folder for successful ones—and carried them over to the tray used for soaking items. I dropped the file folders in it. Searching the chemical closet was the easiest part of my plan. I snatched a large bottle of sulfuric acid from it and toted it over to my soon-to-be victims. With caution, I poured it over the files. After a while, the stack of paper resembled a pile of wet toilet tissue.

You're on a suicide mission, you know that right?

Andrus-infected hospitals lacked security save for general security guards and cameras in the ER or outside the hospital. None of the high security areas allowed cameras or audio equipment. The Andrews had decades of experience weaving themselves into work environments. This required complete enmeshment. The risk of audio and visual equipment, even if their own people monitored it, opened doors for more corruption and blackmail. Recordings have a way of ending up in the wrong hands. Any employee of the Andrus would be more than willing to take a bribe for a glimpse at the experiments. And besides, preternatural creatures had a way of distorting video equipment. It's part of the magics.

After my game of destruction in the lab, I made my way through the ER and checked on a few admitted patients. Nothing out of the ordinary seemed to happen in my absence. A young boy with a broken wrist after a skateboard trick down a flight of stairs, an older woman who fell while getting the mail, and a man bitten by a pit bull was the extent of it. I checked up on the latter. The man had a nice bite mark on his inner thigh. He was happy it wasn't farther north.

Back in my office, I was somewhat astounded at the clarity of my thinking. How I was focused on my task and determined to do my part to let the Andrus know that they were discovered despite the consequences to me. What did *I* matter to them anyway? If I disappeared from here, they wouldn't bother with me. I was as replaceable as the next doctor with a knack for chemistry. I took the files from my office, stacked them up, and began feeding each sheet into the shredder one at a time. My heart thudded in my chest.

When I was finished shredding anything that could potentially contain harmful information, I sat back in my chair and looked around my office. It was sparse, with a few medical books on a shelf and several diplomas on the wall. The diplomas and awards were the only hint of me that actually existed in here, not unlike my apartment. At home I had one trunk full of sentimental items and at work all I had were my diplomas. Not much to show for a rather successful career.

I listened to the sound of the clock ticking, counting down the minutes, and wondered what my mother would think of what I was doing. Would she approve? Would she try to stop me?

I don't know why I'm being so cocky about all of this. I could potentially fail at finding the containment cells and even if I did find them, then what? What is the plan?

I gulped, being reminded of Mal and Caden's plan for rescuing Lost Ones. What if I found a half dozen werewolf cubs? Breeders? Feral-borns? What was I going to do then? Okay, so maybe Caden was not the only one with poor planning skills... But, unlike Caden, I wasn't as lucky. I had already initiated this plan by destroying those files. If Dr. Reynolds came back and found the files destroyed before I was able to help those being held, their lives might be in even greater jeopardy.

Idiot.

There was no going back now.

The hospital was nearly silent at midnight on a Thursday. The weekends were usually busier. There was less nursing staff available and many of the on-call doctors were probably catching a few hours sleep or getting something to eat. I casually went to the private elevator and completed the usual retinal scan. When the doors closed, I examined the number pad. I doubted that the containment cells were going to be on the top floor. I rationalized and hit *B* for *Basement* as my first choice. Taking a deep breath, I began my descent into the unknown.

There were no security guards down here. There was no need; the private elevator only allowed full-access staff to use it. When the elevator stopped in the basement, it opened into something that resembled a warehouse, lit with dim yellow floodlights, some of which were blinking with exhaustion. There were boxes of medical supplies stacked high to the ceiling and a random scattering of old, battered, or broken medical equipment stashed here and there. It was damp and dreary. I nearly jumped out of my skin when the closing elevator door shuddered. With my arms wrapped around myself, I walked the length of the basement between the large boxes and metal towers. It was silent other than a few random drips from a leaking pipe in the distance.

A deep breath calmed me, and I continued walking around, weaving in and out of the aisles, just waiting for the moment when something would jump out and scare the piss out of me. I began to hum softly to help keep me focused. When I made it to the other side of the basement, I found nothing but a cold concrete wall. A heavy sigh escaped my lips, and I decided that maybe the best thing to do was to follow the wall all the way around in hope of finding a door. The basement was nearly the full size of the hospital. When I had walked for a good five minutes, I paused.

"Okay, think, Shawnee. There's got to be an entrance down here. We're only partially underground," I said softly, then the thought struck me. *Partially underground...* The containment cells would undoubtedly be *below* ground.

I started walking again, and this time I kept my eyes on the soiled, damp floor. My sneakers treaded on dust and dirt, making distinct tracks in the shape of their soles.

When I turned the corner, suddenly my footprints were not the only ones on the ground. I hurriedly followed the trail of footprints down the narrow aisle, keeping my eyes peeled on the ground for any hints of shifts in direction when—*Wham!* My head crashed into a tall wooden crate.

"Shit." I rubbed it, blinked a few times, and took a step back to get the trail again. The footprints led right into the crate that I had just walked into. I frowned and looked around it to see if it was moveable, shoving it with a grunt.

Of course that didn't work.

The crate was a good two feet taller than me so this time I tried opening it. I pulled at the corner, then pushed it, huffing when nothing happened. How could footprints lead directly *into* a crate? It was too heavy to move and didn't have a door. And then it hit me. I looked up toward the top of the crate and grinned. I grabbed hold of it and feverishly pulled myself up to stand. I thumped around on top. Surprisingly it sounded rather solid.

Think, Shawnee; remember very large creatures need to fit into this entrance, I told myself.

I walked around on top of the crate until I heard a creaking sound when I stepped on a certain spot. That area was hollow. I bent down and used my fingers to pry it open and nearly fell backward when I heard the sudden hiss of hydraulics releasing. The top of several crates opened simultaneously and the entire structured folded and disappeared into the floor. The now open space revealed a full concrete staircase that went down into a deep dark abyss.

"Clever," I muttered.

I thought about this perfectly disguised staircase that no one would ever think to look for inside a stack of immovable crates. It was probably only a temporary entrance, which validated that the Andrus had only just begun to infest the hospital. I took a deep breath and began my descent, counting the steps down and bracing myself with both hands on one wall. I cursed myself for not bringing a flashlight.

Thirty-eight steps led me downstairs. The width of the chamber was about ten feet across to allow for very large creatures to be carried down. I took my cell phone out of my pocket and used the display screen as a light source. Up ahead I saw a blue light blinking and hurried toward it. The sound of my feet crunching on concrete suddenly changed. A mix of worry and fear sent shivers up my spine. The size of the blue light grew until it was right in front of my nose. My hands guided my chin placement on the spot for the retinal scan. I held my breath, hoping it would work. The blue light scanned my eyes. Simultaneously, the door at the top of the stairs slammed, while a metal door directly ahead opened with a hiss. Bright lights blinded me as the lair came alive. I pocketed my cell phone and walked inside, my mouth hanging open at the sight before me.

The containment area was completely white, kind of like the television room in *Willy Wonka and the Chocolate Factory*. The floors were made up of pristine white tiles that matched the white walls. The surface of the tiles was dull to prevent reflection. It was spotlessly clean and dry. I took a step inside and to my left was a huge gurney and medical equipment similar to that of an emergency room. To the right was a giant refrigeration unit, emitting a low, droning hum. Ahead of me was an endless hallway.

I took another breath and began to walk down it. My belly started to ache. It was silent except for my footsteps. The white walls turned into thick, multilayer matted glass, or something of the sort. Just as I turned to look in one of the glass-covered cells, I heard a loud, threatening growl echo through the entire place. I spun around to see where it was coming from, clutching my chest. I saw nothing and tried to calm my breathing. There were six containment units. I walked toward the growling. Each unit contained either a big mattress and bedding or something of the sort, like stacks of hay. I couldn't smell anything except bleach and cleaners, probably meant to dull the senses of any captive werecreature. The growling continued to grow louder while I walked. The three units to my left were completely empty, as were two on my right.

When I reached the sixth unit on the right side, I screamed as a full-grown werewolf lunged for the glass. I fell backward and scuttled away, using my arms and legs in a crab walk. The werewolf roared, growled, and clawed at the glass. He was standing on his back legs in beast form like both werecats and werewolves do while fighting. They were agile, giant beasts that could walk on four legs or two depending on need. The thudding and banging against the glass was quieter than it should have been, and the fact that the glass was tough enough to withstand the assault of a full-grown, frenzied werewolf surprised me. I had no idea what the material was made of, but it was effective enough to keep this raging wolf captive. I stood slowly and held both hands up to the beast, dropping my head into a bow.

"Shhh...easy. I'm not here to hurt you, but I need you to calm down."

The wolf tilted its giant head to the side for a second before lashing out at the glass again—snapping with large, salivating jaws and bearing its fangs. Startled, I took a step back.

Easy, Shawnee, he's contained. He's contained. I tried to comfort myself and took another step toward the beast. "Shhh, it's okay. I can help you, but you need to calm down," I repeated, and the beast paused its roaring, tilting its head in the opposite direction. "Yes, that's it, listen to me. I'm here to help," I pleaded.

He lowered his head enough to look me in the face. The fur on his back stood straight up—all the way down his spine to the tip of the tail—making him look larger than the ten feet he already was. I took another step closer to the cell when he did so and instead of remaining calm, he tossed his head back again and roared, thrashing angrily against the glass and yanking against the silver chain that was around his rear ankle. I frowned, realizing not only was this beast in a frenzy, but it was probably in a lot of pain too. Pure silver was toxic to almost all werecreatures, but werewolves suffered the most in particular. Wounds caused by silver healed slowly and were usually grossly infected. A werewolf held captive in silver could die over time from the poisoning it caused. The beast balled up his front paw into a fist of claws and punched full force at the glass, which simply waivered at the jolt. I sucked in my breath.

"That's enough!" I shouted, looking him right in the eye. A dangerous and desperate move, to say the least, that could backfire on me if he wasn't weak enough to tolerate a stare down from a Breeder. "Calm down!"

The beast kept my gaze. He stared me down. My shoulders began to slump, my body began to submit.

"No," I said through clenched teeth. "Let me help you. Sit *down*!" I said with a final shout, breaking away from the hunched position and standing straight. I watched him fall backward with a loud thump on the ground. He looked at me, confused but silent. *Did I just subdue a frenzied werewolf?*

Pay attention! Now's your chance.

"That's better." I walked to the glass, putting both my hands on it. "Listen to me, you need to shift. Be human," I demanded.

He narrowed his eyes at me and moved around, sitting on his haunches and crossing his immense arms over his chest in defiance.

"Oh, no you don't. I can't help you like this. You have to trust me!" I said, the reality of time setting in. I had been down here for at least an hour, if not more, and it was getting riskier by the minute.

The beast curled his upper lip, revealing his fangs in distaste, and made a gruff, yarp, grrrup sound while moving his jaws. My brain translated without thinking.

"You should trust me because..." He was right, why

should he trust me? I looked just like the people who had put him here. Then the idea popped into my head. "You should trust me because I am one of yours," I said and pulled up the sleeve of my scrub top, showing him the glyph on my upper arm. He dropped his arms immediately and rushed to the glass. His eyes were wide, and he put both battered paws against the glass in desperation. The sight of my glyph sobered him.

"Yes, yes. Now shift, be human. Please hurry. I know you're hungry and hurt, but I can't help you like this, it's too risky. Please..." I begged. "If you shift, the chain will fall off," I added, getting the sense that the werewolf had been too scared to shift to a more vulnerable form since containment.

I watched as the beast closed his eyes and his breathing began to slow. I pleaded with Gaia to grant him grace and clarity enough to make a quick, painless shift. In less than a minute, there was a naked young man in front of me. He was a pale-skinned, blond-haired twenty-something-year-old who looked scrawny and scared.

"What's your name?" I asked him.

"Bailey..." he said with a raspy voice. "Bailey Owens."

"Okay, Bailey, I'm Shawnee. We're going to get you out of here and get you something to eat. But you need to keep the beast in check until I find food, all right? Get away from that silver," I instructed. I could almost taste his fear.

"Okay," he said and stepped away from the silver, moving as close to the glass as he could.

"Any idea how to open this cell?"

"Yes...yes." He coughed and I watched his hands tremble with the adrenaline that was rushing through him. "Behind that panel." He raised a shaky hand and pointed.

I followed his finger and went to the panel, prying it open. It was behind the same strong glass, probably to protect it from accidentally being triggered.

"Okay. I need to get you food first before I let you out,

or your beast will be tempted. You know this, right?"

He nodded. "Sorry. I'm already thinking about eating you."

"You're forgiven. I'll be right back." I patted the glass to reassure him and rushed back toward the entrance, remembering the large refrigerator and guessing that was where they were keeping the food. I hoped it had food and not corpses. I pulled open the fridge and beamed when I saw large racks of chilled meat, mainly deer and cheap leftover butcher cuts. I grabbed a nearby cart with wheels, started tossing as much meat on it as I could, then hurried back to Bailey with the full cart. When he saw the food, he stood immediately, and I saw his blue eyes flash yellow.

"Ready?" I bit my lip knowing that his beast would have to choose between me and the cold meat. Bailey nodded, salivating as he eyed the meat. I backed away from the glass and left the cart. I pressed the panel button marked "6," and the glass slowly began to descend into the floor. When it was halfway down, Bailey leaped over it and began devouring the meat in human form. Again, he changed into his beast with bones popping and snapping in and out of place to restructure his skeleton. The werewolf tore apart the meat, bones and all, in large gulps at first, then began to slow down. I held my breath and tried very hard not to move. When there was almost nothing left on the cart, Bailey shifted back down to human form and wiped his mouth on his arm, cracking his neck and shoulders from the discomfort of shifting consecutively.

"Better?" I sounded winded, even to me.

"Much. Thank you. It's been a while." He stood a bit straighter, his strength slowly returning.

"We need to get you some clothes, bandage that ankle, and get the hell out of here before they get back. Can you walk?"

"Yes," he answered quickly. "They've been gone for... I don't know. I can't tell how long it's been, but long enough for me to be really hungry."

"At least a week. C'mon." I rushed with him over to the area with the gurney and searched around for some bandages and whatever I could find to sterilize his wound. I found a first aid kit and peroxide. "Sit up on the table. This is going to sting badly, but it's the best we've got."

Bailey nodded and sat down. I poured half the bottle on his ankle, and he sucked in his breath while his chest rumbled. I did my best to ignore it and smeared his ankle in antibiotic ointment and wrapped it in gauze and tape. "Okay. Clothes...clothes." I looked around quickly and saw a single lab coat hanging on a hook beside the medicine cabinet.

"All right, okay, we can do this."

Bailey watched me quietly. I grabbed the lab coat and then slipped out of my scrubs, tossing them to him. "Put these on, and hurry." Bailey slid quickly into my scrubs, and I was left wearing bike shorts and a white T-shirt. I buttoned up the lab coat and tossed a stethoscope around my neck. "This will do for me." I went over and grabbed the scrub-in kit from beside the sink and took out three hair caps and handed them to him. "One on each foot, and then one on your head. Quickly."

Bailey grinned when he understood the plan and hurriedly dressed himself as a surgical assistant. I tossed a few pens in the pocket of his scrubs and put my identification tag on my lab coat. I looked around for anything that would help Bailey blend in more and grabbed a pair of glasses that were lying on a table beside a magnifying glass.

"Put these on your head over the cap. That's good enough. Let's go. Don't stop to talk to anyone, just follow me."

"You're a bossy Breeder. I like it," he teased.

"Thank you. When I tell you to run, you run. I don't care who you have to freak out in the mean time. Just run. Run like your Firsting, got it?" I turned to him, staring directly into his big, blue eyes. My heart leaped. They reminded me of my blue-eyed girl.

"Got it. Run like my Firsting." He slid off the gurney.

I grabbed his hand and tugged him toward the door, which opened automatically when we approached. We rushed up the stairs. Bailey could see perfectly so he ended up guiding me part of the way, and when we came to the fake ceiling, we pushed. The crate top released the hydraulics and swung open.

"Do you have a place to run to? A family? A pack?" I asked as we raced to the elevator.

"Yes, a pack. My family's pack. What's the date?" We skidded into the elevator.

"February 24th." I hit the button for the first floor and dimly realized today was my birthday...

"I've been gone for over a month." He sighed. "They probably think I'm dead."

"You almost were." I looked up at him. "We'll be getting out near the ER and then I'll walk you to my office. Follow my lead. If anyone asks, you're a shadowing intern preparing for a surgical residency, got it?"

"Got it." He took a breath and so did I. When the doors opened, we walked slowly out of the elevator.

"You'll do a rotation in the ER eventually as well. It's always best to have a well-rounded internship experience," I babbled before we disappeared into my office, and then whispered, "Sit in the chair and act interested. The nurses don't recognize you so they're being nosy." Bailey nodded, and I handed him my business card and smiled. We sat for a minute or two before getting up again and shaking hands. Bailey mimicked my expression, and I walked toward the door, waving for him to follow. "I'll show you the way out. Be careful on your way home, it's cold out there." We walked toward the main entrance of the hospital. The nurses had lost interest. I paused and grabbed Bailey's elbow just before we got to the outside surveillance cameras.

"There's cameras. Run, don't look back. Don't come back. Just, go." I shoved him, fully knowing my effort to push a werecreature with the density of a stone wall would be useless.

He nodded and then hesitated. "Thank you."

I nodded to him, crossing my arms over my chest. "Go now."

Bailey turned and bolted from the hospital at whirlwind speed. I held my breath and watched him disappear around the corner of the hospital. If I wasn't mistaken, I could have sworn I saw him do a back flip before he disappeared into the patch of woods at the end of the road.

When I returned to my office, I removed the diplomas from the walls and tucked them into my gym bag. I dropped my lab coat on the floor, then set my name tag, stethoscope, and a note down on my desk...

I resign.

-Shawnee

CHAPTER SIXTEEN

I walked home, wearing only my bike shorts and T-shirt in near freezing temperatures. My teeth chattered. The reality of what I had just done started to sink in. I collapsed on the steps to my apartment and sat there in silence.

What have I done?

I saved a life.

You're just lucky there was only one wolf in those cells.

"I know... I know..."

"Shawnee," I heard a voice from behind me say. "Shawnee." This time it was followed by a hand on my shoulder. "I've been waiting for you."

When I recognized Vanessa's voice, I stood and lunged into her arms, which was something I'd never done before. She caught and held me tight, wrapping my legs around her waist.

"Hey, it's okay. What happened? Where are your clothes?" She picked up my bag from the steps and carried me up to the apartment. One of the tenants leaving the building did a double-take when he saw the slender-framed Vanessa carrying me effortlessly. We entered my apartment, and I looked over her shoulder to see that there were a few black garbage bags outside of Xany's door. Vanessa toted me to the sofa and sat down with me in her lap, rubbing my back and legs to warm me up.

"You're freezing," she said. "And I can hear your heart racing. Tell me what happened, Shawnee, did someone hurt you?" Her voice quivered. I thought she was worried about potentially having to hear another horror story.

"No." My breath rushed in and out of my lungs. "I'm... I'm okay." I spoke into her shoulder. She squeezed me tight and buried her face in my hair, then jerked back.

"Dog! You smell like dog, but not like Xany's dogs." She frowned. "And meat, and... freezer burn."

"I...there was an injured wolf in the ER tonight." I had no idea how I was going to keep all these secrets from her.

"Lie." She frowned as she blew my story out of the water.

"I quit my job." I countered with the truth.

"What?" Her fingers gripped my hips.

"I quit. I... I've been thinking about things, and working there isn't good for me anymore." I told her more of the truth. I hadn't been thinking about it for long, but it was the truth regardless.

"Shawnee...are you sure that was the best decision?" Her voice sounded hesitant, as if she didn't want to sway me one way or another.

"I'm really sure." I held my breath, anticipating her next question.

"Then why are you riddled with fear? And smelling of foreign dog?"

I bit my lip. "Did you mean it when you said you could visit me anywhere, no matter where it is?"

"Of course, Shawnee. I go to Ireland every day." She grinned proudly.

"Promise?"

"Yes, of course I promise." She touched my face for a moment, purring loudly. She let her hand slide down my neck, over the side of my breast and stomach to settle on my thigh. I smiled because it tickled.

I got the idea to distract her, hoping she'd forget about my little, or not so little, lie. "Xany said scars aren't always bad. Mine tickles when you touch it."

"Huh? Your scar tickles?"

"Uh-huh, want to see?" I lifted up my shirt to show her. She shifted in her seat, her eyes lingering on my stomach. She licked her lips before returning her gaze to mine and pushing my shirt down.

"No, Shawnee, I don't want to see. You're avoiding telling me something."

She was right. I was avoiding telling her about the Andrus and about something else. "I think... I think I should go with Xany to Caden's pack."

She took my hands into hers and held them in my lap to stop my fidgeting. "Is that why you quit your job?"

"Yes." *No.*

"Is that *part* of why you quit your job?" She frowned at me again.

"Yes, it's part of it." I took a deep breath.

She hugged me. The sound of the purring in her chest soothed me. She gave up trying to expose my lies when I started to relax. "Tired?" Vanessa placed a firm hand on my back, rubbing in slow circles.

I nodded. "Stay with me?"

"Of course." She kissed my shoulder. "Maybe in the morning, you'll tell me the truth."

I closed my eyes. I kept feeling my body twitch every time I thought about the events of the night. The fear of getting caught, and the fear that the Andrus would hurt Vanessa and Xany if I told them anything weighed heavily on me. I was glad Xany was leaving on Friday. I was glad Vanessa could bend and get away easily. I worried for Bailey and hoped he got home safe, and I worried for the potential werecreatures and people who would be kept in those containment cells in the future. I may have saved one life, but there were a lot more out there that I wouldn't get a chance to help. But one life saved, one warrior of Gaia, was all I could ask for tonight. I fell asleep against Vanessa, and I think she held me all night, hoping that one of my dreams would reveal the truth.

CHAPTER SEVENTEEN

I awoke around 6:00 A.M. As quietly as I could, I attempted to pry myself away from Vanessa and inadvertently woke her up in the process.

"Morning," I whispered.

"Morning." She groaned when the warmth of my body left her and shivered. She curled up on the sofa, yanked the blanket off the back of it, and purred herself right back to sleep. I watched her for a moment before stretching and yawning my way to the door. The bags were still beside Xany's apartment so I tiptoed into the hallway to knock on her door. I had to let her know that I'd changed my mind. I hadn't planned for this. I hadn't planned for anything that had happened in the last twenty-four hours. But I knew that leaving here was the best way to protect Xany and Vanessa—and myself, I suppose.

Xany came to the door wearing her usual boyshorts and tank top, perking up as soon as she saw me. "Hi, Nee! I was hoping you'd stop by after work—is that blood on your shirt?" She scrunched her nose at the dark stain on the shoulder of my white T-shirt.

"Hey. Oh, uh, yeah, probably. Sorry, I should have changed. But listen I need to tell you something..." I added before Xany could cut me off.

"Is it your blood or is it from work? Ooooh, I bet it was something interesting. Was it gross?"

"Xany!" I winced, realizing how loud I was. "Will you be quiet for a second? I'm trying to tell you something."

"Oh." Her giggle reverberated down the hallway. "Sorry, I've been up for a bit. Tell me." She bounced, reminding me of a hyperactive puppy.

"I changed my mind." I hesitated, not sure how to say the rest.

"Good for you." She nodded, grinning. *Clueless.*

I huffed. "I changed my mind about going with you to Utah... I-I want to go."

Xany stared at me with a blank expression for a moment before screaming, "Yes! I knew you would!" She nearly knocked me over in a crushing hug.

"Shh! Xany, it's early!" I tried to quiet her, but it was too late.

At least two neighbors poked their heads out of their apartments and grumbled at us. Vanessa came scrambling into the hallway, hissing wildly and ready to attack. Xany snickered at the entire scene. I sighed at her and waved Vanessa back into the apartment so she'd know everything was fine. She hissed at me and groggily disappeared back inside.

"Chaos seems to follow you." I huffed at Xany again before glancing at my feet and speaking softly. "Can I still come?"

"Of c—" she started to shout so I put my hand over her mouth.

"Use your inside voice, Xany."

She cracked up and supplemented shouting with bouncing. "Of course you can," she said. "Caden and Mal will be here around noon. Have you packed?"

"Um...no, but I don't have much." I forgot about the packing part of moving.

She grinned. "Make the cat help you! I'm nearly done,

then I'll help. I'm gonna go call Caden and tell him you're coming." She giggled again, clearly pleased by the change of events. "I'm happy you changed your mind, Nee."

"Vanessa said she'd visit just like here, and you said there were hospitals there too."

"Of course there are hospitals there." She hugged me again. I returned it a bit stiffly.

We parted ways, and I returned to my apartment to pack while Vanessa continued sleeping on the sofa. I took a quick shower and dressed then gathered some of my belongings. I didn't have much. All my clothes, toiletries, towels, blanket, and pillows fit in my duffel bag. The rolling trunk I kept at the foot of my bed with all my important things had room in it so I put anything that didn't fit in the duffel in there. In a few hours, I had packed every bit of my life into two condensed containers, minus the kitchen stuff which was negligible anyway. The only additional items I would bring would be the television and my laptop.

When I dragged my duffel bag and trunk into the living room, Vanessa began to stir. She stretched. The rumbling in her chest told me that she'd enjoyed the sensation of unraveling her muscles. She rolled onto her stomach and peeked up at me from over the arm of the sofa.

"You're done already?"

"Yes, thank you for your help." I messed up her hair when I walked by, and she tried to swat me.

"You're sure you want to do this?" Vanessa sat up and stretched before leaving her perch on the sofa. She followed me into the kitchen to help me toss some junk into garbage bags. Emptying the kitchen was easy. So was the living room.

"I'm sure." I glanced around the room. "Did I forget anything?"

Vanessa shook her head. "No, you don't have anything to forget."

She was right. I owned less than nothing, without

counting clothes. I didn't really care about objects so the comment didn't bother me much. "I know. Will you take the trash bags down?"

"I will. What time are they coming?" She gathered two bags in each hand.

"Noon." I checked my phone for the time. "Which is in like twenty minutes."

"Be back in a minute." She carried the bags out of the apartment.

I sighed and looked around. I wasn't sure that this was what I wanted to do, but I was doing it. What was the worst that could happen? Even if I didn't like it there I could always come back to Wyoming. I had a ton of money saved up so that wasn't an issue.

Of course you have money saved up, you only buy basic necessities.

I rolled my shoulders, suddenly bombarded by thoughts and fears about being homesick. I wasn't the best at transitioning to new places, especially when strangers were involved. When Vanessa came back, she looked at me with a furrowed brow.

"What's wrong?" She washed her hands in the kitchen.

"Nothing, why?" I met her gaze after shaking off my thoughts.

"You're standing in the same spot like you're frozen." She dried her hands and came back into the room.

"Just thinking," I said. "How long will it take for you to be able to bend to the place in Utah?"

"You'll have to be there first and tell me what things look like so that I don't bend into some random place." She smirked. "Or in the middle of the ocean," she added with a shiver.

Bending was a handy ability but it was not without its limits. In order to bend into a certain place, you needed a guide. The guide was a person who was already there and was able to describe the environment to you so that the Bender could envision what the place looked like. Then the magics kicked in and boom, bending happened.

Guides were not necessary but helpful. If you didn't have a guide, you could bend into an unknown place and get lost. It was best to visit the places Benders plan to bend to by normal travel first; using guides could be inaccurate. The more you visited a place, the easier it was to bend there and the less time it took.

"Caden said it's a cabin, and it is northeast of Salt Lake City," I told her.

"That's a start." She smiled and pulled me into a hug. "Don't worry, you're a good guide. You'll just have to tolerate a long ride with Xany and two wolves."

"Sounds like fun. Can't you bend me with you?" The sarcasm rolled off my tongue.

Vanessa snickered. "Nope. We'll both end up in the ocean or something, and besides you're the best guide I've ever had. Other than my mom, that is."

"You tricked me that time when we went to your parents' house in Ireland for Christmas break in college, didn't you?" Vanessa had a way of tricking me into a lot of things.

"Yes, thank God you fell asleep on the drive to the airport because neither of us had tickets." She grinned.

"You drugged me, I swear. One minute I'm sleeping in a cab, the next I'm in the middle of Dublin in a mansion." I swatted her arm, as she laughed.

"No drugs. A little hypnotism, but no drugs."

"Vanessa!" I laughed and was about to swat her again when Xany burst into the room.

"Hey, people!" She issued her trademark giggle that I was becoming familiar with. "The guys are outside. They're gonna be coming up to get our stuff. Is that all you have, Nee?" She glanced at the duffel bag and trunk by my feet, perplexed.

"Told you I didn't have much." I shrugged at her. "And we can take the TV if you want."

"Of course! You've got a cool flat screen thing. Mine is a fat screen and old. Yours is much better." She began dragging my duffel toward the door.

Vanessa snickered at her. "She's in a hurry. C'mon, I'll help carry," she said.

"Don't let people see you, Vanessa. It's one thing to see two giant men carrying huge boxes, but it's another to see a scrawny redheaded woman doing so," I warned. Vanessa was not the most careful of Changers.

"That's so sexist of you, Shawnee," she mocked, picking up the large trunk under one arm, which just looked down right ridiculous. "Not too noticeable, is it?"

"Vanessa! Just wheel it." I huffed in exasperation and gave her a light shove. Xany giggled from the hallway. Vanessa laughed and set the trunk down, tilting it up on its wheels to roll it out.

"Better?" She exaggerated the heaviness by panting.

"Wise ass. Yes, that's better." I began disconnecting the television from the cable box. The television was relatively light so I toted it out to the hallway and set it outside the door.

Eventually Caden and Mal appeared in the hall and greeted us. Both men seemed very upbeat and excited to begin the drive. In all of fifteen minutes, my stuff and Xany's was loaded on to the bed of Caden's pickup truck. Having three Changers as your moving crew was very helpful. Xany turned in her key to the building manager. I kept mine...just in case.

"It's going to be about an eight to ten hour drive back, ladies, so take whatever you will need from your bags now," Caden said as he and Mal secured our stuff with bungee cords to the bed of the pickup.

I pulled out a blanket and pillow from my bag because I planned to sleep most of the way in order to avoid too much talking. I tucked my laptop under the seat in case I couldn't sleep and needed an excuse to zone out on something. When everything was set to go, Xany and I climbed into the backseat. The guys were way too big for the back so Mal took the front passenger seat, and Caden drove. Xany sat behind Mal and kicked the back of his seat a few times to annoy him. He glared at her. I allowed a small smile at the ongoing antics of the siblings, then jumped when Vanessa appeared outside my window.

"Send me text messages if you need to, okay?" She reached in the window, caressing my cheek. I nodded. I couldn't believe it, but I got pretty tearful when she touched me. I didn't like the idea of not being able to have access to her for ten hours. I worried about freaking out or having nightmares and not being able to control myself. It wasn't like I had a backup plan, and of course I had no beer.

"I will."

The others remained quiet to allow us our farewell. Vanessa smiled softly, seeing my emotion. Her cheeks and nose were red like they usually were when she was feeling emotional herself. "It'll be okay, Shawnee. Xany will be there next to you. I'll see you tomorrow morning, as soon as I can."

"Okay." I tried to hide my sniffle, pulling the blanket up around me. I felt like a five-year-old being shipped off to sleep-away camp for the first time. She leaned into the truck and kissed my cheek, purring in my ear when she tucked a strand of hair behind my ear.

"Have a safe trip."

I leaned into her purr and swallowed the knot in my throat when she stepped away from the truck. "Bye, Ness."

"We'll take good care of her, Vanessa, don't worry." Caden sounded sincere.

She nodded at him. I could tell she knew he was speaking the truth. Vanessa waved to us when Caden started up the truck. Xany waved back and bounced excitedly when she heard the engine come to life.

We pulled away from the curb and started down the road. I craned my neck and watched Vanessa until she disappeared from sight. Somehow, it made me feel better that she stood there watching us too. I curled up under the blanket, tucked the pillow against my shoulder, and closed my eyes. I wanted to block out as much of this drive as I could. I was surprised at how quiet everyone was while we drove. Caden had soft music playing in the background, and within an hour, I was sound asleep.

CHAPTER EIGHTEEN

I woke up at some point during the drive. It was still light out, but we were driving into the setting sun. Xany was asleep in the seat beside me with an empty bag of chips in her lap. Caden was now in the passenger seat, eating a cheeseburger while Mal drove. I sat upright to look out the windshield of the truck to see how far we had traveled. Mal noticed my movement and looked at me through the rearview mirror. He caught my gaze for a moment, and I saw his cheeks lift into a smile. The image of his hazel eyes in the mirror burned into my memory. My cheeks flushed with hotness so I slouched to avoid sharing any more glances.

"Hungry?" he asked, his tone sweet. For some reason I thought he was grinning when he asked.

"I'm okay." I tucked my pillow under my arm so I could see out the side window. We were still traveling along Route 80 West, according to the highway markers. Snowy peaks of the mountains lingered in the distance. At this point, I was pretty sure we were passing through Salt Lake City.

"How much longer?"

"Not long," he replied. "Maybe an hour. Our land is

near Wasatch-Cache National Forest."

"Why are we driving through Salt Lake City? Isn't that farther east?" I was a bit uneasy. Part of me wondered if this trip was an elaborate kidnapping scheme. It wouldn't be out of the ordinary for werewolves to steal away Breeders. It wouldn't be out of the norm for me to be kidnapped either. I didn't have the best record when it came to luck.

"Yes, but we want to enter through Hank's territory. There is a small pack that patrols the northern part and into the Ashley Forest. It only adds about an hour to the trip, but it's worth it to enter safely." He glanced at me again in the mirror so I looked away.

"Shawnee, you must be hungry." Caden turned around to offer me a McDonald's bag full of food. I shook my head no.

"Thanks though."

"More for me then." He grinned and took out another burger.

It was odd talking to both men while Xany was asleep. I wasn't in the mood to carry on any conversation so I curled up under my blanket again and pretended to sleep. Caden and Mal were silent for the remainder of the drive, but as Xany had mentioned once before, Mal could do some mind talking thing. Or Caden could. One of them. I bet they were saying whatever they needed to say privately.

The sun had set by the time the truck slowed down, and the texture of the road changed from smooth pavement to crunchy gravel. The blanket had rolled from my lap so I sat up to gaze out the window. It was nearly pitch black, except for the headlights. We were traveling along a dirt road surrounded by trees and, well, nothing. All I could see was the road and trees. The truck turned right, then left, and began a straight drive into darkness. Eventually Mal slowed down, and Caden bagged up the remaining food. I took that as a sign we were nearly there. We made another sharp right at a fork in the road, and I saw a wooden marker with script that was too small for me to read. After traveling for about a mile, the truck rolled to a stop, and Xany awoke as if the momentum of the moving vehicle was the only thing keeping her asleep.

"Are we there yet?" She blinked the sleep out of her eyes and looked around.

"You betcha." Caden chuckled and got out first. "Let me get the lights, I'll be back in a minute."

Xany and I exited the truck on opposite sides, slamming the doors at the same time. I inhaled the chilled air, catching the scent of wilderness untainted by the smog of the city. I heard a trickling noise that belonged to a nearby stream and the croaking of tree frogs somewhere in the distance. It was slightly warmer here than it had been in Wyoming. Mal killed the engine of the truck and stood beside us in the darkness. Just as the fear over realizing I was in a new place began to climb, light filled the area surrounding us. The floodlights on the roof of the cabin were blinding, and the light from nearly a dozen windows of the cabin blared into view.

"Much better." Xany giggled and hopped toward the cabin. "C'mon, Nee!"

I held my breath as I watched her. My feet were frozen to the ground. Had I really done this? Secretly I had been wishing that this was all a dream.

"Shawnee?" Mal said quietly, lifting his hand to place it on my shoulder.

"I'm fine." I moved quickly away from him toward the cabin.

He followed behind me while Caden grabbed a bunch of bags from the bed of the truck and toted them inside. I went in after him. The vast, bright cabin, crafted completely out of indigenous logs stained in a soft pine color, took my breath away. Big windows allowed for plenty of natural lighting, and the kitchen was the first part of the cabin, split in two by the front door. On the right, there was a refrigerator, sink, and several appliances placed on the wooden countertop with cupboards above. To the left sat a dining table with six chairs stained to match the rest of the cabin. All of the appliances and furniture looked new. The kitchen was open and just beyond the table was the living area. There was a stone fireplace and hearth to the left, a sofa, loveseat, and armchair surrounding a coffee table, and a thick burgundy shag carpet placed in front of the fire. Mal went immediately to the fireplace and began lighting a fire. Caden came into the room and placed my flat panel television on top of the mantel.

"What do you think? Do you want it here or in your room?" he asked. I could sense the excitement emanating from the guys, and Xany was buzzing around the place opening every cabinet and door she could find.

"Um...yeah, leave it there." I chewed my lip.

Caden smiled and started hooking the TV up to the power supply and satellite dish. When he was finished, he shot me a grin before disappearing outside to bring in more stuff. Mal followed him this time, and the two men continued unloading the truck. Xany suddenly appeared in front of me and grabbed my hand.

"C'mon! This place is awesome! Check out the rooms." She dragged me out of the living room and into a hallway that had five doors, four of which led to individual bedrooms. Two of the bedrooms had simple double beds, a chest of drawers, and a writing table. Each room had its own closet.

"These must be ours. The other rooms have stuff in them." Xany bounced around happily. "And check out the bathroom, it's huge!"

I didn't get a chance to process what I saw before Xany dragged me into the bathroom, which was the fifth door at the end of the hall. The bathroom had a stand-up shower, a claw-foot bathtub, and new fixtures. Everything in the cabin looked new, but the bathroom looked the newest.

"Caden and Mal built all of this stuff. It was just a four-walled cabin without any appliances, power, or bathroom.

There's an old outhouse in the backyard." She turned the faucet on and off.

"They built all of this in about a week? How?" I glanced around the room. It was pretty amazing after all.

"Hank owns a contracting builder-uppering-thing company and half of his workers are werewolves. It takes them like a minute to dig a hole and make plumbing and stuff."

"It's a nice cabin..."

"Of course. What did you expect?" Xany bounced over to me again. "Want to see the door to nowhere? Mal told me about it."

"What?" I blinked out of my daze.

"C'mon." She waved for me to follow her, bringing me back out to the living room. A few feet from the hearth, just before the hallway, was a door on the east-facing wall. She opened it, and I gasped when I saw that the door had a few planks of wood that dropped off into nothing with plastic sheets hanging to block the door from the cold. She moved the sheets aside, and we were looking out into woods. The ground below looked freshly leveled.

"This is probably for an addition."

"Uh-huh, but I kind of like having a door to nowhere." Xany grinned. We went back into the kitchen where Mal and Caden had brought in every item from the truck.

"Wow, you guys should start a moving company." Xany giggled then carried some of the stuff toward the bedrooms. "Nee? Do you want the first room or the second?"

"It doesn't matter, Xany, really." I wrapped my arms around myself. I was beginning to seriously question my decision to move out here. Everything was nice, but it seemed like I was ridiculously exposed and almost vulnerable. I didn't know these people, these wolves, and the reality was starting to set in. The weight of my phone in my pocket reminded me to call Vanessa. I wanted her to get here fast so that I could stop feeling so...so... I had no idea what I felt. I wanted at least one familiar face around.

"Okay then, you take the first." She looked pretty perky and dragged a box into the second room on the right.

I went over and wheeled my trunk into the other room. Mal followed me with the duffel bag and set it down on the floor. "Thanks," I murmured, and he left the room with a chuckle. I sat down on the bed. The mattress was firm and new. Both my bed and Xany's had fresh white linens and a pillow. I tossed my pillow on top of the one there and laid back on the bed, pulling the blanket up over me. There was a window by the head of the bed, and I could see the crescent moon peeking out from above the trees. I smirked at the silvery light filling the room and took my phone out of my pocket.

"Hello?" Vanessa sounded groggy.

"I'm sorry I woke you. We just got here," I whispered.

"Mmm, Shawnee, hi. That wasn't too long. What's it like there?"

I could hear her shifting around in bed. The clock on my phone said it was nearly midnight. "It's..." I paused to think about it. "Not bad. The cabin is like all new and stuff."

"Describe it to me." She grew quiet.

I spent the next ten minutes or so telling Vanessa about every single detail of the drive here, the cabin, and my room. I felt myself growing tired and relaxed hearing her soft purring over the phone. By the time I finished describing every inch of the place, I had fallen asleep with the phone on my shoulder. That night, I had a dream that Vanessa's mouth traveled to Utah to snicker in my ear.

CHAPTER NINETEEN

I left Vanessa asleep in my bed and ventured out for my first trip to the new bathroom in the middle of the night. To my surprise, Xany, Caden, and Mal gathered by the hearth where they had a fire crackling. I tucked myself close to the wall in the hallway by the bathroom door. I didn't want them to see me, but I couldn't help my curiosity over what they were saying about me behind my back. And about Vanessa.

"She's sleeping already." Xany giggled.

"That's not a bad thing, Xee," Mal said.

"He's right. It's going to be an adjustment for her." Caden unpacked a few more random items from boxes, placing them around the room. "This cabin has no decorations. Xany, that's your new job, to decorate."

"Gimme money then." She grinned at Caden and held out her hand. He chuckled and slapped his bank card into it.

Mal shook his head. "Bad move, bro. But back to Shawnee, I don't think it's going to be as big of an adjustment for her as we think." I was surprised to hear Mal's assertion. What did he know about my adjustment?

"What do you mean?" Xany asked, slipping Caden's

bank card into her back pocket and settling down on the sofa. I saw the clock on the cable box, which read 1:20 a.m.

"Shawnee grew up on a reservation in a pack. Caden was right when he said she knows more than she lets on. I imagine living in the city was more taxing," Mal presumed. How could he know that? Did I have it tattooed on my forehead or something?

"She does know a lot. I wonder how this will play out. Xee, we should go food shopping in the morning too. Want to split the work? You hit the frilly, girly decoration shop, and I'll get the food. Mal can hang back here with Shawnee and finish digging out the fire pit and unpacking some of the other stuff," Caden said.

"How do you know she knows a lot?" Xany asked, then added, "It's a deal."

"You can tell by how she reacts to us. She reads our body language and gestures before we even speak or move near her. That takes practice and a lot of exposure," Mal said.

Damn. And here I thought I was good at hiding.

"He's right about that. On the day we met, she knew exactly what I was as soon as she entered the room. I bet she even knew I was a dominant." Caden crunched on a few cheese puffs.

I did know that. He reeked of wolf. Not in a bad way, though. Was I really that obvious to these people? I wonder if they would have found me out without Xany having seen my glyph.

"How can she know that? I didn't even know that," Xany whined. "I grew up with a pack too."

"Yeah, but ours was small, and we didn't live on a reservation. We went to public schools and lived in a residential neighborhood. Reservation packs are closed off, and everyone grows up together. There aren't many reservation packs left these days, maybe three or four." Mal chowed down on a cold cheeseburger.

I watched Mal while he spoke. His eyes flickered in my direction more than once. I can't help but wonder how he knew all of this. Clearly, he wasn't from a reservation pack, why did he know this about me? I pulled my sweater tighter around myself. I didn't like being exposed, and I surely didn't like people knowing more than they should about me.

"Reservation packs? Is that like something different than a regular reservation or a pack?" Xany looked between the men.

"Very different," Caden said, then allowed Mal to continue telling the story.

"Packs are packs. Members can live separately all over the same town without having much contact unless needed. Reservations are as they've always been. Small communities managed by a specific tribe or few mixed tribes. Shawnee is part Cherokee like you said, so I imagine her reservation was predominantly Cherokee with some others. There is a large reservation in Wyoming that's recognized but that one belongs to Shoshone, I think, or something like that but that's not the one she's from." Mal downed another burger.

He was right. My reservation pack was mainly Cherokee and a smattering of other tribes mixed in. My mother was pure-blooded Cherokee, which was rare, to say the least. My father was mixed. I don't really care to think about what mix. Maybe it messed with his head, like interbreeding dogs too closely. Maybe that's why he was such a terrible, deranged person.

"How can you know this stuff? She hardly speaks." Xany frowned. I imagined that she was annoyed because the wolves had more information than she did.

"We have other senses, Xee," Caden said.

"You still didn't answer my question!" She crossed her arms over her chest and huffed.

"You interrupted. Such a brat." Mal let out a low growl at Xany who merely turned her nose up at him. When he growled, a shiver ran up my spine. I gripped my sweater tighter. It was easy to forget that a man as gentle and sound as Mal had a voracious beast living just below the surface.

"Reservation packs," he continued, "are not only small tribal communities but small tribal *werewolf* communities dominated and controlled by the Chief Alpha. They're strict and secluded. The children are born, raised, and educated there. Most of them function pretty well as an independent unit, and the Changers and Breeders live happy existences, protecting their people and Gaia." Mal smirked.

I scoffed. Not all Breeders lived happy existences. I was proof. His smirk told me that he knew the same.

"Most?" Xany frowned.

"Some, well, aren't as good. But that's with anything. It depends on the leaders and how much influence the Tainted Ones have on them and such." I could tell Mal was clearly minimizing the situation. My original pack family was more than touched by the Tainted Ones; they wove their way inside us. Inside our elders. Destroyed us from the inside out.

"You think Shawnee had a not-so-good one?" Xany asked, continuing to frown.

Mal lifted a brow at her. "What do you think?"

I clutched my chest, begging the panic to stay at bay so I could continue to listen in on their conversation. I wanted to know what they assumed about me, how they would treat me. I wanted to believe Xany that Mal and Caden were good. Not domineering but respectful, protective wolves that followed Gaia's calling. I really wanted to believe that.

"So in a way, yes, this will be an adjustment for her. But at the same time she'll be at home. That's the assumption. I mean...she changed her mind pretty quickly. Something must have provoked it—" Caden started.

I swallowed the lump in my throat. Sometimes I forget

how intuitive werewolves could be. Something definitely provoked it, but I could never tell them. I couldn't tell Vanessa either. I'd endanger all their lives. Maybe I already had.

Mal interrupted, "I smell cat." He leaned up with his nostrils flared. I looked over my shoulder and realized I left the bedroom door open. Of course they could scent her anyway, but I just made it easier.

"It's the redhead. A bending redheaded weretiger." Caden chuckled. "She's not a threat, bro." I wondered if Caden was even sure of that comment himself. Vanessa was a pretty big threat once you got to know her.

Mal grumbled. "Cats are trouble."

"Did you really think that that cat would let her out of her sight for long?" Xany giggled.

"No," Caden said. "Just leave her be. We need to alert Hank first thing in the morning and bring something with Vanessa's scent over to them or we could have mayhem."

"No kidding." Mal sighed. "Though I bet that cat could take out half his pack."

I'm starting to believe Mal has the best instincts of everyone.

"She is a tough one." Caden began cleaning up the junk food mess.

And maybe Caden too.

"Again! Leaving me out of things. How can you tell?" Xany huffed and puffed. Sometimes I wanted to just throw something at Xany. She reminded me of dopey cheerleaders from high school.

Caden chuckled, but Mal answered. "She's cocky and confident. How many weretigers have you known to sit calmly purring with her head in the lap of a Breeder while surrounded by two dominant wolves?"

I smiled hearing this; my cheeks grew warm because Vanessa was my werecat.

"None, of course. So that means she's strong?" Xany queried.

"It means she can take care of herself," Caden said.

"And mind you she just popped into known pack territory without a thought. That says something."

I looked back to the room door. Part of me wondered if Mal sensed that I was awake and listening to the conversation.

"Note to self, don't piss off the fire-crotch cat." Xany pretended to make a checklist on her hand.

Caden chuckled. "Or insult the cat."

"Who me?" Xany smiled.

As I disappeared into the bedroom, Mal's glowing eyes stared in my direction down the hall.

CHAPTER TWENTY

It was the rising sun that woke me the next morning. The warmth of its rays plunging in through my window when the sun broke through from behind the thick trees caused me to stir and squint at the brightness. I kicked off my blankets and knelt on the bed to look out the window. The view was something unexpected. My window overlooked an area of forest that was broken by the shore of a lake. When I saw the snow-capped mountains cascading in the distance several miles beyond the lake, my stomach leaped in delight. The lake itself was probably a quarter of a mile away from the cabin, and it seemed as though the trees stepped aside to create a pathway from my window.

I unpacked some of my clothes and chose an outfit and towel to take to the bathroom with me. The cabin was dimly lit and quiet at this time of morning. I heard someone in the kitchen before I disappeared into the bathroom. It was nice to shower with the new fixtures. Everything was clean and untainted, so much so that I didn't have the urge to over scrub my hands and body. I must have taken a long shower though, because when I entered the kitchen, Caden and Mal were talking about food and Xany was impatiently waiting to get into the bathroom.

"About time, Nee! I was going to bust down the door!" She giggled and disappeared.

I smirked at her, then went over to join the guys.

"Morning, Shawnee," Caden said, though his eyes were on Mal who was cutting up some very fresh meat into cubes.

"Hey there." Mal grinned. I watched him for a moment before moving closer to see what he was up to. There was a metallic odor coming from the meat. As I stood beside him, the heat of his body radiated as if I were next to an open flame. Despite the warmth, it gave me goose bumps, and I had to take a step back.

"Hunting?" I asked, staring at the meat.

"Hope you like elk," he said. "Caden hasn't gone shopping yet." He paused, watching me as I looked down at the meat. He spoke like he knew what I was thinking. "The hides are out back drying along with useable bones, the blood and organs returned to Gaia under the vultures nest in the forest," he finished, looking over his shoulder at me with a raised brow.

I gave him an approving nod, appreciative of his proper care for the animal. "I like elk."

He smiled, and I watched him continue to prepare the meat.

Caden chuckled at us. "He's got his wits about him, Nee, don't worry."

"One of us has to," Mal shot back.

After a short while, Xany emerged from the bathroom with her wet hair pulled back into a tight braid. Mal had just tossed some of the meat into a skillet when she looked over his shoulder.

"What's that?" Her nose scrunched up.

"Elk."

"Did you hunt it?" She gulped.

"Yup." Mal tossed a raw chunk into his mouth.

"Gross! I am not eating that!" she shouted, huffing and puffing. "Caden, let's go shopping now."

The guys laughed at her, and I gave Mal a sharp elbow in the side before taking a few dishes down from the cupboard, trying very hard not to join the guys in their laughter.

"Are you sure you don't want to eat first?" Caden asked Xany, standing up because he already knew her answer.

"Hell no. I have no idea where that boy got his crazy ideas about hunting and cooking. Mom and Dad used the cold meat section at the grocery store just like every other normal person in the world!" Xany stomped toward the door. Caden couldn't help but laugh at Xany's exaggeration and nodded to us before ducking out the door with her.

"You're not very alike," I told Mal and set the plates down on the table.

"Who?" He added some seasoning to the skillet while flipping the meat.

"You and your sister." I set napkins and utensils beside the dishes.

"True. Our family was pretty assimilated into white culture. I didn't think it was right to abandon our heritage for the sake of fitting in." He put aside some very rare pieces of meat and continued to cook the rest.

I smirked hearing him. Hadn't I done that? Didn't I abandon what I was for what I could become? Maybe it was just avoidance. I watched him while he cooked. I couldn't help but let my eyes wander over him. He seemed so comfortable, so relaxed in his body. Like there was nothing in the world that would bother him, but I knew different. Mal was a feral wolf, and that meant his beast was close to the surface. I was intrigued by him, ironically enough. Usually I'd be scared of a big-muscled Indian man, but for some reason Mal didn't scare me. Caden did though, which was pretty normal.

"Our mother was part Cherokee, and our father was part Navajo all mixed in with white ancestry as well. My mother was a Changer like me and taught us the language when we were young. Xany understands more than she speaks though." He spoke in the presence of my silence. Mal brought the cooked meat over to the table, setting the rare pieces on his dish and splitting the well-cooked meat between the two of us.

"My mother was Cherokee, my father was Cherokee and Sioux, I think," I told him while he placed the food in my dish, nodding in thanks.

"Your mother was a Changer, right?" He took out two bottles of water from the fridge and placed them by our dishes.

I nodded again, avoiding eye contact as the anxiety began to rise in my chest. I didn't like talking about my parents. I didn't really like talking about much of anything having to do with my family or my past. I opened my water bottle and took a sip to try and settle my nerves. Mal watched me before sitting down to eat. I toyed with the meat on my plate for a moment before taking a bite.

"What do you think of it here so far?"

I was glad he changed the subject. He didn't pressure me, and I liked it. I was able to lift my eyes to him again when the anxiety began to quell.

"There's a lake outside my window."

"Yeah. It's a small one but nice. It's recently started to thaw. When we were out here originally, it was frozen over."

I smiled, sensing his enthusiasm about the lake. "I was thinking about going to see it later, maybe."

"Not a bad idea. Be cautious though when you venture out. Hank's pack is local, and they travel these woods frequently. The young ones won't recognize your scent yet," he warned before chomping on a chewy piece of rare meat. I wasn't surprised that Mal liked his meat almost raw; most feral werecreatures did. The taste of the blood satiated some of the desire that roared through them. I imagined that Mal was the type of wolf that had to hunt often. Caden struck me as one of those wolves that didn't. He seemed to always be in control of himself. I ate the food along with him. It was tasty and well prepared. It had been a while since I had eaten freshly killed meat.

"Tell me about Hank's pack," I requested.

Mal finished every bit of meat on his plate, then began speaking. "His sept is larger than most. There are a lot of Indians, of all mixes and tribes, white folk too. His wife runs a small trading post shop in town that carries a lot of Southwestern and handmade items like pottery, and weaving, and the like. Hank himself owns a contracting company that a lot of his Changers work for, and it's pretty successful. Imagine how long it takes twelve werewolves to build a house." He shook his head, smiling. "His sept members are involved in all parts of government in this area; from the police to the forest rangers and such. That's why it's worthy of being called a sept. There are, like, small little sub-packs within the larger one."

I finished eating while listening to him. "That's pretty involved."

"It keeps his people safe. He's allied with Caden's father's pack in California, minus the politics. The two cover a lot of territory together when needed."

"I should tell Vanessa to not wander too far from the cabin when she visits." I put the dishes in the sink.

He nodded, then began washing them so I offered to dry. He passed me the warm, wet plate, and I ran the cloth over the ribbed edges. We worked in silence for a few minutes, the monotonous task ongoing. After a while, Mal handed me a plate that was still soapy.

"Hey," I protested, waving the sudsy dish at him.

"Just seeing if you were paying attention." He grinned. I laughed a bit and handed it back to him. This time after he rinsed it, he splashed me with a bit of water. I flinched and swatted him with the rag. My cheeks were warm, and I tried to distract myself from it.

"Caden's told Hank that we have a feline ally that is

often around. He's going to bring something with her scent over so they can identify her. But for now she should be careful." He stopped and smirked at me.

"What?"

"I've never met a cat who was so devoted to, well, anyone." The smirk became a full-blown grin.

"Vanessa is different, I guess." I paused, watching his expression. "What's so funny?"

"Nothing." He chuckled and rinsed off the last dish.

"Don't lie, what's so funny?" I frowned.

"Fine, fine. I had a thought that went something about a pussycat being pussy-whipped."

I tried to be angry about it, crossing my arms with a bit of attitude, but I couldn't help laughing when I thought about it. "You ass."

"I couldn't pass up the opportunity." Mal laughed and shook his head, and we began putting the dishes away. I grinned and took the dry glasses to the cupboard. While reaching up and placing them on the shelves, I glanced over my shoulder at him. There was something about him that was different. Something that didn't make me afraid of him. His movements were slow and deliberate. He placed the dishes in the cabinet without making a sound. He wasn't your typical, clumsy wolf. In a way, he reminded me of Vanessa's subtleties.

Distracted by my thoughts, I closed the cupboard with one of the glasses teetering on the edge of the shelf. When the door hit the glass, the weight pushed the door back open. The glass clipped the edge of the counter, went flying to the floor, and shattered into a million pieces around my boots. The noise of the breaking glass echoed in my head. I began to tremble and gasp for breath. I saw Mal rush over and pluck me up from the floor away from it. He said something inaudible to me like he was submerged underwater and sat me up on the counter. I screamed when I couldn't see him anymore...

"Dirty dishes are for dirty girls!" I hear my father yell. I am

under a kitchen table crying. Glass is shattering around me.

I hear myself say, "Stop, stop!" and scream when a sharp piece of glass ricochets off the floor and hits me in the arm. I feel the warm blood emerge from the gash, and I pull the glass out of my skin, throwing it away from me.

Just as two big hands reach under the table to grab me...

"Shhh...shh...it's okay."

Mal's voice pierced the haze that had washed over me, bringing me to the surface until I could see him again. His eyes were blazing though his hands were soft, holding me in place. The pressure of his stomach was on my knees while he leaned against me. Tears streamed down my cheeks and Mal cupped my face, lifting my chin so that he could look me in the eye.

"Hey...hey there," he said when I began to calm down.

Sobbing, I clenched my teeth. My heart was pounding in my ears. Mal looked like he had a golden halo around him for a few seconds before it went away and I was left with the knowledge that I freaked out in front of him again.

You're so stupid, Shawnee. How could you let this happen again? It's your own fault that you dropped that glass.

"Shawnee?" he asked, but I struggled against him a little, wanting very badly to dig a hole and bury myself in it. "Stop." His voice was firm, and he had one hand on my cheek.

My body relaxed at his command, and the creepy crawly feeling on my skin disappeared. I held my breath, but I couldn't stop myself from crying. He held me in his gaze, and I didn't have the strength to look away.

"You're okay. No one will hurt you here..."

I gripped his arm tightly as the shame washed over me like an itchy woolen blanket. The color drained from Mal's bronzed complexion. His chest began to rumble, and I heard the distinct grinding of his teeth. He was tuned into what I was feeling. The rumble turned into a growl, and I put my hand on his chest.

142

"I'm sorry," I whispered to him.

"Don't ever be sorry. You did nothing wrong." His voice was coarse when he spoke through his growling.

For some reason I took comfort in his aggression. I sniffled and wiped away the tears on my sleeve. My sobs faded and so did the rumbling in his chest. When he nudged my chin upward, his dilated pupils returned to normal, and his hazel eyes became vast again. I heard the echo of eagles crying from somewhere inside me. He smiled and traced his thumb over my bottom lip.

"What do you see when that happens?" he asked.

"Bad things..." I told him. In my slouched position against the cupboard, completely surrounded by Mal's largeness, it seemed like there was no one else in the world except us.

"You scream like it's happening now."

"It feels like it is. Everything disappears, and I'm back there in those bad things," I whispered to him like I was telling him a secret.

"Next time take me with you."

I thought about that for a moment and imagined what it would have been like if he went back to that moment with me, to be the one who lifted me out from under the table.

"I'll try," I whispered.

"That's all I can ask for."

CHAPTER TWENTY-ONE

Caden and Xany bustled through the front door with loads of bags from their shopping trip. They had interrupted our conversation, and Xany froze, seeing me sitting on the counter with Mal leaning into me. She looked between the two of us for a moment before setting the bags down and rushing over.

"What happened?"

Caden continued to carry items into the house, listening to the conversation. I had no doubt that he could hear every word even when he was out by the truck. Mal took a step back when Xany pushed her way through.

"She got upset when a glass broke, but she's all right. Be careful there, we haven't gotten to it yet." He gestured to the glass on the floor, then started cleaning it up.

"Are you okay, NeeNee?" She smoothed my hair a bit.

I ducked away from her fussing and slid off the counter to help Mal. "I'm fine."

"Good, because we bought half the market and fancy girly things to decorate this place, and we'll need your help." Caden carried the last of the packages inside and shut the door.

Xany huffed at me, unconvinced that I was actually

fine. Mal and I finished cleaning up the glass, and then all four of us unpacked the groceries. All the while I tried not to think too much about the memory that popped up. It wasn't the first time I'd remembered it, but I hoped it would be the last.

By the time we were finished unpacking, the refrigerator was stuffed, and the pantry was full of prepared foods, snacks, and cereals. It reminded me how much werewolves actually ate.

Sometimes Changers hunted to supplement their diet, but many preferred to just eat normal food. Changers and Breeders were notorious for maintaining healthy body weights. Changers were usually very muscled with little body fat, and Breeders could usually eat whatever they wanted without having to worry about gaining ridiculous amounts of weight. In a way, it went along with the fact that both Changers and Breeders were immune to the diseases that usually caused health problems for regular humans. We didn't get things like cancer or diabetes. This was part of the reason that the Andrus studied us. Well...Changers mainly. Breeders could usually get away with being under the radar because we were not much different than humans, except for the gifts, the ability to pass on Changer genes, and the immunity. I guessed that was a little more different than I thought.

The Andrus' ultimate goal was to capture the immunity of Changers and create vaccines to support cures for diseases in humans. All for financial benefit, mind you, not to actually help people, and they didn't care who they had to destroy in order to get it. Thankfully, their experiments hadn't worked yet.

A pang of guilt pressed in on me. How could I have gone so long working for them? Deep inside I knew what I was doing, and choosing to deny it was my own fault. I'd potentially hurt just as many Changers as the Andrus. I shook my head and distracted myself by screwing a lamp shade onto the new lamp Xany had bought.

She bought new curtains, area rugs, blankets, pillows, and a bunch of other stuff to make the cabin feel homier. Caden was putting together a thick bookshelf, and Mal was installing blinds on each window. Xany and I carried some of the new items to the bathroom where the washing machine and dryer were and began tossing some of the blankets into the washer.

"What happened today when we were out?" she took the opportunity to ask while we were alone. I got the feeling it'd been gnawing at her.

"Nothing. I mean... I just freaked out a little. I'm fine now, okay?" I poured in some laundry soap.

"We can't have secrets here, Nee. You know that." She turned the button that started the cycle.

"Mal knows, and so does Caden by now I imagine. And I just told you. So see? No secrets." I wanted to dismiss her. It really wasn't any of her business. It seemed like it wasn't anyway.

"Fine. Technically." She crossed her arms, letting out an exasperated puff of air.

"I'm going to lie down for a while."

I left her in the bathroom and went to hide out in my room, plopping down on the bed with a sigh. I wasn't used to having so many people wrapped up in my business. Vanessa was one person, but *three* more? It was overwhelming. Snow fell in heavy drifts outside my window and I watched it from my sprawled out position on the bed. A gust of cool air rushed in when I reached above and opened the window. Everything always seemed quieter when it snowed. Quiet and still. I looked out toward the lake and wondered if anyone would miss me if I snuck out the window for an evening walk.

"Don't even think about it," said a purring voice from the foot of the bed.

I gasped as I tried to ignore the strange thrill that resonated through my body at the sound of her voice. "Vanessa! You spoil all my fun."

She snickered, grabbed me by the waist of my jeans, and slid me down the bed toward her, purring vibrantly.

"That's my job," she stated with a grin.

"Hey! I'm delicate!" I swatted at her playfully.

"Delicate?" She laughed, leaning down to nuzzle my neck and shoulder.

I wrapped my arms around her in a tight hug. It was getting easier to be with Vanessa lately. Cats were always ridiculously affectionate, and after being friends with one for twelve years, you had to either get used to it or run away. Wolves were affectionate, too, but not as overwhelmingly as cats. Touching Vanessa made me feel...well, it made me feel something. Another cool breeze rushed in through the window and gave me a chill. Vanessa shot upright, pressing her hand on my stomach, holding me down. She sniffed the air, then froze.

"What's wron—" She put a finger over my lips, then growled deeply when another soft breeze entered the room. She reached across me swiftly and slammed the window shut.

"Where's Caden?" Her eyes shifting from their usual emerald to an intense yellow.

"He's in the main room." I sat up. "What is it?"

Her chest continued to rumble. She bolted toward the door. I rushed after her and into the kitchen where both Mal and Caden were immediately reactive to Vanessa's aggressive presence. Mal crouched, and Caden suddenly looked larger than usual.

"Cat." Vanessa's voice was raspy.

Mal growled, and Vanessa crouched with him. A covering of fine, white fur began to melt over her skin. My heart raced seeing the Changers react, and I instinctively moved toward Xany, who was standing on the coffee table as if that was going to help the situation and make her look bigger.

"She smelled something when I had the window opened," I told the others and stood up on the coffee table

147

with Xany because, what else was I supposed to do?

"There's bobcats out there." Xany squeezed my hand.

Caden seemed the calmest. He cracked open the front door and sniffed the air. His shoulders broadened, and he nodded to Mal. It only took a few seconds before Mal transformed into his wolf form. His ears were perked, and he stood in the pile of clothes that were now in a heap at his paws. He padded toward the door with the hair down his spine standing on end. Vanessa, however, had a harsher change. Her bones snapped and popped wildly, her body contorted into her feline shape, and her dress disappeared. The fine fuzz that was covering her skin sprouted into the full coat of a white tiger with black stripes streaming across her massive body. She roared forcefully and bound over the sofa toward the front door where Mal was standing. Compared to Vanessa's feline form, Mal's wolf seemed dwarfed. He was able to fit almost completely underneath her without having to crouch. He did a double take when he saw her and even Caden stared for a moment.

"She doesn't ask questions, Caden," I warned, biting my lip and stepping down from the table. For a moment I didn't realize I was tugging Xany down with me.

Caden nodded. "Stay here with Xany."

"Why can't we go? That's not fair," Xany whined at him.

"Shawnee will explain," Caden said.

Vanessa nearly shoved him out of the way to get through the door. Mal leaped down the steps to get ahead of Vanessa, who was clearly driven toward whatever "cat" was out there. All three of the Changers disappeared out the front door without a word more, leaving Xany and me inside.

"Whatever cat was out there wasn't just a normal cat," I told her and rushed over toward a window in the kitchen to look outside. I frowned when I saw nothing. "I can't believe Caden allowed Vanessa with them. She'll take out half the forest including the cat if he can't convince her otherwise."

"What do you mean not a normal cat?" Xany climbed up on the kitchen counter to look out the higher window. "I can't see them. Let's go out and look."

"It was a trespassing cat. I think it was a Changer by the way they all reacted." I joined her in kneeling on the counter. "We can't go out; Caden said to stay."

"So? They might need our help!" Xany turned to me with wide, pleading eyes.

"Yes, that's exactly what three Changers need." I lifted a brow at her.

"What? It could be true."

"We shouldn't go out, Xee, Caden told us to stay here." I shook my head at her.

"Oh, c'mon. If it's just another Changer, nothing will happen to us." She hopped off the counter, grabbed my wrist, and tugged me along with her. "C'mon!"

"Xany! We'll get in trouble!" I jerked my arm away, but I had to agree. I was curious, not to mention concerned that Vanessa might cause a heap of trouble. There was a better chance she would listen to me anyway.

"What's the worst that can happen?" Xany grinned in a mischievous fashion. "We'll get a timeout? C'mon."

Xany and I hurried outside, curving around the eastern side of the cabin where my room was and following the trail into the woods.

"We should have taken a flashlight, Xee." I flailed around until she took my hand again. I was beginning to wonder why I always seemed to find myself in need of a flashlight lately.

"Oh. Yeah. I forgot about that. Which way do you think they went?" she asked, looking around through the darkness, the light from the cabin fading in the denseness of the trees.

"I dunno. Probably east since that's the way my window faces and the wind was blowing in when Vanessa smelled it."

"Which way is east?" Xany stopped and tilted her head back, as if the overcast sky would give her a clue.

I sighed. "I have no idea. We should go back—" I began to say when a loud roar echoed through the woods to our right. "This way!" I dashed toward the roar.

Xany ran with me, and we both skidded to a halt when the roars grew louder. A few yards ahead of us was a white mass crouched low to the ground, facing a pair of glowing eyes. We drew closer and could see Caden standing in human form a few steps behind Vanessa with Mal positioned at her hip.

Simultaneously, all four sets of eyes looked our way. Vanessa popped up from her crouch and growled at me, swatting the air in a "stay back" gesture. Mal chuffed, and Caden crossed his arms over his chest, looking stern. The small bobcat pulled back its upper lip and hissed. I gulped at the less-than-warm welcome. Xany, however, seemed oblivious to it.

"What's going on?" she asked and waltzed right over to Caden.

He stepped somewhat in front of her, and Vanessa gave the bobcat a swat on the side of its head. It hissed. Mal trotted over to me and gently pushed me backward. I followed his urging, but he chuffed and whined at me regardless, reprimanding me like a cub. I bit my lip and knelt down beside him. He positioned himself in front of me. His tail swayed which made me think that he wasn't all that unhappy about being so close to me. From the vibes that Caden was giving off, it seemed like he was being entertained by the cats.

"Caden, what's going on?" Xany whined again. I shook my head at her.

"Shh, Precious, just watch." He nodded toward the cats.

Vanessa roared at the bobcat. It snarled and growled right back. Caden chuckled at the measly attempt by the bobcat to stand its ground against her. Vanessa gave the little cat another swat on the side of the head before bowing low. She rose slowly, snapping her head back and emitting a deafening roar. The bobcat made a *wah-wah* sound back at her and stood upright before turning and walking a few yards away. Vanessa's claws dug into the ground before retracting and she, too, took a few steps backward, having said her peace in overpowering the little cat. The bobcat moved into the shadows, and a few seconds later, a human male emerged. He was naked except for a loincloth draped across his thighs, and he looked like a teenager. He frowned at us.

"That's what you get for being nosy, cat." Caden spoke to the werecat and stepped toward him. Vanessa stood her ground beside him.

"I was just seeing what all the movement was about. This land has been empty forever and now suddenly reeks of dog. Where the hell did you get a tiger?" the young man said.

"We have our allies. This is pack territory, which I'm sure you know by now," Caden said.

"Yeah, yeah..." the man grumbled. "I get the point."

"You're lucky she let you keep your throat," Caden chastised. "I'd be cautious if I were you, sneaking around like that."

"Sorry," he said, begrudgingly.

"Go back to your pride," Caden instructed as he gestured at the woods behind the werecat.

"How do you know I have a pride?" He sounded offended.

"I can smell it on you. Get going." Caden nodded toward the woods.

The young man grumbled, shifted back to his bobcat form, and hissed at Vanessa once more before darting off into the woods. She swatted after him and gave a growl of warning before padding over to Mal and me.

"That wasn't all that exciting." Xany crossed her arms

and thrust her bottom lip out as she pouted.

"Well now, it could have been had you two gotten lost out here or met up with the bobcat first. You both are going to be a handful, aren't you?" Caden said.

Xany grinned and bounced on her tiptoes beside him "Yep."

Caden chuckled, slid his hand around her waist, and led the way back to the cabin. Vanessa nudged Mal out of the way and bumped her head right into my hip.

"Hey," I protested as I stumbled, looking down at her. She hissed and yowled, twitching her eyebrows then her whiskers at me.

"I am not a bad kit." I frowned and huffed like Xany would.

Mal gruffed at Vanessa for bumping him and took a few steps aside before shifting back to his human form. With Vanessa in between us, he stood up wearing absolutely nothing, not even a loincloth. His lean, muscular body rippled in the light of the moon. He was confident and comfortable with his nudity, as most werecreatures eventually became. My cheeks heated and I kept my eyes on Vanessa, only glancing at him when necessary. Vanessa's purring grew affectionately louder when she saw the naked man, her eyes lingering momentarily on his maleness.

"You speak cat too?" Mal asked.

"A bit." I whined when Vanessa bumped me again. "Stop that."

"You're in trouble now." Mal laughed, and we walked back toward the cabin.

Vanessa followed in stride beside me, her paws thumping lightly on the ground. She curled her tail around my leg, not letting me stray far from her. She twitched her nose after eyeing Mal's ass, looking up at me and making a chattering sound with her teeth.

"Don't you dare," I whispered.

She mewed.

Once inside, Caden sat in the armchair by the hearth, and Xany joined him by sitting on his lap. He grunted which made Xany giggle. Mal took a seat on the sofa after picking up his shorts from the floor and redressing. Not all Changers had clothing when they shifted in and out of form. Some were able to choose one item of clothing that would travel with them through their transformation, and a loincloth was the most common. Our ancestors had made those things easier to take. I wondered why Mal didn't have anything travel with him all the time. Vanessa, however, had to be different; her green velvet dress went with her when she shifted. She liked to stand out and show off her powerful magics. I sat down on the sofa, only for a moment though because Vanessa took my jacket into her massive jaws and tugged me to the floor.

"Vanessa!" I shouted, landing with a thud and making everyone laugh.

"Told you that you were in trouble." Mal grinned.

Vanessa nudged me onto the carpet and began licking my hands and face. I squirmed when her sandpapery tongue tickled in certain spots. She put her paw firmly on my stomach to hold me in place. This gesture was a form of "discipline" that many breeds of cats used to tame their kits when they were naughty.

"What the heck is she doing?" Xany laughed as she watched us.

"Putting her in her place for disobeying Caden." Mal continued to grin.

"Huh?" Xany glanced at Mal before looking back at us.

"It's like when a mother wolf holds her cubs in her mouth when they're getting too rowdy," Mal explained.

"Oh... That seems more normal."

"Course it does." He laughed at his sister. "You're not a cat."

I squirmed under Vanessa but didn't necessarily mind her feline attentions. I ran my fingers through the snowy fur she always kept pristinely white. Her stripes made sensual designs across her coat, and her eye color had changed back to the casual light blue that often went along with a relaxed white tiger. After a few more licks along my neck, she thumped down on the floor beside me and purred, resting her head on my stomach. I petted her ears gently and listened to the others talk.

"She's huge," Xany said. "And a little scary."

"You think she's huge now, wait until you see her beast," Caden said. "Weretigers are notorious giants in beast form. She'll tower at least two feet over Mal and I."

"That's scarier." Xany shuddered as she continued to stare at Vanessa. "No wonder she's confident."

Vanessa looked at the others, lifted her upper lip, blinked both eyes, and twitched her nose.

"What did she say, Nee?" Mal asked.

"She said 'thank you.'" My lips curled into a smile.

"You're welcome. Did you have fun?" Caden asked while laughing.

Vanessa nodding her big head before using her nose to nudge my shirt up and began licking my stomach, which of course made me laugh.

"*Tla.* Stop."

Vanessa gave me a toothy grin and placed her paw on my stomach, doing that gentle kneading type thing that cats often do. Mal smiled at me when he heard me say *"tla"* instead of "no." Every so often I could feel her claws pinch my skin, but I didn't mind.

"So what do you say I whip up some fried chicken and Mal makes some of his famous potato salad?" Caden suggested.

"That sounds yum. Can I help?" Xany asked.

"Of course." Caden grinned and patted her hip for her to stand.

"I have a famous potato salad?" Mal asked, his expression lost.

"Well, no. But you're making potato salad." Caden grinned.

Mal laughed and joined him and Xany in the kitchen while Vanessa and I lay by the fire. After a few moments of listening to her purring, she shifted back to her human form, her green velvet dress melting back into place. She smiled at me and pulled me closer to her. I was calm and at ease with the atmosphere in the cabin. Vanessa's presence was no longer a source of anxiety for the wolves, and she obviously didn't feel threatened by them. I wondered if the calm would continue. Maybe Vanessa would be able to visit like this more often, out in public with me instead of hidden away at night in my room.

CHAPTER TWENTY-TWO

Time seemed to pass more quickly than I remembered. An entire month had gone by since I left Wyoming. The spring thaw came earlier in Utah, though it was subtle. My laptop was stowed away in my trunk. I plopped down on the floor in my room to unearth it from the depths of my cluttered belongings. Not only had it been a month since I moved, but it had also been a month since I checked my e-mail or thought about work. Vanessa suggested that I take more time off. I was not sure how I felt about that. I mean, I still had plenty of money, and Caden had finally let me contribute to the household expenses. I didn't necessarily need to work right now, but work was what I did, wasn't it? I was a doctor—the more time away from work I spent, the less people I helped. Not that I was helping that many people during the times I was in the lab being a minion for Doctor Reynolds.

That jerk. My anger surprised me. I placed my laptop on the bed and dug around for the charger.

Now that everyone had settled in, Caden worked a few days a week at Hank's contracting company. I thought he did it to keep busy rather than for the money. Mal would join Caden occasionally though he seemed content being around the cabin and completing projects. He made a lot of handmade items for Hank's wife to sell down at her shop. The last thing I saw him make was a dagger created completely from the bones of the elk he hunted. It was impressive.

It seemed that Xany and Caden were sort of an item, as if that wasn't bound to happen, and Xany was looking into courses at the state school nearby. She was talking about taking some culinary classes to expand her menu beyond breakfast foods.

In a way, I was the stagnant one. Caden had driven me past the local hospital a few times, but I had yet to send my résumé or make any contact with the administrators. It was like I couldn't move forward and couldn't go back. I was stuck in place.

After emptying out half the trunk onto the carpet, I sighed and abandoned my quest for the laptop charger. I began putting papers and notebooks back into the trunk, clumsily dropping some of my loose drawings on the floor. Xany stopped short when she burst into my room, nearly stepping on them.

"Whoa, what a mess. Whatcha up to?" She bounced over and knelt down beside me.

"Just looking for the computer charger thing..." I gathered the scattered artwork as fast as I could.

"It's on the table there." Xany waved at the small writing table in the corner and picked up one of my drawings off the floor. "Did you draw this?"

I frowned at the charger for eluding me, then snatched the sketch out of Xany's hand. "Yes."

"Hey!" She pouted and sifted through a few more of the drawings, most of which were sketches of wolves, Vanessa, or little children.

"They're really good, Nee, I didn't know you could draw."

"Yeah, well... I can." I flinched when I heard the snark in my own voice. I didn't want to come across mean, but I was getting tired of Xany invading my privacy. I snatched those away too.

"Why are you being rude again? I was just saying that you're a good artist." She huffed and quickly grabbed up another sketch that was farther away from me. Her expression fell.

I got up, tossed the sketches back into the trunk, and stalked over to Xany. "Give me that, it's not for you to see."

"What are these?" She jerked away from me so I couldn't grab the last two in her hand. "Is that you?"

"Xany! Give me those now!" I nearly knocked her down when I went to grab them again.

She moved away from me. "No, Nee. What is this?" she asked and turned the pictures toward me so I could see them.

One of the pictures was a self-portrait that I had drawn of myself looking like a decaying zombie and the other...the other was the one that upset me the most. I hated seeing the drawing of myself, tied up in a tree with coyotes nipping at my heels. My father's darkened image laughing in the doorway of the trailer. Blood covered my arms and legs where I'd been bitten. I was ten. Something rose up inside me and over my shoulders like a hot burning volcanic wave, and I lunged for her. Xany emitted a surprised "oof" when I tackled her. I shouted and wrestled with her, trying to grab the sketches away. The rage engulfed me. Everything seemed red and black.

"Shawnee!" she shouted, the sketches lying forgotten on the floor.

I struggled against her grip. She held my wrists so that I couldn't swing at her. Her legs wrapped around mine, and she flipped me so that I was now on the floor. I screamed and continued to struggle, fighting and kicking at her, at Vanessa, at the floor, at the world, at my father, at everything. Rage seemed to erupt inside me like a pressure cooker left on too long. I'd never been so angry before in my life. I hated everything and everyone, and I wanted to scream, which of course I did. Again Xany manipulated my body. She kept a hold on my wrists, except now I was sitting up against her, and my arms were pinned across my torso.

"Shawnee, calm down...it's okay." She spoke quietly in my ear.

I jerked left and right to get away from her, clipping my knee on the metal corner of the trunk. A sobering pain shot up my thigh and brought tears to my eyes. The royal red rage slipped away and left me in a different type of haze filled with guilt and self-loathing. Xany cautiously let go of my wrists, but kept her arms around me until I stopped moving altogether and sobbed.

"I'm sorry, I shouldn't have looked at your pictures," she said against my cheek.

When she apologized, I hugged her arms. "Scared," was all I was able to say to her.

"I know you're scared, and I bet your knee hurts too." She was talking to me like I was a five-year-old, and I knew I'd been acting like one. I sniffled and looked down at my knee that was bleeding through a small tear in my jeans.

"Yes."

She kissed my cheek and began rubbing my arms. "My ass hurts, too, thanks." She giggled, but it sounded forced.

"I didn't mean to push you. I'm sorry too." The guilt was consuming, engulfing me like a black hole deep inside my soul.

Some helper you are. All you do is hurt everyone around you by causing them pain and distress. You deserve to be hurt... You deserve...deserve...

"Hello? Where'd you go, Nee?" Xany interrupted the painful echoes.

"Huh? Oh, sorry." I winced at the pain in my knee when she helped me up.

"Let's go take a look at that knee."

I limped to the bathroom where the first aid kit was

tucked under the sink. "I can do it, it's all right."

"You don't have to be a doctor to put on a bandage." She smiled and nodded toward the vanity. "Hop up there."

I sighed and sat beside the sink, bending my knee to take a look at the damage through the hole in my jeans that was now pretty saturated with blood. "What did I hit?"

"The corner of your trunk. The metal bit." She placed the kit beside me and took out the alcohol, antibiotic ointment, and a bandage. "You can't roll them up that high." She grinned when she caught me trying to pull my pant leg up rather than take them off.

I sighed as I unbuttoned my jeans, sliding them off before sitting back down. "This is embarrassing. I can really do it myself." I laid my jeans across my lap to hide my thighs.

"So? You get to sew up people's brains and stuff, let us average folk have a lil' fun and play doc for a bit." She rubbed her hands together.

"Fine, go ahead then, *average folk*."

Xany cleaned the gash on my knee and watched as it kept on bleeding. I winced as the alcohol touched my wound, causing it to sting. To drown out the pain, I decided to focus on something I could do, something I knew like the back of my hand.

"Want to stitch it? I'll teach you."

"Stitch it? Won't it hurt?" She stared at me, her expression horrified at the suggestion of stitching my body.

"Not anymore than it does now. Put more alcohol on it and then apply pressure, it's still bleeding too much," I instructed, and she did just that, holding a clean gauze to my knee and pressing. I smiled at her when she was eye level to me.

"Will stitches leave a scar?" she asked, pushing a bit of my hair from my face.

"It'll leave a scar anyway. I'll just add it to my collection of scars."

"You don't have any scars on your legs." She glanced them over again, as if reconfirming her statement.

"The collection is a full-body." I tried to keep the remark neutral. To make it sound like I didn't care. *Oh, it's just another scar. No big deal.*

Xany smiled sadly at me, brushed a strand of hair off my shoulder, then peeked at my knee. "Is it done bleeding?"

"Yes. Now get the suture kit from the box." I pointed it out to her, and she took the small hook with black thread-like material out of the packet, and the surgical sutures.

"It's like a hook! Ewww." She held it away from her, treating it like a living vermin.

"And now you use the sutures to slip the pointed part through the skin flap, then I'll teach you how to tie it. Two stitches will be enough." I laughed at Xany's squeamishness. "Ew! No way. I can't sew your skin!" She did the I'm-completely-grossed-out dance and turned in a circle.

I laughed harder at her antics before taking the sutures from her. "Okay then, watch me." I leaned over and put two small stitches in the gash to close the wound, then tied each stitch slowly so that Xany could see how it was done.

"There, easy. We need to get new tools for the first aid kit now though, since we can't reuse them."

"Shawnee, that was nasty... But fun! Maybe next time I'll try." I realized she'd crept closer to stare at me while I was tying the knots.

"Okay, Xee, next time I injure myself in a flailing incident, you can stitch me up."

"Cool!" She grinned. "I'll put the bandage on!" I leaned back against the mirror to let her finish the bandage. "Do you like being a doctor?" she asked.

"Very much." I tried to fight back the wistful sensation that tugged at me.

"Vanessa thinks you need a break." She applied the ointment, gauze, and tape to my knee.

I raised an eyebrow at Xany's words. "Oh, does she now? She told you so?"

"Uh-huh, I heard her say it when she was talking to Caden the other day." She finished the bandaging and tugged my soiled jeans away from me to toss them into the wash.

"She was talking to Caden?" I frowned now that I was only wearing a T-shirt and my undergarments. "Why?"

"I dunno. She said you worked like a million hours a week in Wyoming and that she thinks you should take a break for a while." Xany shrugged and rested against the washing machine.

"I've taken a month's break. She has no right to suggest that to Caden. What if he says I'm not allowed to work?" I didn't like being controlled by anyone. Immediately I was put off, and Xany narrowed her eyes as she seemed to pick up on my fears.

"She has a right to say whatever she wants, Nee, you know that, and Caden won't make rules like that. Stop being all defensive." She strode over and poked me in the side.

"Hmph." I crossed my arms and glared at her.

"'Hmph' right back at ya." She grinned, absently rubbing my thighs. It made me cringe and suck in my breath.

"Don't...don't touch—" I stopped myself. "Don't touch too high up," I corrected and pushed her hands gently back toward my knees.

"What?" she asked, confused until I nudged her hands back down. "Oh." She giggled and even had the decency to blush a little. "Sorry, you just have soft skin. Why did you draw yourself looking so scary like that?"

Her question bothered me. I didn't want to talk about it. Not my past, not my father, not the drawing or myself. "I just did. I should get dressed."

"Do you think you really look like a zombie?" She persisted, leaning her hip casually against the counter where I was sitting. She continued to rub her hand around my knees in a manner that a mother would do to soothe a child who had just fallen and gotten hurt.

"Maybe at one point," I lied. I still thought I was some sort of monster, but she didn't have to know that.

"Well... I have to say, for a while there back in Wyoming, you looked like you were wasting away but now you're back to beautiful, Nee. I know the guys think so." She wagged her eyebrows. I grew quiet listening to her. I had nothing to say in response to her compliments. Nothing she said could make me feel pretty or beautiful or acceptable in any way.

"And Vanessa too," she added in a quiet voice.

"Oh please, you've seen Vanessa, she's gorgeous. How can she think anyone can compare to that?"

"That doesn't make any sense. Do you really think Vanessa is that conceited?"

"She's not conceited!" I stopped, realizing I'd gotten caught up in my own words.

"You just said she doesn't think anyone can compare to her." Xany tried to hide a smirk. "Or is that your own messed up thinking?"

I grumbled at her.

"C'mere, I wanna show you something." She grabbed my hand, tugging me from the counter. I was beginning to believe that Xany was going to be tugging me around forever. I imagined that if we were sisters, I'd be the little sister who got bossed around and tricked into taking all the blame for everything.

"Careful! I'm injured." I took a few wobbly steps before limping alongside her.

Xany giggled and led me to her room. "Good thing the guys aren't home or they might make something of you walking around without pants."

"Hush up, I'm uncomfortable enough as it is."

Xany's room was set up similar to mine except hers looked more lived in. She had pictures on her bureau of what I imagined to be her parents and a painting someone had done of her name hung on the wall. Her blanket had a flowery pattern, as did the pillowcases and sheets. I smiled because in a way, her room was suiting of her personality. It was bright and cheery, just like Xany.

"We're not playing dress-up, are we?" I hoped to hell it was something else.

"Nope, not dress-up." She closed her bedroom door. A full-length mirror hung on the back of her door.

"Is this an in-house kidnapping?" I crossed my arms over my stomach when she shut the door. With effort, I reminded myself that I was not trapped. Wounded? Yes. Behind a closed door in a room that was not my own? Yes. Trapped? No.

"Um, well, maybe a little bit. But it's only temporary." Xany took me by the shoulders and guided me toward the mirror behind the door.

"Don't freak me out, or I might tackle you again." I resisted a bit, digging my heels into the carpet.

"Better watch it or I'll make Vanessa groom you again." She grinned at me in the mirror, looking over my shoulder.

"Noted." I couldn't help but laugh and shove her hand off my shoulder.

"Okay, we're gonna try something, but you have to trust me okay?" Xany met my gaze in the mirror. My stomach gave a nervous flip-flop.

"Sure, no problem."

"Easier said than done, I know." Xany smiled and held her arms out to me. I bit my lip but walked to her cautiously. She wrapped her arms around me.

"It's weird when you hug me. I don't usually let that happen."

"I know. Nee, I know you've been through a lot of shit in your life, and it's okay to get angry and stuff, but there's one thing that I just can't sit back and let you believe."

"What do you mean?" I tilted my head, puzzled by what she could be talking about.

"You walk around here hiding yourself, totally clueless of how everyone really sees you because you're too caught up in how you see yourself," she said. When she saw my confusion, she explained further. "I'm gonna show you how the rest of us see you."

I did *not* like where this was going. "How?" I tried to keep the cynicism from my voice.

"That's where the trust comes in."

I avoided actually looking at myself and continued to watch Xany through the mirror.

"If it gets too scary, all you have to say is 'stop' and we'll stop, okay?" Her brow softened, as did her smile.

"Okay, stop." I glanced at myself before returning my attention back to her.

"You have to say it when you're really scared, not when you're scared of getting scared." She swatted my arm hard enough to leave a small welt.

"But Xany—"

"That's the rule." She smiled and nuzzled my cheek. "Now, I want you to look in the mirror..."

"I am." I was looking in the mirror just at Xany's greenish eyes, rather than myself.

"At you, not at me." Her breath puffed against my neck

"Xee, I don't want to do this..." I turned around when tingling panic snuck up on me again.

"You can do it, Shawnee, I promise." She nuzzled me again and wrapped her arms around my middle so that her hands were on my stomach. "Look at yourself in the mirror and watch my hands. Can you do that?"

I chewed the inside of my mouth, nodding through my discomfort. Xany started by running her hands slowly up and down my arms.

At first I was uncomfortable, then I noticed the different tones of our skin. "I'm a little bit darker than you."

"Mhmm, just a little." She smiled at me in encouragement.

I watched her hands caress me. In the mirror, I saw a flash of Vanessa's hands replacing Xany's and blinked away the weird vision. She ran her hands over the top of my thighs because they were the next exposed area of skin. I gnawed my lip and drew my gaze away from myself and looked at her in the mirror instead.

"Don't be afraid," she whispered. "Watch my hands and feel what they do. No hurting, right?"

"No."

"Your skin is soft and your muscles are toned from all the walking you do, can you see that?" she asked.

I watched her hands on me and held on to her arms. My heart thumped loudly in my chest, but remained at a steady rate rather than escalating. I nodded to answer her question.

"Now it's going to get a little trickier okay?" Her hands gripped the bottom of my shirt and slowly lifted it up. I made a noise of protest, and she stopped. After a moment to allow me to get used to the idea, she removed my shirt, and I pressed back against her, closing my eyes. She was right; this was trickier. I didn't like seeing myself naked or even partially naked. Xany dropped my shirt to the floor and left me standing in my bra and panties. She lifted my chin and turned me toward the mirror.

"Open your eyes, NeeNee, and take a look."

I listened to her and looked at myself; my stomach churned. My beliefs about myself threatened to turn me into a grotesque zombie. My eyes welled with tears, and my thoughts crept up on me, but then Xany spoke.

"Tell me what you're thinking." She tilted her head; the soft gesture reminded me of my mother.

"How can you tell I'm thinking?" I focused on her cheekbones. When she made certain expressions, I could see the relation between her and Mal.

"I can feel it. Say it out loud."

I hesitated. I didn't want her knowing my private thoughts. I didn't want anyone to know them. She gave me a nudge, and I gave in, probably a bit too easily. "You're an ugly good-for-nothing little bitch. I'll break you. You deserve to die. Let me teach you how." I whimpered.

"Those aren't your own thoughts. That is what someone told you once, right?"

I nodded as a few tears ran down my cheeks.

"Look at your stomach, there's no scars here. Your panties cover the big one. It's smooth and tight." She rubbed her hands on my stomach like Vanessa did. "And your softly curved figure and hips." She traced them. "Most women would kill to have a figure like yours."

I watched her hands move around my torso. She was right. I didn't have any visible scars. Why did I think there were so many? Suddenly I didn't feel as uncomfortable gazing at myself. The image of the mutilated zombie melted away only to be replaced by the body of an average woman. I couldn't believe it was me.

"And here..." She reached behind me and unhooked my bra, letting it drop to my feet, "Your breasts are soft and supple, not too big or too small." She spoke quickly before I was able to get too nervous and moved on when she sensed my discomfort. "And your long, soft neck and defined collarbone that makes lovers want to kiss it all night long." She gave me a gentle kiss on my shoulder. "And your sweet-smelling hair. Dark brown but not black, almost black though. The only thing that hints of your mixed ancestry. Your hair always like shampoo." She giggled and ran her fingers through it, which made me smile. "And your beautiful face—the sharp bone structure of a Cherokee woman—prominent cheekbones, long lashes, plump lips, and the most gorgeous amber eyes I think I have ever seen."

I made eye contact with her through the mirror before glancing back at myself. My face appeared more filled out than it had the last time I paid attention to myself. I didn't look like a sunken, grayed shell of a person. I was...healthy, and my face didn't have scars either. I reached up to stroke my cheek. I knew there had once been a scar there; I was certain of it. Teachers used to stare at it when I was in school. The most visible scar; it was the biggest source of pity in my life. Where had it gone?

"Can you see yourself yet?" she whispered. I was leaning back against her more fully, in the manner of a shy child. "Only one more piece to the puzzle," she warned before pushing my panties down my thighs to the floor.

I squeezed her arms, knowing I was going to have to see the hideous scar. She let me hold on to one of her arms while she used the other to trace my scar. It made me jump with the familiar tickling.

"Look at your scar, NeeNee. It's not as big as you think it is."

Hesitantly, I listened to her. My scar was a lighter color than the rest of my skin and was not as pronounced as I had thought, not when I was seeing my entire body in the mirror anyway. It was only a tiny percentage of my whole being. I looked at Xany through the mirror again.

"So you see? You have one...err...well, now two scars if you count the soon-to-be-scar on your knee." She giggled. "And even so, people have markings, Nee, good and bad." She poked the glyph below my right shoulder for emphasis. "But they don't define us. They're just decorations, like sprinkles on an ice cream cone." She grinned. "You're a beautiful woman, and everyone here knows it. Hopefully soon you'll realize that the way you see yourself isn't right." She kissed my shoulder again, hugging me from behind. I could tell she was finished with her demonstration.

Normally I might have been completely freaked out by standing naked in the mirror with a strange woman holding me from behind, but I wasn't. This was different. Xany pushed my limits and took a lot of heat from me over the past several weeks, including being an unwilling party in a girl-on-girl wrestling match. She had nothing to gain by telling me this. Why would she lie? What was in it for her? There were no answers for these questions. I was left with the responsibility of accepting the possibility that Xany was telling me the truth.

CHAPTER TWENTY-THREE

Xany left me to think about my experience in front of the mirror. I sat alone in my room. An unfamiliar silence surrounded me. The voices, or echoes, I usually heard when I was by myself seemed to have retired for a while. The calmness was foreign. It made sense when Xany said that some of the things I thought about myself weren't truly my own thoughts but something that someone once told me. It was true. And the voices I heard in my head weren't my own either. Most of the time it was my father's voice that said all those things. I guess that's why I called them echoes sometimes. I used to wonder all the time if I'd gone psychotic and the voices were some sort of symptom. I tried my hardest not to think about that. It was just too scary to take in. I thought about Eloise and some of my other patients who had come into the emergency room while symptomatic. My illness wasn't like that. I'd always believed that my illness came from my soul.

I got dressed again in non-bloody clothes and cleaned up the rest of the mess I had left on the floor after Xany and I wrestled over my sketches. I set my laptop on the table by its charger, remembering to glare at it for causing all this trouble to begin with. It was still unbelievable to me that anyone could see me as a whole picture rather than a series of messy divides. If I learned anything at all today, it was that not all injuries create hideous scars, and not all scars are on the outside.

The cabin was quiet late in the afternoon. Xany and Caden had gone out for their usual shopping trip and pizza as they did on Friday nights. Vanessa was working late because the kids at her studio had a recital. I was left to my own devices. I knew that Mal would be in the house. Caden never really left me alone. He made sure of it because he worried like any Alpha would. I wandered from my room into the living room where I found Mal seated on the floor by the coffee table. A fire burned in the hearth. He looked very involved in whatever he was doing. As I got closer, I saw that he had a beading loom on the table and trays of seed beads here and there.

"I figured you'd be here," I said as I approached.

"Hey, just doing some beading." He smiled at me.

I knelt down on the floor across from him to see what he had been working on. "Do you work with seed beads often?" I admired the pattern on the loom. The diamond shapes, and bold colors reminded me of my mother. She'd taught me to bead and sew when I was little. It was something we did together. Often in the woods under the glint of the moon, or in the wheat fields on a summer day. She'd even taught me once how to make beads out of clay, and we'd spend time painting them together.

"Sometimes, they're really small and frustrating. My big ol' hands flick them all over the place." He grinned. "Hence the mess on the floor." He laughed, gesturing around us. Sure enough, there were random scatterings of beads in the carpet and on the floor.

"You're doing well. You can use salmon bones for needles if it gets too tricky, but they're just as small." I started picking up a few of the little beads and placing them back into his trays.

"Why am I not surprised that you know how to bead?"

171

He lifted a brow at me, a grin tugging the corners of his lips.

"Because good Cherokee girls know how to weave, says Momma." I couldn't help but smile at him. Mal was a hard person not to be happy around. He made me feel normal, in a way, and reminded me of the good things in my past. It was a familiarity I could see myself getting used to.

"I bet she does." He chuckled. "Can you sew as well?"

"Yeah, but I've always preferred making dream catchers or mandala type things. Or painting on hides." I sat back and watched him continue to work.

"It sounds like you've learned a lot," he grumbled as he sent another little bead flying across the room. I laughed at it.

"Yeah...my mom was a good teacher." My voice caught in my throat, and I swallowed a back a lump of sorrow.

"She'd be welcome here, you know. That is, if she were still living and needed a pack." He was casual about it, and I appreciated it. I wondered what it would be like if my mom were alive and able to live here with everyone. I thought she might like it. Mal rubbed some beeswax on the end of the threads and prepared to fasten the findings.

"I know. And thank you...for offering and all." I watched his fingers fumble a bit with the sinew. "Careful, it's going to slip." I shot up and caught the end of two of the threads that escaped the loom.

"Your mom has returned to Gaia, and thank you for catching that." He carefully took the threads from me, his fingertips brushing over my hand. My skin tingled when flesh met flesh as if his very touch left an imprint on me. The fluttering sensation in my stomach following the gentle brush caught me off guard.

"Welcome." I tried not to stutter. I watched him remove the slender bracelet from the loom. It had a black, orange, yellow, and white diamond in the middle with purple and white mixed in toward the ends. He'd done a really good job. I hadn't seen a bracelet like that since I'd left the reservation. Mal tied the threads tightly and secured the finding with the necessary steel clasps, then held it up for me to see. He wouldn't have used silver findings for obvious reasons. Silver would be toxic for him to work with, even if it was in such a small quantity.

"What do you think?" he asked.

"I think it's perfect." The thought of such a feral wolf creating delicate beadwork was kind of ironic.

"Excellent." He reached across the table and draped it across my wrist. "I think it belongs to you."

"What? Me?" And before I knew it, he'd fastened the bracelet on my wrist. Nervousness tightened my stomach but in the back of my mind I knew that I would never take it off. My face was hot, and it was difficult to look at him.

"Yes, you. See? It looks perfect." He smiled and leaned back with his elbows on the sofa.

"*Wa-do*," I thanked him quietly, grateful that my complexion would hide most of my blush.

"*Gv-li-e-li-ga.*" He gave the typical response when thanked.

I looked up at him not realizing I'd thanked him in our language, but I sure as heck noticed when he spoke it. His eyes lingered on mine. The fire blazing in the hearth reflected in his pupils and, again, the echo of a crying eagle sounded from somewhere inside me.

"You remind me of an eagle..."

"An eagle? Funny, I thought I might remind you of a wolf." His grin was soft, engaging.

I bit my lip. I didn't understand why I didn't feel threatened by him. Surprisingly, I wondered what it would be like to move closer to him.

"That too, but your eyes make me think of eagles." I couldn't help but smile at him. Mal watched me, his own smile enduring. I didn't understand why he reminded me of eagles, and I tried to think about what my mom would have said if I told her about it. I imagined it would be something like "in time, Gaia reveals all" or something

173

cryptic like that.

Mal was about to say something when Xany came barreling through the front door.

"We brought food! And visitors!" she announced. I tore my eyes away from Mal only when the smell of pizza wafted through the room.

"Pizza and visitors?" Mal stood, offering me a hand, which I gratefully took.

"Uh-huh. Hank stopped by with some packmates to get a good sniff of us." Xany grinned, and Mal hurried over to help her with the boxes.

"A lot of people?" I bit my lip and moved closer to Xany. As a general rule, I wasn't very comfortable around people, especially werewolf people. I'd been around enough wolves, both dominant and submissive, who had attitudes that I just didn't care for. Though, I had to have some faith in Hank if Caden did. After all, Caden wasn't an overbearing Alpha, and I imagined his fellow werewolf peers would share his style.

"Just a few." Caden walked in the door with arms full of bags.

Mal brushed passed him to gather the rest of the groceries from the truck outside. I heard him stop and greet our guests. An immediate ball of unease stirred in my belly. Xany looked over to me and ran her fingers through my hair.

"It'll be okay, Nee, they're really nice," she tried to console me. I was seriously beginning to doubt her claims of not being an empath. She seemed to pick up on my emotions quicker than I did.

"C'mon in, Hank, and meet Shawnee!" Caden called out the door and waved everyone in. Mal carried in the last of the groceries and after him came Hank. He was nearly as large as Caden, though somewhat older. He had long, dark hair pulled into a ponytail, and was dressed like a lumberjack—red flannel shirt with dark blue jeans, the whole bit. He was light skinned and jolly looking. I smirked at the irony of his appearance. Hank, like Caden, was a clear dominant wolf and not only was he a pack leader, but a sept leader, which meant he had control of several smaller packs within the area. He had to be pretty powerful to control all of that. Behind Hank came an average-sized woman with long, black hair and fair skin. She had on an ankle-length skirt and carried a young child on her hip. I guessed she was Hank's mate.

"Hank, Imogene, this is Xany and Shawnee." Caden introduced us, and we all shook hands. "And this of course is Cote." He gestured to the young boy in Imogene's arms, who turned away when he was introduced.

"Nice to meet you again." Xany giggled. I nodded and shook their hands, watching the little boy act shy.

"It's nice ter meet ya two ladies as well," Hank said, with a thick accent that I couldn't even begin to place and a bright smile. "Caden, I kin smell the cat ya spoke of."

Caden chuckled and nodded toward me. "Shawnee carries her scent mainly."

"Hey, boys, c'mon inside fer a darn minute," Hank shouted out the door followed by a hearty chuckle. A few seconds later, two young boys bounded into the house. They looked around twelve or thirteen years old. Both had short hair that was spiked with some sort of product.

"These are two more of my sons, Achachak or Jack as he prefers, and Mato."

"It's Mat, Dad," huffed the younger one, who immediately looked to us and stuck out his hand. "I'm Mat."

Xany shook his hand first. "It's nice to meet you, handsome." She grinned, and it made Mat blush.

"Well met, Mat." I shook his hand quickly before he ran off. Even at such a young age, I could tell that he was going to be a pretty powerful werewolf once he had his change. Jack was the quieter of the two; he sniffed the air around us and looked up at Hank with a frown. "There's cat here."

"Yes, there is, an' you'll be right to respect the cat you just scented, boy." Hank clapped his son on the back, looking between all of us. "He's about prime for his Firsting," he explained.

Most adolescents who were close to their Firstings often exhibited hot tempers and poor behavior, which didn't distinguish them at all from regular adolescents. It was the fever you had to look out for. Werewolves had a body temperature that was higher than average, but children near the time of their Firsting spiked a fever around one hundred and four degrees.

"I can smell it on him." Caden laughed a bit. "It's all right, Jack, and the cat you smell is an ally."

Jack didn't seem convinced as he shook our hands firmly. "Can I go now, Dad?" he asked. Mat might have the promise of a dominant wolf, but Jack had the attitude of an Alpha in the making.

"Be off wit' ya, be off." Hank waved the young ones outside.

Cote remained in his mother's arms, hiding from all the eyes in the room. He was absolutely cute and was wearing a leather vest over his T-shirt and jeans. I knew he couldn't be a werewolf just by looking at him. But if he was, I imagined he'd be a rather submissive wolf. Caden, Xany, Hank, and Imogene started talking some business about allies, and cats, and cautioning about some of the cubs that were close to their Firstings. Caden reassured Hank that Vanessa would be able to hold her own if anything should happen, but that he would warn her anyway. Hank didn't seem remarkably moved by Caden's trust of a feline. I continued to watch Cote nibble on bits of his mother's hair.

"You like kids?" Mal asked from behind me. He tugged me from my daydream, and I turned to face him.

"Yeah. They can be terrific. I like working with them. It's rewarding to make them feel better. The look on their little faces is priceless." I crossed my arms over my stomach. The discomfort over being around strangers was overwhelming at times. Especially when I was talking about intimate things like family, kids, and work.

"I imagine that at times like that, being a doctor is rewarding in itself." He put his hand on my shoulder, which was a brave move by any sort. The last time he tried to touch me he had a second thought. His wolf probably didn't take well to the rejection that he saw coming. Most wolves don't. Being skin-to-skin was important for them, and affection was part of communication.

This time, however, he didn't stop himself, and to be honest, I didn't mind as much as I thought I would. A strange shiver ran down my spine. I could only take it for so long before I had to move away. I twisted away from him to open one of the pizza boxes on the table. "It is. Hungry?"

"Always. Caden knows a guy at the pizza place in town who puts all sorts of meat on the pizzas for his werewolf friends." Mal grinned. "And pepperoni for the non-beast folk."

"Caden must have all the good connections then."

"Amen." He handed me a slice of pepperoni on a plate before dishing some pizza out to everyone else.

In effort to distance myself from the chatting strangers, I took my pizza over to the sofa. When Mal gave Xany her plate, she said something to him and nodded in my direction. He came over and joined me on the sofa, sitting a bit closer than usual. Normally this would bother me, but I was able to swallow down my worry along with a bit of pizza.

"Did she tell you to come over and keep me company?" I asked.

"Nah, she said I should bring you a soda." He handed me a can.

"Thank you." I smiled at him, but I had to admit I was a bit skeptical as to whether he was telling the truth.

"My pleasure."

After a while, Hank and Imogene bid everyone good-bye and left for the night. Caden and Xany joined us by the fire with the pizza, sodas, and bags of potato chips.

"Hank seems nice," I told Caden as he sat in the armchair. Xany sat down on the floor at the coffee table so she could add garlic powder and parmesan cheese to her pizza.

"He is. He and Gene have about nine cubs." Caden chuckled. "She's a quiet spirit, but you should see her in the home with the cubs. She's got them all in line."

I smiled, listening to Caden as I finished the last bite of my pizza.

"Nine cubs? Damn, that's a lot of kids running around." Xany shook her head while taking two slices of pizza and making a pizza-sandwich with them. I laughed at her.

"What are you doing?" I asked.

"It's less calories this way!" She grinned and took a huge bite. I laughed again and shook my head at her.

"Your cat is here," Mal announced as he helped himself to a second slice of overly meaty pizza while rolling his eyes at his sister.

Caden grinned at Xany then glanced to my bedroom door, waiting for Vanessa to appear. She sauntered out of my room wearing a full-body, black leotard that had a cropped oval neck, long sleeves, and a sheer green skirt that hung loosely at her hips. She had her hair up in a ponytail, but as she walked toward us, she removed the bauble and let it fall loosely. Every eye in the room was on her when she swayed her way over to us. The sensation in my stomach made me feel kind of fidgety so I reached for my soda and took a sip.

Caden cleared his throat before speaking. "Nice outfit there, Vanessa."

She purred when she saw me but grinned at Caden. Xany glared at her for the faintest second before glancing at me with a perked brow, rubbing her stomach.

"Hey, Ness. Hungry?" I always liked when she wore her dance outfits; it made her subtle feline movements more prominent.

"Hi. Not yet," she said, purring louder as she knelt down in front of me, burying her face against my stomach. She nuzzled me with affection typical of a feline, getting reacquainted with me in the same way she usually did after spending a significant time apart. Except it wasn't usually my stomach that she nuzzled. It was most often my neck.

A sudden surge of something rushed from my belly button downward, then up my spine. I lifted myself up to stop the feeling from continuing. I pushed at her shoulders a bit, and she looked up at me.

"What's wrong?" she asked, her expression guarded.

"I dunno. It felt funny when you did that." I urged her upward into a normal hug.

She hugged me tight and wormed her way in, sitting between Mal and me. He was grinning at her, enjoying her quirky behaviors and near obliviousness to the other people in the room. Xany looked kind of annoyed and had moved to take a seat in Caden's lap while she ate her food.

"You make quite an entrance there, Red." Mal chuckled at her.

She hissed at him, though she followed it with a grin that made him laugh. For some reason my face was flushed, and only got warmer when Vanessa nuzzled my neck. I sat up a bit.

To avert any reaction from her, I hurriedly asked, "How was the recital?"

"Good. One little girl did fall off the stage by accident but"—she shot us a mischievous grin— "I caught her and put her back on stage."

Caden chuckled at her story. "Did you use your super agile cat speediness to do that?"

She grinned boastfully, and her purring grew even louder. It sounded more like wheezing now, making her voice sound rattley. "Maybe."

"Vanessa, you need to be more careful," I lectured and pushed her bangs off her face.

She merely mewed at me like a pathetic kitten. The sound made me melt, and I nuzzled her. Xany was oddly quiet and leaned over to whisper something in Caden's ear that I couldn't hear, but Vanessa must have because she looked over at her with a risen brow. Xany sunk back into Caden a bit, and he patted her hip reassuringly. Mal broke the tension.

"We have lots of pizza, Red, if you're hungry."

Vanessa lifted her gaze to him for a moment and twitched her nose once. Even in human form, her behavior always seemed more catlike. Mal tried to mimic the nose twitch, which made him look like he was about to sneeze.

"Sorry, I don't speak cat."

I laughed softly and poked Vanessa in the side. "English, bad kitty..."

She mewed at me again and gave me a gentle nip on my neck. My face felt like it was about to burst with the embarrassment brought on by Vanessa's overt public display of affection. This time Xany couldn't help but giggle a little bit. "She's like a real kitty."

"She is a real kitty, Xee." Mal decided that the nose twitch meant yes and served Vanessa a piece of pizza. She took it and lifted her chin to him in thanks.

"I think we'll all be speaking cat eventually," Caden said.

Vanessa grinned and took a bite of her pizza, turning around to lean against me while she ate, and put her bare feet up alongside Mal's leg. I draped my arm around her middle habitually. Xany watched us again. This time she caught my gaze for a moment before giggling.

"What?" She was acting strange, and it bothered me a bit.

"Oh, nothing really," she said in a singsong voice before reaching for another slice of pizza.

"You're up to something again." I frowned to express my displeasure.

"Me? I'm never up to anything, right, Caden?" Xany bat her lashes at him.

Mal nearly spit out his soda as he laughed so hard his entire body shook. After a moment, he finally gathered himself enough to say, "Xandrea Wade, you are the biggest troublemaker I have ever met."

Caden laughed and kissed Xany's cheek. "Of course, precious. You're the best behaved of all."

I laughed upon hearing Caden purposely feed into Xany's good girl act, and Vanessa seemed to enjoy listening to everyone while she ate. Xany grinned at Caden and stuck her tongue out at Mal who shook his head at her.

"So, Red, think one day you'll dance for us?" he asked casually.

"Maybe." She finished her pizza and set the plate on the table before stealing my soda for a sip.

"What kind of dancing do you teach?" Mal continued to talk with Vanessa, which I appreciated. I was surprised that she was able to answer his questions so directly. Whenever she was in a room full of people, her social skills all but disappeared.

"Irish Dancing." She slouched a tiny bit, her shyness peeking through. Her hand fell to my upper thigh, and she began doing a gentle kneading motion with her fingers. It reminded me of a common house cat when she did that.

"She used to compete when she lived in Ireland. She has medals and stuff." I joined the conversation to distract myself from Vanessa's wandering hand. For some reason, I was uncomfortable with her affection. She was always touchy and affectionate with me, but it was usually in private. Maybe it was the presence of other people in the room that fed my discomfort.

"Really?" Xany asked with peaked interest.

Vanessa nodded, slouching a little more to rest her

head on my shoulder. Even though Vanessa took pride in being the center of attention, she never seemed to like being the center of attention that required Q and A.

"For such a confident cat, you're being awfully shy," Mal said as he watched her. He seemed intrigued by her interesting demeanor as many people often were.

Vanessa mewed at him, then snickered. "I'm not confident," she said, which made everyone laugh.

"She's very modest," I said through my laughter, which earned me a swat from Vanessa. Xany giggled and seemed to be struggling with whether or not she was entertained by Vanessa or put off by her.

"You want to stay and watch a movie with us?" Caden asked. I imagined it was his way of casually including Vanessa. He had a subtle way about him that, even though he was large and scary, made people feel welcomed and comfortable. He was a strange dominant, a strange Alpha, and a strange wolf. So was Mal for that matter. Who would have thought a wolf would ever be sharing a couch with a cat? Xany was right; Caden and Mal were different. Their inclusion and acceptance of Vanessa as an ally, without knowing her from Eve, proved that. Vanessa nodded to Caden. I smiled at him, silently thanking him for inviting her to stay. He gave me a subtle wink, and Xany hopped up to the stack of DVDs on the mantle.

"I get to choose!" she shouted, then selected *Dracula* this time. I got the feeling she had a thing for vampire flicks.

Mal laughed at his sister, grabbed a few blankets off the back of the sofa, and tossed them out to everyone. Vanessa turned on her side, and I wrapped an arm around her. She slipped her hand up my shirt and rested it on my bare stomach. A bizarre flutter wiggled through me under her hand. It made her grin. I didn't quite understand all the things that my body had been doing lately. Between the hot flashes in my face and strange stomach lurches and gurgles, I didn't know which was worse. If I wasn't a doctor, I'd probably think I'd had some sort of disease. But knowing what I knew, I doubted there were any diseases where the main symptoms were hot flashes and belly gurgles.

We all watched the movie together; however, I could have sworn Mal, Caden, and Xany were all sharing some sort of silent conversation with each other because every once in a while I would catch them glancing or nodding toward one another. I imagined that it was either Vanessa or I as the subject of their discussion...

CHAPTER TWENTY-FOUR

I woke up the next morning later than usual after having a ridiculous dream about a version of Dracula that sucked mercury out of thermometers. Rolling over to stretch, I found myself alone in bed again and frowned. Sometimes I liked when Vanessa stayed through the night, and for some reason last night was one of those times. I got out of bed and went about my showering routine before heading into the kitchen. Xany was there by herself, taking out a few items from the fridge to start breakfast like she usually did.

"Need any help?" I asked.

She perked up, greeting me with an excited hug. "Sure, NeeNee," she replied with a smile. "We can make an omelet, home fries, and sausages. I think we have all of the stuff for it."

I returned her hug this time without much thought. I was starting to get used to her affection. "Yum! Yeah, let's do all that."

Xany appeared tickled by my sudden enthusiasm. "The guys are outside finishing the fire pit, and they'll be hungry soon."

I smiled, and we got to it. We fixed a ham and cheese

omelet, seasoned home fries, and plump sausages. I set the table, and Xany squeezed some fresh oranges for juice. She was proud of our collateral work, and frankly, so was I.

"So, where's your kitty today?" she asked as we set the food on the table.

"I dunno. Most of the time she leaves before I wake up in the morning." I shrugged, placing a plate of sausages in the center of the table.

"Really? Why?" Xany looked over her shoulder at me.

"She just does." I turned to face her, not understanding what the big deal was about Vanessa leaving. She always did; it's just how she was. Maybe it's just how cats were in general.

"You want her to stay, huh." She grinned, but I could tell she was trying to hold back a girlish giggle.

"Sometimes, yeah, I do. She falls asleep with me almost every night, then when I wake up, she's gone." I poured the juice into glasses as we conversed.

"Maybe it means something to her by staying all night and waking up with you," Xany suggested, tapping her lip and looking at me with a risen brow.

I got the feeling she was trying to plant a seed that I was sure I didn't know how to sow. "Maybe."

Mal and Caden came into the house, covered with mud and dirt from digging out the fire pit. It wasn't a very deep hole that they'd have to make so I wasn't sure why they were so dirty. Maybe they decided to roll in it or something.

"Hey, ladies... Wow, it smells good in here." Caden sat down at the kitchen table.

"Of course! Nee and I cooked." Xany grinned, before her expression suddenly changed into a stern look, both hands on her hips. "Oh no, you don't, Mister Lionsong. You get your sexy ass in there and clean up before you even think about sitting down at my table." She pointed toward the bathroom.

Laughing, Mal snuck off to the bathroom first to clean

up while Caden got reprimanded. Once they both were clean, everyone gathered around the table. Mal was smiling when he sat. "Damn," was all he said before he started serving everyone, Xany and me first, then Caden and himself. I lifted a brow at him when I saw the serving order.

"We don't have eating ranks in this pack. Ladies first," he explained with a grin.

"The man speaks the truth. Alpha eats with his pack here, not before." Caden gave me a nod and only started eating once everyone had a plateful. I smiled at them and looked to Xany. ·

"Told you." She shrugged, smiling proudly. "They're different."

While we sat together and ate, Mal told me of his plans for the fire pit and how he decided to dig it out a few yards from the front of the cabin. The fire pit was a place where everyone could hang out on cool nights, have ceremonies, cook, and sometimes simply make S'mores.

"What do you say since you girls cooked, Mal and I clean up?" Caden offered.

"Good plan, I'm game!" Xany giggled.

The guys cleaned up the kitchen relatively quickly while Xany and I decided to saunter off to the main room to turn on the TV.

"We should check the weather, Nee. It said there was going to be a series of thunderstorms heading our way." She flipped through the programs until she got to the news channel that warned of severe thunderstorms.

"I like storms," I commented while listening to the forecast. Mal sneaked off to the bathroom and Caden joined us while he waited his turn.

"Hank said his men will be back out here at the end of the week to finish the addition now that the ground isn't as frozen," Caden said.

"What are they adding on?" Xany asked.

"Two more rooms. One I thought would be good for a

library or office type area, and the other can be a spare room or guest room or whatever we want it to be. They're also going to add a second bathroom at the end of the addition."

"A second bathroom will be perfect. That way Nee can take as long a shower as she wants without me bothering her when I have to pee."

I laughed and bopped Xany with a pillow from the sofa. Caden chuckled and sniffed the air. "The resident cat has returned."

"Does he always announce my presence?" Vanessa asked as she strolled into the living room from the doorway of my room. She had gone back to wearing her usual green velvet dress. My mood lightened when I saw her. Her hair was down, and she smelled of sweet shampoo and fabric softener, which were my two favorite scents. She was barefoot as she almost always was, and she purred while nuzzling my cheek in greeting.

"Every time." I returned the gesture, closing my eyes briefly and enjoying the contact with her. While I was distracted, Caden glanced to Xany who giggled softly.

"What if I wanted to sneak up on you?" She sat on the arm of the sofa beside me.

"Unless you have a gift that makes you scentless, it'll be pretty hard," Caden said.

Vanessa snickered and peeked over at Xany who continued to giggle. She lifted a brow at her and slid her hands to her hips. I looked over to Xany to see what she was up to.

"What's so funny?" I asked.

"Oh nothing..."

I shook my head at her antics. "Ness, you want something to eat?"

"Milk?" Vanessa asked, keeping her eyes on Xany.

"Just milk?"

"Mhmm. Or cream." Her purring was low and subtle. She watched Xany, who was unrelenting with her giggling

187

MAX ELLENDALE

and grinning as she toyed with Vanessa.

Caden watched the interaction silently. Just as I got up to get the glass of milk, Mal returned from his room dressed in his typical jeans and T-shirt. His shirt was tighter than usual, which made me do a double take and bump into the kitchen table. He looked at me with a risen brow. I smiled innocently and hid behind the door of the refrigerator until he went to sit in the main room with the others and nodded a greeting to Vanessa.

"Xany, what are you doing?" he asked when he saw Xany giggling and Vanessa eyeing her.

I came back to the living room and handed Vanessa her milk. When I went to sit down on the sofa, she slid quickly under me so that I ended up sitting on her lap. I shook my head though I smiled. She held me close and scooted around until she was comfortable. Vanessa was such a typical cat sometimes. When she could tell I was in a good mood, she always made the extra effort to get as much affection out of me as possible. I didn't mind.

"Oh, nothing," Xany said in a sweet singsong voice.

"I think you're right, bro. She is a troublemaker," Caden said.

Vanessa sipped her milk, then handed it to me to place on the coffee table as she silently watched the exchange.

Xany continued to put on her innocent act. "Am not."

Mal nodded to Caden, and Xany huffed. "It's not my fault she let her secret out," she said, baiting Vanessa whose entire body tensed.

She glared at Xany with such force that I imagined if her eyes were laser beams they'd go right through my body like butter. "What secret?" Vanessa's voice was low and quiet, threatening.

It is common knowledge in the preternatural world that cats are notorious seekers of secrets. They love to keep them, have them, and find them out. Telling a cat you have a secret or know a secret is a sure way to rile or upset them.

"Xany, that's not very fair. She's just teasing you, Vanessa, relax." I watched her emerald eyes fixate on Xany, flashing yellow bits, and her pupils became slender.

"Neither one of us is going to protect you, Xandrea Wade, when Vanessa kicks your ass and ties you upside down from the ceiling fan," Mal warned. Caden laughed lightly, but I could tell he agreed with Mal. Xany grinned at having a one-up on Vanessa and shrugged, pretending not to care.

Vanessa grew increasingly tense. I turned in her lap, straddling her legs to face her. Vanessa's hands went to my hips, digging in with a force that was ever more crushing. She continued to glare at Xany with her cattish eyes. I took careful hold of her chin and guided her to look back at me.

"She's baiting you. Don't bite."

She hissed at me, then frowned. Her posture slouched, and she turned fully away from Xany. In the language of cats, Vanessa had just expressed the depth of her displeasure. To be ignored, not just mentally, but physically, was the greatest of insults.

Caden gave Xany a chastising glance which only made her pout. "I was just having fun."

I ran my fingers through Vanessa's hair and then glanced at Xany. Vanessa smiled at me when I touched her hair, and her purring returned slowly. She tugged me closer so that my stomach was nearly pressed against hers. I didn't think twice about sitting like this. It wasn't unusual for us, in private anyway.

"Mom would have tanned your hide for that," Mal reprimanded his sister.

"But Mom's not here." Xany bobbed her head from side to side with each word.

"Even if you do know a secret, it's not fair to drive the cat crazy over it. Play fair." He lifted his lip as if to snarl at Xany. The flavor of his discourse was so thick I could almost taste it.

Xany huffed and went to sit in Caden's lap. He, of

course, babied her but didn't disagree with Mal's lecturing. Neither of them agreed with hitting below the belt. The room grew quiet until Vanessa's purring was the only sound. Suddenly there was a crack of thunder outside. A deep grayness overshadowed the previously bright tree line. I watched out the window, waiting for more lightening to come.

"Your favorite," Vanessa whispered, her eyes swirling back to their usual green.

"Mhmm. I like storms." A flash of lightening illuminated Vanessa from behind. Her hair seemed to shimmer for a moment.

"Me too. They're especially strong up here," Mal said. I drew my gaze over to him.

"Think we'll lose power?" My brows flicked upward though I tried to hide my excitement.

"Maybe." He grinned. "You like that?" He mimicked my lifted brows which made my cheeks flush.

"Yeah. Everything stops, and we're stuck in total nothingness with no distractions. It's pure. I love it." I smiled at him. I could tell Mal was the kind of man that appreciated the simple things in nature.

Caden was sitting there with a smile on his face. I could feel Xany's eyes on me while I interacted with Mal. For some reason she kept watching the two of us like hawks lately. I didn't really understand why, but maybe she was feeling protective of her brother. Caden looked pretty goofy sitting there smiling for no reason.

"I hate rain." Vanessa shuddered.

"You hate water unless it's a shower." I poked her stomach.

She grinned and leaned into me, pretending to bite my shoulder. I laughed and tried to wiggle away.

"Naughty."

She snickered and relaxed back against the sofa as her eyes wandered over me. I watched her until a flash of lightening lit up the window. It sent a shiver up my spine.

Vanessa chewed her bottom lip. I wasn't sure if she was nervous or holding back something she wanted to say. Vanessa purred louder, until she was making the wheezy-sounding kind. She slipped her hands up my shirt to rub my bare stomach.

I glanced at the others, worried that all eyes were on us without the distraction of a movie. My slight discomfort turned into full-blown embarrassment that burned my cheeks. My stomach jumped and warmth rushed through me, starting from behind my navel.

Vanessa's expression made the slightest of shifts, but she continued to gaze me. I could tell Mal was watching us. I glanced over at him. He seemed relaxed. Xany and Caden were quietly kissing by the fire. I tore my gaze away quickly and looked back to Vanessa.

"You smell different," Vanessa said, still chewing her lip.

"I...what? How do I smell different?" Her odd statement caught me off guard.

She rubbed her hands on my stomach again. That weird flutter behind my navel returned. A wave of shyness suddenly caught hold of me. I hugged her to escape it, which ultimately gave her less access to my stomach.

"When the storm is over, what do you all say we head down to Imogene's shop in town? Mal has a few things to drop off, and it might not be a bad idea to get out a bit tonight." Caden's voice seemed to appear out of nowhere, but I was secretly grateful for it.

Mal was the only one who seemed to be enjoying the ambiance. Vanessa wrapped her arms around me and nipped my neck and shoulder. Occasionally, I could hear a quiet inhale as she sniffed me. I didn't understand what she meant by saying I smelled different. Nothing had changed. I still used the same soaps, and detergents, and everything else. Worry struck my core. I didn't want to smell different to her. I wanted to smell the same. What if the smell was gross or something?

I wasn't ready to deal with the feelings in my body or the worry over my sudden scent change so I decided to be the first to volunteer for the outing. "I'll go. I want to see her shop."

"Me too," Xany said. "Maybe she'll have some cool stuff for the house."

"How about you, Vanessa? Want to come along?" Caden's grin was daring.

"Will it be messy?" Vanessa asked, mischief twinkling through her eyes.

"Maybe," he replied with a chuckle. "Up for it?"

"Mhmm..." She issued him a wicked grin.

"Caden! And you say I'm the troublemaker!" Xany exclaimed.

"What can I say? I learn from the best."

CHAPTER TWENTY-FIVE

The raging storm lasted longer than we expected. The heavy wind, rain, and golf-ball-sized chunks of hail spewing from the sky were fabulous. The cabin lost power for a few hours, which didn't really affect us all that much. Mal kept the fire going, and we still had running water. The guys cooked hot dogs in the fireplace that tasted perfectly charred, and Xany made dip to go with our chips. The lull of the rain beating down on the roof made me relaxed and tired. Twice I dozed off on the sofa.

"I'm going to go lay down for a while," I said.

Xany and Caden were lying on the floor by the fire. She was resting her head on his chest with her eyes closed, her hand moving in a gentle caress. Vanessa purred contently while sitting sideways in the armchair, dangling her legs over the arm. Mal sat on the floor, whittling a piece of wood. He looked up at me. "Feeling all right?"

"Just tired. The rain makes me sleepy." I got up, giving Vanessa a pat on the knee as I walked past, then disappeared into my room. She reached out to let her hand drag across my waist. She didn't follow me, which was a little bit surprising. Maybe she was feeling a bit self-conscious.

I pulled back my blankets and curled into bed, cracking the window open to listen to the rain and the rumbling thunder outside. I hugged my pillows and melted into the comfort of my bed.

***

I could hear myself screaming, and my body was shaking so hard that I couldn't get a grip on the bed to push myself up. Mal dived onto the bed and plucked me up from my hiding spot where I was huddling in the corner. The screaming was so loud I had to cover my ears.

"Shawnee, shh... It's okay, you were having a dream." He brushed his fingers against my cheek, his tone soothing, as he tried to calm me.

Mal's quick movement abruptly stopped my screaming. All I could hear was the familiar underwater sound emanating from him when he spoke until I heard, "*Take me with you.*" Mal's voice injected into my brain like a cool liquid, calming and surrounding me.

Caden and Xany stood in the doorway of my room, and at nearly the same time, Vanessa appeared in front of them. She paced beside the bed, growling and snarling at Mal. I opened my eyes just as Mal pulled me into his lap. When she saw that he wasn't hurting me, Vanessa knelt beside us. Tears trickled down my cheeks. I was like a five-year-old being coddled after a nightmare. It was embarrassing and confusing to have everyone in my room. I wanted to push Caden and Xany out the door and scream at Mal and Vanessa to get away from me, but I didn't. I sobbed and collapsed against Mal's chest, covering my face. Vanessa's growling stopped when she came closer to stroke my hair.

"I hate this," I muttered through my sobs. "I hate it so much."

Mal rubbed my back and rested his chin on my head. He sucked in his stomach, holding his breath. I wondered if that's how he squashed his emotions because sometimes that's how I squashed mine. Vanessa caressed my cheek and tugged my hands away from my face. I glanced between her and Mal, feeling my stomach drop and sullenness wash over me.

Energy left my body, and I went limp, reduced to nothing more than a silent, teary mess. Mal wrapped his arms tighter around me while Vanessa tilted her head back and closed her eyes, fighting her own tears. I'm not sure how, but it was like she sensed my defeat. Caden squeezed Xany, and his throat made a wolven gargling sound. Xany was holding on to him like she'd gotten weaker over the last few minutes.

"Shawnee." Mal was the one to break the silence. "You-you have to think about some of this. It's been a while since you've had a nightmare or flashback like that—at least a week. When you first moved here, it was nearly every day, sometimes more than once."

I listened to him. His flesh burned into mine as if in some strange way we were melting together. Vanessa's cheeks and eyes reddened with sadness. Her body writhed in a silent agony that I couldn't understand. It was like it was hurting her to not be the one comforting me.

"Mal is right, Shawnee," Caden chimed in. "Even if it doesn't feel like it, you've gotten better. I can sense it in you." His chest puffed up as if he was pressing some sort of energy outward. His power filled the room, and it took my breath away.

I guess a marathon runner might describe it as something like catching a second wind. It gave me the energy to move again, but that energy turned into anger.

"I hate this so much." I clenched my teeth and sat up in Mal's lap. I talked to Vanessa because she was the one that was in front of me. "It's not fair I have to deal with this. I have no control over anything I do, and then suddenly I wake up and people are holding me in place or caressing me to make me feel better. It's not fair. I want to know what happens to me. I want to know why you're holding me and touching me." My voice got louder as anger surged through me. "I want to feel it while I'm awake and not in some disgusting place where my father is raping me or beating me. I want to have memories of things that are good and not drowned out by alcohol or loud music and bad men." Hot tears continued to trickle down my face and my breath heaving while I shouted.

Mal seemed to breathe with me as he tapped into my rage. We rode it together. Vanessa took my hands in hers, nodding to me, as if she had been waiting for me to react like this for some time.

"I can't stand it anymore."

Only you can change your life...

I heard the echo of Vanessa's voice in my head. It was an old one, and I closed my eyes, trying to remember where it came from. Her voice sounded younger, firmer. I couldn't remember ever hearing Vanessa's voice so strongly in my head. Usually it was my father, or sometimes Mom. Then the memory struck me. My shoulders slumped down by the sudden weight of guilt that I couldn't place. I watched Vanessa, trying to understand her voice and the feelings. I touched her face. Suddenly her hair was shorter, and she had makeup on. I had to blink away the imprinted image to focus again, seeing her as she was now.

"I need to take a bath," I said. My voice sounded distant, like I was reading a line in a play. I knew exactly what I was supposed to say because I'd said it before. A sudden sense of *déjà vu* washed over me. The color drained from Vanessa's already pale complexion. She knew her line too.

"*Only you can change your life,*" I mimicked the echo as if she could hear it too. At that moment, I was slammed with a memory.

"What does that mean?" Mal asked.

My vision grew hazy, and his voice was a distant whisper...

"How could you bring that asshole back here, Shawnee?"

Vanessa's voice rings in my ears.

"It's not your business," I shot back. Suddenly I am in our old dorm room. Vanessa is standing in front of me, wearing a bright red dress with a torn sleeve.

"You look awful. Have you seen yourself lately? Don't you even care?" She asks and takes a step toward me. I shove her, ineffectively, before storming off toward the bathroom.

"Go fuck yourself, Vanessa. I know my life is fucked up, but it's not for you to pass judgment."

"Only you can change your life, Shawnee," she says. I slam the door in her face.

I blinked out of the memory. Everyone was staring at me, though still standing in the same place so I knew that I hadn't lost that much time.

"What—" I started to ask before Mal interrupted.

"Welcome back. Want to fill us in on why you just told Vanessa to fuck off?"

I was sitting sideways in his lap in a way that allowed me to see everyone. I looked between him and Vanessa. "I...what?" Vanessa was still holding my hands and kneeling in front of me. She was shaking harder than I was.

"'*Go* fuck yourself, Vanessa. I know my life is fucked up, but it's not for you to pass judgment,'" Mal quoted.

I sighed. It was getting harder to contain myself lately. "It was a memory..."

He waited for me to continue. When I didn't, he spoke. "None of this is going to get better until you start talking."

"No, no...she doesn't have to tell this one," Vanessa said suddenly, dropping my hands and running her fingers through her own hair. Her complexion had gone from pale to gray. I had no idea why she would defend me shutting down. Normally she was the one who encouraged me to take control of my memories. But then it hit me. She must know something that I didn't. I frowned at her. Whatever it was that I'd forgotten must have been pretty big, or maybe even humiliating.

Xany decided it was her turn to direct the traffic. "You can't keep her secrets for her, Vanessa. She has the right to know."

Vanessa moved away from the bed and hissed at Xany for her continuing to bring up secrets.

"What secrets? What else did I say?" I asked. Now I was getting angry at both of them for potentially hiding something.

"She doesn't remember so what's the point of bringing it up now, okay?" Vanessa's voice quivered. I'd never seen her act this way before, and it was starting to scare me. She glanced at Caden. He looked stoic, which to me meant he was going to let this play out.

"I have to agree with Xany this time," Mal said as he looked at Vanessa. "Shawnee, what do you remember?"

"I dunno... I guess I brought a jerk home that night, and Vanessa was pissed about it. Her dress was torn. She told me to look at myself because I looked horrible, and I told her to fuck off like you heard. She told me that it was my job to change my life, no one else's." I glanced at her because that was all that I remembered. She watched me, wringing her hands together while she waited for me to continue.

"Then I slammed the door." I shrugged; the memory didn't seem very exciting. "She was right, though. I just didn't want to hear it I guess."

"There's more you're not remembering," Xany said, glaring at Vanessa before looking back to me. "She knows it, can't you tell?"

I glanced between the women. "Is that true?"

Vanessa hesitated. She'd started pacing back and forth before sitting in the chair by the writing table. She watched me and gave me a faint nod, drawing her eyes away with a pain-filled expression, to gaze out the window. The rain was streaming down the glass.

"Think about it, Nee." Xany moved to the bed.

"Ness?" I scooted forward so I could put my feet on

the floor.

Vanessa didn't look at me; she just shook her head. Her reaction freaked me out so I turned to Xany, chewing my lip. The anxiety pressed on my chest, making it difficult to breathe. If whatever happened that night was affecting Vanessa this way, I wasn't sure if I wanted to know after all.

"I know you're scared, NeeNee, but it's not Vanessa's job to tell you what happened. You have to at least try and remember." She tucked a bit of hair behind my ear.

She was right; I was scared. I had never seen Vanessa behave like this before. Had I done something to her? Had I hurt her or someone else? Who was the guy? Did he hurt her? I watched Vanessa as she put her head down on her knees. I looked around at everyone. They were all expecting me to tap into a blocked memory, and apparently, it was a badly blocked memory.

"Try," Xany said encouragingly.

I nodded. If anything I owed it to Vanessa. I closed my eyes and thought about the scene I'd just remembered. I heard the door slamming over and over again in my head. I knew it meant something. I focused on the door.

Take me with you. Mal's voice jumped into my thoughts. I opened my eyes to gaze at him; his lips weren't moving. He nodded to me. *I'm here. Just go.*

Relief filled me when I heard him inside my head. I'd heard many voices over the years and many echoes to go along with them. His voice was soothing, something I wanted to hang on to. Something I thought I could listen to forever.

"I keep hearing the door slamming over and over," I told Xany. "But I was already in the bathroom. I think Vanessa left."

"Did you?" Xany asked her.

Vanessa nodded into her knees without looking up at us.

"Keep going, Nee. You went into the bathroom and

slammed the door at Vanessa. Then she left and slammed the door at you..."

I concentrated on that concept and tried to imagine myself in the bathroom. I thought about what the bathroom in the dorm looked like. It was small and had cosmetics scattered in and around the sink that belonged to both Vanessa and me. There was a bathtub to the left and the toilet behind me.

"The bathroom was red, like the light in there was red."

"Ness?" Xany checked in with Vanessa again. The werecat shook her head. "'No' what?"

"The light wasn't red," Vanessa said. She wiped her eyes, then went back to staring out the window.

"Okay, Nee. Just keep going, maybe it will make sense later," Xany pressed.

I nodded and kept trying to remember what the bathroom looked like. Above the sink was the mirror that Vanessa and I used to do our makeup in. Just as I thought about the mirror, a flash of memory made me jump.

"Zombie. Zombie," I gasped.

"Where is the zombie? Look at me, Shawnee. Everyone here is with you, and you're safe."

I turned my attention to Xany and tried hard to slow down my breathing. "Me. In the mirror."

Xany thought quickly about what I was trying to say. "You saw yourself in the mirror, and you looked like a zombie. Remember when you and I were in the mirror? Remember that?"

The image in my head changed, and I remembered when Xany and I stood in the mirror together. My breathing slowed down naturally. "I wasn't a zombie then."

"That's right. And you're not a zombie now. You saw yourself as a zombie back then, that's why you drew it, remember?" Xany tried to put pieces together for me.

It helped, and it gave me a small confidence boost. "Vanessa said I looked horrible that night. She was right. My face was sunken, and my makeup was running. I had a bruise on my cheek. I don't remember how it got there."

"You didn't know back then either," Vanessa croaked.

"Let's not worry about that piece then. Keep going, what else do you see?" Xany asked.

"Nothing. I mean, just me..." I paused. "I don't see anything, but I hear a lot of things..." I trailed off.

"What do you hear?"

"I hear... I hear my dad. He tells me I'm disgusting and useless. That he would kill me if he could, but people would notice if I had gone missing." I reached up and touched my ears. "I tried to cover my ears." The words began to pour out of me now, and it became effortless to try and remember. "'Die, you dirty bitch, die. Do it yourself if you have to. No one wants you around, you worthless piece of shit. Just like your mother.'" My voice dropped an octave as I mimicked what I was hearing.

Vanessa watched me intently. She didn't seem to know this part of the story. My eyes burned with tears. It'd been a while since I'd heard my father's voice that clearly. It scared me. Parts of my body started to ache with the physical echoes of his abuse. My legs, my scar, my cheek.

"What happened next?"

You're safe now, Shawnee, remember that. Mal's voice rang into my head. I took a deep breath and let his words wrap around me like a warm blanket.

"He said...he said I should do it myself. I saw myself in the mirror and decided to listen to him. He was right, I deserved to die." I was stuck between remembering and being in the room with my packmates. "There was a razor. On the sink." I shook my head. I didn't want to continue. Instinctively I knew where it was going. My head ached from tapping into the deepest depths of my mind to remember. I didn't want to.

"Go on," Xany urged.

"I grabbed it and snapped it in half so that the blade was exposed. My mind was clear. It was like I was making the right decision and that everything would be better. I couldn't change my life but I could end it. I was powerful—at least in that moment. I felt like I finally had control of something. So I filled up the tub and got in it. I remember what I was wearing. I had on black heels and tight jeans that were torn in different places and a bright red shirt. I looked like one of the Go-Gos." I glanced up at Xany and made a face. "What an idiot."

"No distracting." Xany smirked as she chastised me.

I looked over at Vanessa who was crying quietly, and she put her head down on her knees again. My heart broke for her as the rest of the memory poured from my lips.

"I got in the tub, Xee. I got in, and I took the razor, and I slit my left wrist. I remember screaming at the pain, and then suddenly it was gone. I saw the blood pulse from my vein and run down my arm. I took the razor and slit my other wrist. I was shaking, but there was a sense of calm. I wasn't scared anymore." I had to pause there to catch my breath through my sobs. "I thought about my mom and wondered if she would catch me when I fell, and then I thought about Vanessa... I got so tired. I couldn't hold myself up anymore, and I slipped down into the water and watched the bubbles rise from my lips. I opened my eyes and everything was red from under the bloody water. Everything..."

Then I realized why everything looked red when I first thought of the bathroom. I tried to kill myself in the bathroom that Vanessa and I shared without a single regard for who would find me. I knew why this memory was one she didn't want me to share. She was the one who found me. It had to have been. I wanted to scream and break things. I looked over at Vanessa who remained folded against her knees.

"I woke up in the hospital," I told Xany. Caden looked like a statue, and Mal was seething at the forces that had pushed me that far. "I never remembered anything else except the hospital." I was clenching my teeth so tightly that it was making my jaw hurt.

I slid off the bed to kneel in front of Vanessa. She startled when I touched her. I pried her hands away from her head. She sobbed, looking at me with a tear-stained face, crying harder than I had ever seen her cry. Her eyes were bloodshot, and she was scared.

"Tell me what happened when you found me." It was a difficult thing to ask, and I knew it would be even more difficult for her to answer.

She shook her head and reached out to touch my face. Despite her pain she still tried to comfort me.

I grabbed her hands and held them in mine. "Please."

"I could smell your blood down the hall. I ran back." She sobbed. "I took down the door. There was so much blood. Your heart was still beating. I took you out of the tub. Your heartbeat was getting slower." Her tears dripping onto our laced fingers. "I couldn't let you die, Shawnee." She met my gaze. "I licked your wounds. Both of them..." She turned my wrists over and ran her thumbs over them. "No scars!" Her voice became deep, and she spoke through her growling.

I looked down at my wrists, and she was right. There were no scars. Some cats have powerful gifts, and Vanessa had just divulged one of hers. Her tongue had the power to heal.

"I tasted your blood and breathed into you. Your heartbeat steadied, and you started breathing on your own again. I called our friend Jaxon, and we took you to the hospital." She sniffled and closed her eyes. "They couldn't figure out how you had become so anemic. We never told. You couldn't remember anyway, so what did it matter? You were alive."

I grabbed her, pulling her into a crushing hug. She melted into my arms, and I held her, burying my face in her hair to cry along with her. "I'm sorry, Vanessa. I'm so sorry."

When I apologized, she wrapped her arms around me and nuzzled her cheek against my neck. I didn't deserve her forgiveness, or anything she had given me over the past ten years or better. I heard the others leave the room and the door close, leaving us alone to process the expulsion of a very big secret.

CHAPTER TWENTY-SIX

Vanessa and I spent the better part of an hour on the floor, tangled up together. After a while, our crying ceased, and her purring slowly returned. I ran my fingers through her hair, and she did a gentle kneading motion on my thigh.

"At least now I know why you always interrupt my showers," I whispered in her ear. She looked at me with a faint smile. I caressed her cheek; her eyes were soft emeralds. "And why I don't have any scars anymore."

She glanced away for a moment. "They made you unhappy," she whispered.

"I thought healers could only heal open wounds and battle scars." I brushed my lips against her cheek.

"Those *were* battle scars." She purred harder with my affection.

"How could you stand me after that? That was a horrible thing to do. I had no regard for you because I was too caught up in my own pain." The guilt became nearly too much to manage. "Promise not to keep any more of my secrets?"

She nodded, leaning in to nuzzle my neck. She rested against the bed and plucked me off the floor to sit in her lap. I straddled her legs to face her. Her purr was strong, vibrating through me like one of those rocking baby chairs. She rubbed my thighs while both of us sat in a silence that could only be described as awkward despite her purring.

My mind seemed at war. Part of me had a huge sense of relief while the other was wrestling to get control of the guilty feelings I suddenly harbored. The only person other than my mother to care about me and take care of me was the one I hurt the most. I didn't mean to hurt Vanessa, but the fact that I had totally disregarded her feelings without thinking of how it would affect her bothered me. What other horrible things had I done to her?

"Stop thinking," she said.

"I can't help it. You were always good to me and never left me. Ever. You still don't. And I turned around and did something like that."

"Shawnee..." She slipped her hands up my shirt to rest on my stomach. "It was a long time ago and you were really sick back then. More sick than you have ever been. It was my choice to stay with you after that. It was my choice to try and help you have a better life. If anything, it taught me how much help you really needed."

"It shouldn't have had to be that way. I could have asked for help." I shivered. Her hands were cool against my overheated skin.

"Stop that. You didn't know how to ask for help. You still don't," she stated with a smirk. "You can't judge yourself back then. It's just not right. Hell, Shawnee, you can't judge yourself about how you acted six months ago, let alone six years."

It was hard *not* to judge the fact that I came across as a blind and selfish person. "I'll try."

"And besides, you had some help. You didn't make the decision to die on your own. When you spend half your life being told that you should die or kill yourself, eventually you might believe it." She frowned, her eyes drawing away to stare out the window. "I hated your father."

"Me too." I tucked a strand of hair behind her ear.

She smiled and touched my face, brushing her thumb over my bottom lip. I surprised her by trying to bite her thumb. Her entire face lit up as if she'd suddenly been given a breath of life. She always liked when I was playful. "Hey!"

"What?" I laughed at her reaction.

"Oh, nothing. Shawnee, even if you can't forgive yourself, I want you to know that I've forgiven you. A long time ago I forgave you." She slipped her fingers behind the waistband of my jeans. It made my stomach jump.

"But you've still carried it with you." Out of sheer curiosity, I placed my hands on her stomach. I wasn't sure why she always had her hands on my abdomen, so I returned the gesture. Her stomach flip-flopped under my touch. The velvet of her dress was soft and fuzzy. "I saw how you reacted today."

"Maybe. But no one has ever asked us about our secrets before. It was more about that than the actual event itself. You've never talked about anything, Shawnee. Not until you came here at least. I'm always afraid of how pushing issues will set you off. So it was kind of a bit of each of those things," she explained, biting her lip when I kept rubbing her stomach. Her purring became wheezy sounding, like it did when she really enjoyed something.

"Do you think I'm getting better? Like the others said?" I ran my fingers around her stomach, leaving little trails in the velvet. I'd never really noticed what her dress felt like before.

"Honestly, yeah. I do," she said. The more my fingers moved, the more she responded. Her stomach kept fluttering, and she shifted her legs around a bit. "You sleep through the night now without waking up a hundred times crying or shaking. It only happens once in a while. I know you've been here only a few months, but it's noticeable. Maybe it has something to do with being a part of a pack, or maybe because it's given you time to actually work on things in your own life instead of drowning yourself in work at the hospital."

"Which is why you told Caden that you think I needed more time off?" I realized I still felt a little bitter about her saying that, though I didn't know why.

Her cheeks looked flushed. "Yeah. And I almost killed Mal when I saw him on the bed with you. I thought he was the one that made you freak out."

"He didn't. Mal actually... I dunno, he doesn't scare me. Caden does a little still," I said. "I think Mal heard me scream."

"I heard you scream, and I was by the lake." She smiled at me gently and ran her finger from my cheek, down my neck, between my breasts, and back to my stomach.

My entire body shuddered. This time I couldn't ignore it. "What was that?"

"What was what?" She looked confused.

"That feeling." I gestured at my stomach, uncertain how to describe it.

"What feeling? I can't feel what you feel."

"When you did that thing." I mimicked and showed her how she ran her finger down my middle. "It made me feel funny."

She did it again, but this time she went slower and used most of her hand rather than her finger. A shiver rushed down my spine, and warmth was building in my lower belly.

"Yeah, that." I bit my lip in effort to keep the pleasure from my face.

"Enjoyment, I imagine." She grinned, her eyebrows flicking upward.

"I should at least know what those things feel like."

"How can you know if you never learned?" she asked, purring and returning to rubbing my thighs.

"Good point. I feel a lot of funny things lately that I don't understand," I admitted.

"Why do you think that is?" she asked, though she probably already had the answer.

"I dunno." I shrugged. "Maybe because I've been feeling better lately. Even though I still sleep a lot sometimes."

"You need to sleep, Shawnee. You used to avoid it at all costs then sleep for two days straight. That's unhealthy. You sleep more normal now. And I agree; I think you're feeling things because you're better and relaxing."

"It's just weird I guess." Unshed tears began to burn in my eyes. I blinked them away, trying to understand why I wanted to cry over being better. It was scary to think about being better and feeling things. I've never known what *better* meant. After spending all these years being fucked up and messed up, I had little frame of reference for these things.

"Why the tears?" She nudged my chin up.

"Just a little scary I guess. I don't want to feel too much—the bad stuff hurts so much sometimes. I hate waking up with that feeling." I sniffled, and she wiped away my tears.

"What feeling?" She tucked my hair behind my ears, then lifted my arms and placed them on her shoulders so that we were forced to stay in position.

"The pain in my body, it feels so real," I said. "I don't want to feel that."

"That pain, Shawnee, is like..." She paused to think about it. "Echoes. It's like, you can feel it, but it's not really happening. It's like a memory echoing in your body."

I thought about that concept. That's how my thoughts seemed sometimes and the voices I heard; it might be the same for my body. "My thoughts can be that way too," I told her.

"We'll keep an eye on that and tell me when it happens again, okay?"

I nodded and hugged her. Her body was warm, and her arms around me were safe. She leaned me back a bit and rested her forehead against mine.

"No more tears."

I smiled when her eyes were bright and playful again. It'd been a while since I'd seen her fully enjoying herself. Maybe she was getting better with me.

"No more tears," I repeated.

She laughed and brushed her lips against mine in a delicate, nuzzling gesture. I tried to ignore the fact that my stomach was doing all sorts of weird, fluttering stuff. My body and sensations were in control, leaning me toward her. She jerked back, apparently surprised by my response. When she had brushed her lips against mine in the past, I just let her do it without responding or thinking about it. This time, however, my body responded for me. Her eyes searched my face in an awkward dance, probably trying to decode what was happening. I stayed as still as possible.

When she realized she had my full attention, she brushed her lips against mine again. This time though, I mimicked her movement. Her lips were silky and delicate, and I pulled back at the unexpected sensation. She leaned toward me again, and this time she let her lips linger just a bit. Feeling her warm breath, I moved into it—the sensation rising in my stomach drove me to do so. She closed the small distance between us, and our lips touched completely. She guided me into a gentle kiss that only lasted a few seconds but seemed like minutes. My heart thumped in my ears, and my whole body grew warm and tingly. I broke the kiss. Her pupils were dilated and her lips red with arousal. My face blazed with warmth. She simply smiled at me, pulling me into a crushing hug. Instead of the gentle halfhearted hugs I often gave, I squeezed her tight, not only with my arms but my legs as well.

"Life looks good on you, Shawnee," she whispered in my ear.

CHAPTER TWENTY-SEVEN

The pack was growing more and more connected. Caden and Mal were becoming more attuned with Xany and me with each passing day. It was how it worked when a pack lived together. The Alpha had a growing sense of each member of his pack. If the connection continued to expand, he would be able to employ a gift similar to Mal's where he could communicate with us privately. It was not the same as Mal's in that he can speak to each of us individually. It was more of a pack-wide thing. It was useful in battle and in sticky situations. The way that Xany and Caden acted lately, I couldn't help wondering when he would officially choose her as his mate. Things will change then. The pack would be stronger. The pack was always stronger when the Alpha and Beta choose mates.

Vanessa left after our talk to go to work. I didn't want her to go, and she didn't want to either, but it was necessary to part ways for a little while. I didn't think too heavily on the kiss we shared. Cats are notorious for their overt affection, and I thought now that I was growing more comfortable around her, Vanessa was able to be herself and let her true nature show. I was more surprised than anything.

I knew that the others were stewing in the main room with no idea what condition we would emerge in. I could sense them waiting, especially Mal. I wanted to go and soothe them, but I decided to take a shower first.

I took my time in the shower to think about what had happened between Vanessa and me this afternoon. I was afraid of how many other events I'd forgotten about or blocked in my life. It killed me to know that my selfish, hopeless decision hurt Vanessa. We were both young at the time, but no young person deserves an experience like that.

I let the water cascade over my face and down the front of my body, running my hands over my skin as I looked down at myself. I remembered a few places where there had been scars such as my left arm where the piece of glass got stuck. There wasn't a mark on my skin anywhere except my stomach and the small scar on my knee. Vanessa healed every single one of my scars and saved my life with the very same gift. I owed her so much.

As I rinsed the shampoo from my hair, I remembered how Vanessa's lips felt against mine. The soft, delicate flesh of our lips mingling and the taste of—I think it was strawberries. I jerked myself from the uncomfortable thoughts and hurriedly finished my shower. Before today, I had forgotten what kissing felt like. I had no memories of kissing anyone at all. Sex and anything in the realm of it was something I often pushed from my thoughts. I never enjoyed it. I never cared to be with people in that manner. Even though I had been known to entertain many men throughout the years, it was never for me.

The part that confused me the most was that it'd been Vanessa. Cats don't usually kiss, as a general rule. It was all about affection and sex. I'd gotten used to Vanessa's mild affection and was never surprised with the numerous men she'd brought in and out of our lives, but kissing was something totally different. Maybe she thought it was part of an affection I'd appreciate because after all, wolves kiss just fine. It couldn't be anything else. It just couldn't. I couldn't bear thinking about it anymore. I finished up in the bathroom then joined the others in the main room.

Three sets of eyes followed me as I sat down on the sofa. Xany came over and sat beside me. "Are you okay, NeeNee?" She stroked my wet hair.

"I'm fine, Xee." I let her baby me for the moment in an attempt to soothe her. She was obviously worried and needed to feel useful.

"Are you sure?"

I nodded, then decided to tell her what was still bothering me. "Yeah. It just makes me wonder how many other really big things I've forgotten."

"Well, you remembered that one with just a little help," she said encouragingly. "You can probably recover most if you tried, and if you wanted to."

"I think so. At least I know I wasn't crazy about the scars. I did have a lot, Vanessa healed them all. She said that they were battle scars..." I trailed off, trying not to think deeply on the concept.

"Did you know she had a healing tongue?" Mal asked.

"I didn't. The thing that makes me the saddest is how much I've disregarded her. I was only fooling myself. I knew she was a cat the moment I met her and just chose not to acknowledge it." I fought the urge to curl up in a ball of misery and guilt.

"You can't change the past, Shawnee, only go forward," Caden chimed in, and I appreciated it.

"I know...I know." I looked to Xany. "I really did kind of look like a zombie you know."

"I believe you, NeeNee, but you don't now." She pulled me into a hug.

I returned her hug genuinely. I bit my lip, feeling the urge to suddenly talk to her more, but I didn't want to in front of the guys. I thought of all people I knew, she would have the most insight into the relationship stuff that only confused me.

"Is Vanessa okay?" she asked.

"Yeah, she had to go to work. She seemed okay..." I trailed off. "Are we still going to Imogene's shop?" I didn't want to talk about the fact that Vanessa seemed more than okay.

"You're so cute, NeeNee." Xany giggled, tackling me into another hug.

"Ack!" I laughed. "Why am I cute?"

"I dunno, just because. We'll go to Gene's now." Xany let me go to bounce over to Caden.

Mal chuckled at her and watched me for a moment before standing. "That was a fast recovery," he said.

I shot him a look. "Let's just go shopping."

***

On our way to town, Caden drove with Xany in the front passenger seat while Mal and I sat in the back. He was squished so tightly that he had to keep his legs pulled toward his chest.

I watched the scenery as we drove down the dirt road and onto the main road that led to town. The trees were nearly in full bloom, and there were all sorts of flora and fauna scattered about. The mountains in the distance were still snow-capped, which offered a bit of irony to the view. It was warmer today, in the lower sixties, which made the scent of wildlife stronger. The air smelled sweet and fresh without the taint of exhaust, and the wet leaves on the ground had a subtle decaying odor as they dried out after spending a long winter buried in snow. Mal caught me gazing out the window.

"Have you gone exploring yet?" he asked.

"Not yet. Just outside the cabin every now and then."

"Hmmm," he said thoughtfully. "I think you'll like what you find if you venture out a bit."

"I think I will too." I smiled while toying with the bracelet I was still wearing. Lately I'd been feeling shyer around him, and I couldn't explain it. Every time he looked at me, it was as if he were peering beyond just my eyes. It didn't freak me out like I expected, but instead I was more exposed to him, more open. He chuckled suddenly and held his arm out to me. At first I didn't understand the gesture, but after thinking about it, I moved closer to him, and he wrapped his arm around my shoulders. Sometimes I surprised myself.

"Here we are," Caden announced twenty minutes later.

He pulled the truck around the side of a short building where the car park was tucked. We exited and headed toward the main street where all the shops were. It was a small town with one main road that had a few cars parked on it. The sidewalks were narrow in front of each store and disappeared at the bus stops on either side of the road. There was a little coffee and bagel shop, an office supply store with electronic devices on display in the window, Imogene's shop, and a tavern-like bar on one side. On the other side there was a family restaurant, department store, auto parts shop, and a pizza place.

Caden and Xany led the way into Imogene's shop. It was late in the afternoon at this point, and there were no customers inside. Imogene was sitting by the register rocking a fussing baby in a bassinette, and Cote was playing on the floor with some Kachina dolls. There was a door behind the checkout area that led to a room with sounds of children echoing from it.

"Afternoon there, Gene. How's my favorite married woman doing today?" Caden smiled and greeted Imogene. Xany grinned proudly as she listened to him flirt with the older woman. She waved to Gene and ran off to go look at some of the items.

"Caden." Gene's voice was delighted and she leaned across the counter to shake his hand. "I'm glad you all came for a visit. It's been a quiet day, at least as far as customers go."

"It happens. You remember Shawnee." He gestured to me.

I shook Gene's hand with a smile, then waved to Cote

215

who kept peeking at Mal. Mal shook Gene's hand and stood beside me. He placed his hand on the small of my back. I didn't expect it, startling at first until the tingly heat of his touch ran up my spine. His touches seemed to be getting braver lately. I tried not to pay it too much mind.

"Nice to see you all again." Gene grinned.

"You too." I glanced to the children then back to her. "They're adorable."

"Thank you." She beamed at the compliment.

I smiled at her, then broke away from Mal to walk around the shop. There was everything you could imagine: steel, platinum, and turquoise jewelry, handmade leather dresses and clothes, T-shirts and fleeces, dream catchers, mandalas, beaded jewelry, headbands, bow and arrow sets, bone jewelry and knives, moccasins, purses, and so on. The only thing missing from Gene's shop was anything made out of silver, for obvious reasons. All silver products were replaced with steel or platinum. The relaxing scents of fresh leather and sage filled the shop.

Caden continued chatting with Gene for a while before heading off to find Xany, who was browsing the clothing section. Mal followed me over to the area with handmade moccasins and loincloths.

"I bet these are handy for all the Firstings around here," I said.

"Very," he agreed with a laugh.

"Did you make these?" I asked, noting some of the bone jewelry and recognizing the knife he had worked on several weeks ago.

"How can you tell?"

I grinned and pointed to the artists' name tag attached to one of the items. "I'm psychic."

Mal laughed and suddenly hugged me from behind. It took me by surprise at first, but I held his arms. "I think you might be."

I grinned, and he led me over to the area with the dream catchers and medicine shields. There were dozens of different types with individual weaving patterns in the webs of the dream catchers. I pointed to a few that I liked and then paused when I saw the large medicine shields. They had stretched hides in the middle of the big ring, and one of the hides had a portrait of a wolf painted on it.

"This is beautiful," I murmured in awe.

"It is." His voice was soft.

I looked closer at the medicine shield, then frowned. "That's imprinted on, not painted," I said, disappointed.

"Good eye. Imogene has to order these; they're the only unoriginal thing in her shop. Not many talented painters in the area it seems," he said.

"Hmmm..."

Mal walked behind me and dragged his hand along the small of my back. It made me shiver in the same way that Vanessa did when she dragged her finger down my middle. He grinned and disappeared behind a rack of clothes. I think I accidentally opened a can of worms by starting to accept his affections. Touch was really important to wolves and packs, and I knew both Mal and Caden would have the urges for affection from all of us. Me, being the most unwilling participant until late, would prove a finer delicacy toward the advances of the wolves. They liked the chase. And maybe, just maybe, I liked being caught.

The baby that Imogene had in the bassinette started wailing, sucking in breath through heaving gasps. Right away I could tell that the cry wasn't normal. It sounded like the baby was having breathing problems. Without thinking, I rushed over to the counter where Imogene had the baby on her shoulder, patting her back. Mal saw me and hurried after me.

"What's wrong?" he asked when he saw me approach Imogene.

"She's started having colic two days ago," Gene answered.

"How old is she?" I asked.

"Nine months," Gene responded, patting the screaming

baby on the back to try and soothe her. Cote had disappeared into the back room, covering his ears.

"Have you taken her to the doctor recently?" My heart pounded in my chest as the baby's screaming escalated. I did everything I could to stop myself from tearing the baby away from its mother to check on her. Caden appeared at my side, tugging Xany along with him.

"Hey, why am I being dragged off, what's going on?" she demanded with a huff. The guys looked on.

"She's been. He said it was colic. Why?" Imogene's eyes narrowed, and her posture suddenly became protective.

"She's too old for colic." I moved around the counter without bothering to ask, which was a dumb move by any sorts. Had Imogene been a wolf, she would have torn my head off.

"Shawnee's a doctor, Gene." Caden added the disclaimer when she held the baby closer to her like any mother would when a stranger approached so closely. I nodded after hearing Caden. Of course, I'd forget to mention that little detail. The bassinette was the only thing separating myself and Gene.

"You think something else is wrong?" Panic filled Gene's voice when she asked.

"Her cries sound painful, and she's gasping. Will you let me take a look?" I used my doctor voice, the kind one reserved for scared patients and children. *Trust me*, my voice soothed, *I'll make it better.*

She nodded and slowly handed me the screaming child. I rocked her gently, cooing to her before setting her down in the bassinette. "Does her crying always sound like this?"

"No. That's why I took her to the doctor," she answered, clutching her chest and giving Caden a terrified glance.

I unbundled the baby carefully, removing her clothes and leaving her in her diaper. Her skin looked slightly pale. I pinched her fingertips gently and pressed a bit on her stomach.

"Do you have a flashlight, Gene?" I was calmer now that I was examining the infant.

Gene reached into the drawer under the register and handed me a small flashlight. I checked the baby's ears, eyes, and nose with little problem. As she cried, I looked into her mouth. The baby screamed more and began gasping for breath again. I picked her up, placing her stomach in my hand and lifting her up so that I could put my ear against her back. I heard wheezing every time she sucked in a breath of air, and a rattling sound when she breathed out.

"Has she been eating?"

"Not much. She cries so hard she vomits." Gene continued to clutch her chest. "Is she all right?"

"Her breathing is labored. Xee, I need your help."

Xany came around the counter. "What can I do?" she asked.

"I need you to hold her like this." I handed the screaming baby to her so that she was facing outward. "Hold her securely and keep her head from moving. She might vomit, but I need to see in her mouth."

Gene heard this and began crying. Caden climbed over the counter and put his arm around her. "Shawnee will take care of her, Gene, don't worry."

"Like this?" Xee asked as she held the little one tightly.

I nodded and looked in her mouth using my finger as a tongue depressor. In the back of her throat something reflected the glare from the flashlight. I set it down, then as quickly as I could, slipped my finger into the baby's mouth in a scooping motion to dislodge what was wedged just in front of her tonsils and against her uvula. The baby immediately gagged and vomited. I caught the foreign object as it was ejected from her mouth. After a few cries of distress, she quieted.

"Feel better?" I asked her with a smile as I took her from Xany and set her on my hip. The baby cooed, and I turned back to Imogene, who had her arms out for the little one. I handed the baby over and then opened my hand to show her the small wheel from a toy car that had lodged in the back of her baby's throat. "This was stuck in her throat. She could breathe just enough, but it was painful and would eventually get lodged lower."

Gene cradled the now quiet baby, who was sticking her finger into her mouth. I could tell she noticed how much better she felt. "My God. Thank you, Shawnee."

I smiled at her and patted her shoulder lightly with my vomit-free hand. "Of course. I would call her doctor and tell him what happened. He clearly didn't do a thorough exam, or he would have caught that easily."

"I will," she said. As she looked up at Caden, her smile was radiant. "Excuse me a moment." She held her index finger up and walked into the back room. A few seconds later, we heard her shout, "Clean up the floor! All the little pieces. You nearly choked your sister!"—followed by a bunch of scrambling.

Xany giggled when Gene reprimand the kids, then stepped over the mess on the floor to go back to Caden. "NeeNee's a hero, TB."

"I'll show you where the bathroom is, Shawnee." Mal smothered a laugh at hearing Caden's nickname.

My cheeks were burning with a deep blush at being labeled a hero. At Mal's offer, I nodded and hurried after him, needing the sanctuary of the bathroom. It wouldn't hurt to wash my hands and boots too.

"You got all that information just by hearing her cry?" he asked, as he stood in the doorway waiting for me.

"I could tell by the way she cried. Babies have distinct cries for pain, hunger, and discomfort. That one was pain, and then I heard her breathing all wacky." I dried off my hands with some paper towels.

"Well, aren't you just amazing," he said, grinning as I walked toward him. He moved out of my way and leaned against the door frame while I leaned against the other side facing him. I laughed as I tossed the paper towel into the trash.

"Yes, I'm quite the *hero*," I said, stealing Xany's word to make light of myself.

"I'm serious, Nee, that was pretty amazing."

"I'd like to smack that doctor who said the baby had colic. A nine-month-old child with colic? What an idiot."

"C'mon, I can hear Hank." He smiled and held his elbow out to me.

I perked a brow at him and took his elbow. We walked back over to the others where Imogene was filling Hank in on what happened. Caden was talking with them, and Xany was bouncing happily, chiming in every now and then.

"Shawnee!" Hank said, rushing over and hugging me suddenly. I sucked in my breath and held it for a second until he let go. "Thank ya much for helpin' out our lit'le one."

"Of course, Hank." I offered him a smile.

He continued to sing my praises until we were out the door. Embarrassment kept the heat in my cheeks for ages. It wasn't an act of heroism to me, it was just my job. I helped people and saved lives. That's what doctors do.

***

Xany had purchased a few items at Imogene's and convinced Caden to stop at the department store for some more things. Mal and I decided to stay outside and wait for them. There was an outdoor café by the pizza place so we sat down at a table there. We were quiet for a few minutes as I took in the sights.

"This is a nice little town." I toyed with a bottle cap that was left on the table.

"Yeah, it's comfortable here," he said distractedly, watching me twirl the cap on its side.

"Is there an art store around here?"

"Hmmm...not sure. We might have to drive into the city for that, but you can order most stuff on the Internet these days. You thinking about the medicine shield?"

"Yeah, it's a shame to have printed images on hides. Painting is so much more natural."

"Are you a good painter?" He gazed at me with open curiosity.

"It depends on how you look at it." I shrugged.

"Good point." He flicked the bottle cap out of my fingers and laughed.

"Hey!" I said, swatting his hand without thinking.

"Just like a cat." He laughed more.

"I'm no cat." I huffed but couldn't help smiling.

"It depends on how you look at it." Mal wagged his brows.

I swatted him three more times for that. He gripped my chair suddenly and dragged me closer to him. I squealed, and he wrapped me up in a tight hug. I leaned into the embrace. The warmth of his body wrapped mine and enveloped me, making it seem like my body was melting into his.

"I like when you're relaxed. You're a lot of fun," he murmured against my hair.

"It's you that helps me relax. Caden still scares me a bit." I leaned against him and watched the moon rise from behind the buildings across the street.

"He's a big teddy bear, as Xany calls him, or TB." He laughed at the thought.

I craned my head back to look at him. "Oh God, she really calls him TB? She loves the nicknames doesn't she?"

"Yeah. That's Xany for you." He paused. "Tell me something honestly?" He met my gaze and his playful expression melted away only to be replaced by a stiller, more serious look.

"You can tell when I'm lying anyway." I tried to hide my worry over the sudden change in affect.

"Maybe, but sometimes I like to hear someone commit to honesty." He sat back in his chair, leaning his elbows on the arms of it.

"All right, what?" I couldn't help the smile that was

tugging at the corners of my mouth. His body language was open and inviting.

"How do you like it here? At the cabin with Caden, Xee, and me?" He gestured toward the street, but I knew he meant in general.

"I like it. No one bothers me. I'm not scared all the time like I used to be. And Vanessa seems more comfortable here, too, despite the fact that every day she waltzes into the territory of werewolves."

I watched as he placed his elbows on his knees, his hands dangling between them. He looked up at me, his eyes shimmering with the reflection of the setting sun.

"We like having you here. Caden says the pack has grown stronger." He nuzzled my neck. A brave move when he knew that any moment I could reject his touch. Secretly I knew I wouldn't.

"I can tell. I can sense where you are, I mean, like if you're close or far away. That type of stuff," I confided in him.

"Caden and I can tell too."

While we continued talking, Xany and Caden emerged from the department store with a few bags of stuff.

"Aww, Xee, look how cozy they are together," Caden teased.

"Ohhh. Ooo la la." She grinned at us teasingly.

"Shush up, both of you," I said, standing quickly and heading toward the truck.

Mal followed me, grinning at Xany. He walked passed her and pinched her arm before whistling and walking away quickly. Xany went to chase after him, but Caden caught her by the back of her jeans.

The lighthearted clowning around continued all the way back to the cabin. For the first time I was somewhat grounded and...almost happy. Helping Hank's baby feel better and having fun with the others was satisfying. Maybe tonight I would consider mailing my license fees to practice medicine in Utah.

CHAPTER TWENTY-EIGHT

More thunderstorms returned that night, though this time without interrupting the power. Xany chose another movie for us to watch; Caden ordered Chinese for dinner. There weren't very many ethnic restaurants in the area so Caden had made it a habit to bend into Salt Lake City for all our take-out orders. It put a whole new meaning to the term fast food. I made popcorn slathered in butter and salt. Mal lowered the lights before taking a seat on the sofa, and Caden unpacked the cartons of food. Xany started the movie and our night in began.

I was becoming accustomed to this routine. It was comforting in a way. I never really imagined myself relaxed while surrounded by a bunch of people, especially when two of them were off kissing and touching all the time. Barely ten minutes into the movie, Caden and Xany were necking on the chair. I tried hard to ignore them and keep eating my rice. Mal seemed oblivious. I guessed he'd gotten a lot of practice ignoring both his best friend and his sister. I bet that if it were anyone other than Xany, he might be entertained.

Halfway through my rice, Vanessa sauntered into the room. I heard her purring before I saw her. She took a moment to watch the kissing before she joined me and Mal on the sofa, sitting between us. Mal greeted her by lifting his chin. He was picking up on cat language with ease.

"Hey, Ness." I set my dish down on the coffee table.

She purred louder when I said her name, then leaned over to nuzzle me. Her eyes lingered on the others until Caden's hand started to wander up Xany's shirt. I was ridiculously uncomfortable over the scene, which made no sense because I wasn't involved in it. Without warning, Vanessa slid into my lap, straddling my thighs in the same way I usually sat in her lap. I laughed a bit.

"Well, hi to you too." I was secretly grateful that she was blocking my view. She smiled and hugged me. I gave her a squeeze. My affection for Vanessa had grown tremendously over the past few weeks, and I was beginning to enjoy her closeness rather than just feeling safe around her. Out of the corner of my eye, I could see Mal smirking while he demolished a rib—bone and all.

I had to shift my position so that Vanessa could sit more comfortably in my lap. I envied how easy it was for her to move me around. I guessed that was one of the perks of having werecreature strength. She gave me a gentle nip on my shoulder before sitting up again. Her eyes glistened in the soft light tossed off by the television. A smile tugged at the corner of her lips, coated with a film of mischievousness.

"What are you up to, cat?" I lifted a brow at her. My hands had been flat at my sides, resting on the sofa. I didn't know where to put them so I just left them there.

She snickered. Her purring turned into the wheezy sound again, and she nuzzled me, this time resting her forehead against mine. Feeling her breath against my lips reminded me of our encounter this afternoon. I bit my lip. Had we really kissed? My stomach churned, and I saw Mal's gaze draw from the TV to linger on us.

"Ness," I whispered, breathing in her breath, conscious

of the fact that other people were in the room with us, and to the fact that I was feeling something funny inside me.

"What's wrong?" she whispered back.

"I..." I graduated from biting my lip to gnawing. I didn't know what was wrong. I was just suddenly aware of the people in the room, something that never seemed to bother me until lately. She backed off after sensing my hesitation and sat quietly in my lap, purring and running her fingers through my hair. It soothed me and I glanced over at Mal. He tilted his head at me. I shrugged at him and let my hands rest on Vanessa's sides, finally getting up the courage to move them.

This is the second time I've seen you stop her affections. Mal's voice suddenly popped into my head.

I jumped a bit which made Vanessa look at me curiously and stroke my cheek. I concentrated on my words and thought them instead of speaking. *That's the point. You can see us, in public,* I told him.

Does it really matter? He lifted a brow at me. *We can all sense it...from her and you.*

Well, that just sucks! I tried to hide the heat that rose in my cheeks by slouching in my seat toward Vanessa.

Shawnee, you need to do what feels right, not what you think is right. Just like what you did for that little girl today.

That was different, I said.

Vanessa was catching onto my distraction. She cupped my face, so that I would look at her.

No, it isn't.

"Shawnee?" Vanessa finally spoke.

"Sorry," I whispered. "Got scared for a minute."

The smile that touched her lips was gentle, like the kiss we'd shared. "Want to switch?"

"Yeah, actually."

She laughed a bit and slid from my lap, scooting around so that she was sitting beside me and I was able to rest my head on her shoulder. "Better?"

I nodded. She kissed my forehead and wrapped her arm

around me. Everyone's attention returned to the movie except mine. I kept thinking about Vanessa's affection. Part of me wanted to understand it more, and part of me was terrified to find out what lay at the other end of it. I kept balling up my hand to avoid touching her.

You'll contaminate her and cause her pain. Just like you always do.

I squeezed my eyes shut.

You've caused her so much hurt.

I shrunk against Vanessa while I endured the vicious attack of my thoughts. Xany looked up from her kissing, her gaze digging into me. I narrowed my eyes at her. She smiled. I reminded myself that I needed to have a talk with her tomorrow. Bullshit she wasn't an empath.

What is it? Mal's voice interrupted my thoughts. I was relieved to hear his voice in my head instead of the insulting ones that had been gone for nearly a full day. I glanced at him from over Vanessa's chest. Caden seemed distracted by the movie and so did Vanessa, which to me meant that Mal was somehow tuned into me in a different way.

I'll hurt her, Mal. I will, I told him, trying very hard not to become emotional or shift my position and tip off Vanessa.

The only thing you can hurt her with is a silver bullet. I got the impression he was laughing mentally.

No, I know I'll hurt her or make her messed up like me. I got teary eyed and hated myself for it.

Irrational thinking for the win. He quirked a brow.

I don't want to cause her any more pain, Mal, physically or mentally.

Has she ever caused you pain, physically or mentally?

Well...no, she makes me feel better. I thought about what he was getting at. I knew that a lot of my pain was perceived and feared rather than actual. Of all the people in my life, Vanessa would be the last person to hurt me. I was beginning to believe that Mal would be the second to last.

My fear over injuring Vanessa was getting in the way of being close to her, and I had the inkling that Mal was trying to point it out.

So follow her lead, he instructed. *If she's done something to make you feel okay, or better, return the gesture. What's the worst that can happen? She tells you to stop or tells you what else she likes?* Again, he quieted.

When Mal talked to me like this it seemed like I had a conscience, but not in the moral kind of way. He was a guide, sort of, who tapped into the logical part of me and helped me think instead of react.

Vanessa pretended to bite my nose when I looked at her, and she lifted her chin to me. I laughed and bumped my forehead with hers. I considered what Mal had said. I'd always enjoyed her playfulness, the few moments I was sane enough to enjoy it. I thought about this afternoon and the kiss that we shared. It made my belly warm and tingly. Her affection calmed me and gave me a sense of belonging, like I was welcomed in her life instead of just tolerated. I remembered when she ran her hand down my body and how it had a similar feeling. I glanced at Mal and decided to experiment a little.

Very carefully, I reached up and brushed a bit of hair from her cheek, then slid my hand down her neck, over her prominent collarbone, down between her breasts to rest on her stomach where I rubbed in slow circles. Her T-shirt shifted. Her body lifted toward my hand, and she squirmed when a shiver ran through her.

"What was that?" I asked her, whispering.

"Enjoyment," she replied with a smile. She'd known exactly what I was up to. I blushed when reminded of what she helped me decipher this afternoon.

I glanced at Mal, who gave me a wink. He looked to Xany who was huffing and puffing, for who knows what reason this time. Caden was rubbing her thigh to try and distract her when she suddenly looked at Mal. After a few seconds, she shrunk into Caden as if Mal had reprimanded her somehow. I imagine it was something along the lines of "don't you dare interrupt them."

Vanessa turned her attention back to the movie. It was coming to an end, and the action scene was loud with the surround-sound. When she was distracted, I touched her cheek, then slid my hand down to rest on her chest for a moment. Her purring increased with each touch as I caressed her soft, long neck. When I moved my hand down her body toward her stomach, again her body arched up, then relaxed. I paid close attention to how my touch affected her and rested my hand on her stomach. She didn't seem to be in any pain. *Enjoyment* was the word that slipped from her lips, and I wanted to see what else I could try. Knowing Mal was with me, telepathically, some of my fears seemed to slip away.

I continued to mimic the gestures she often did with me and decided to slip my hand up her T-shirt and caress her bare stomach. Her abdomen was firm with muscles that twitched when I tickled her. Daringly, I let my fingertips graze the waist of her skirt and felt that distinct flutter in her belly. My stomach had done that a few times, and although I didn't really understand it, I knew it wasn't a bad thing. Vanessa looked like she was chewing her tongue. She nuzzled me since I had drawn her attention away from the television when I started touching her. I had to admit I was more nervous when I knew she was alert.

"Is it okay?" Suddenly I found myself dreading the thought of rejection. I imagined it was something similar to what wolves experience when mates pull away.

"Very okay," she whispered, brushing her lips against mine like she'd done this afternoon. I breathed in her scent, tensing my fingers against her stomach. I'd done it before, and it wasn't difficult this time. I closed the gap between us. She accepted and guided me into the most sweet, tentative kiss I'd ever experienced.

My stomach trembled like it was going to explode. *It'd*

be pretty horrible to puke from nervousness right now.

Her delicate lips parted mine.

The others had disappeared. Mal remained in the room, pretending to watch the end of the movie. Some may have thought that his staying was voyeuristic, but I was very glad that he'd stayed. In a way, I needed him to.

Vanessa engaged me in the kiss for a short while. I broke it when my heart started to race, afraid that it would get too fast, and I would black out again. I rested my head on her chest and heard her heart racing nearly as fast as mine. I rubbed her stomach again, smiling when she squirmed. I accidentally moved my fingers too close to her side and tickled her. She grinned, licking her lips as if savoring the lingering taste of mine. She purred eagerly and allowed me to explore her body.

I began a cautious search for that fluttering sensation I'd felt before. Deliberately, I moved my hand past her navel toward her lower belly, sneaking my fingertips again into the waist of her skirt. Her thighs parted automatically, her arousal growing. I'd be stupid if I didn't notice the invitation to continue. Her chest rising and falling rapidly.

She urged me on as if testing to see how far I would go. I hadn't felt the flutter yet. Suddenly, she took hold of my hand and pushed it right into her skirt until only half of my hand was visible. She sucked in her breath, shuddering at the same time. Finally, her belly clenched and fluttered against my hand. It was then that I was sure she liked what I was doing.

"Shawnee..." Her voice was breathless.

I started to worry that I'd hurt her. "I'm sorry." I went to remove my hand, but she caught my wrist and held it in place.

"Don't stop." Her hand trembling on mine as she closed her eyes.

Don't stop? Don't stop what? I started to panic and looked over at Mal. If it were possible, he looked distracted and attentive at the same time. He nodded toward Vanessa as if saying, "Ask her."

She opened her eyes when I hesitated. Her eyes flashed from deep green to bright yellow, and she gripped my hand, pushing it lower down her body until my fingertips reached the top of her panties.

My heart was pounding so fast I thought I might die right there. I held my breath. We were both frozen. I had no idea what I was doing, and I imagined she was afraid that I was going to pull away, but I let her guide my hand down into her panties. The warmth of her arousal engulfed my hand as flesh met flesh. She guided me farther until I reached silky, slippery wetness that blossomed from her delicate folds. Her breath caught in my ear.

I shuddered as the unease in my belly turned to an unfamiliar fire that navigated downward and seemed to emulsify into my skin. She took my hand and guided me to stroke her—a gentle, barely moving kind of stroke. Her legs trembled. She tilted her head back and rolled her pelvis against my hand, pressing me to her. When the throb of her need ached against my fingers, my concerns melted away. Right then I knew what she'd wanted all this time, and I decided I would give it to her. I was in this completely for her. I wanted to please her.

My fear tumbled away like loose-fitting clothing, and I began moving my hand against her on my own. Her hand fell away, and I was left to discover her by myself. I was intrigued by her slippery wetness, which was something I had never experienced before. When her delicate lips parted against my fingers, she sucked in a quivering breath.

The firmness of her clitoris pressed into my hand when she rocked her hips. She held me close to her, gripping the sofa cushion at the same time. Her breathing quickened. I could hear her heart racing and tiny beads of sweat formed on her neck and chest. I kissed her neck without thinking and continued using my hand to please her. She began moving her hips faster, gyrating until suddenly her entire body arched and a soft moan escaped her lips. The subtle tension and release of her orgasm surprised me, as did the additional wetness that seeped from her. She rolled her hips against my hand before finally relaxing back on the sofa.

Her purring was louder than I'd ever heard before. She wrapped both of her arms around me, pulling me close and pressing her lips to mine in a breathy kiss. I returned it and removed my hand from her panties. My smile interrupted the kiss. I hadn't noticed that Mal had left the room.

"Hi," I whispered to her. The blush in my face seemed eternal, and I seriously wondered if it would ever go away.

She curled up against me, draping one of her legs over mine. She hid her face against my chest. "Hi."

"I'm sorry I never knew what you wanted before." I continued to whisper while running my fingers through her hair. I kissed her cheek and forehead several times, unable to satiate my desire to touch her.

She melted into my affections like she'd been waiting for it forever. Her smile was endless as was the warmth radiating from her body. "Just you, Shawnee," she said into my shoulder. "Just you..."

CHAPTER TWENTY-NINE

Vanessa stayed with me until morning. She was up before me as usual, and I awoke to the sensation of her running her fingers through my hair. She smiled at me when I blinked to focus.

"Morning." Her voice was barely a whisper. The light coming in through the window told me it was just after daybreak.

"Hi." I poked her cheek playfully. "You stayed."

"Of course." She nuzzled my hand, and then I hugged her. It made her smile and playfully bite my shoulder.

"I like when you stay."

"Me too." She leaned her forehead against mine. I pressed my lips to hers in a tender kiss. Her hand slid down my side to rest on my hip and my body quivered. I rolled onto my back so that she could put her hand on my stomach like usual. This time she pushed my shirt up to expose my stomach. I closed my eyes and let her caress my bare skin. I started thinking about how things suddenly changed between us, or at least it seemed like they had. She rested her head on my shoulder, and I twirled her hair around my finger. She smelled sweet, like fresh air and lilacs. My stomach tightened as I paired the gentle touching with her scent. I never realized how my stomach played a role in my reactions to her. Maybe that was why she was always touching it. I wondered what it must have been like for her—a playful feline being unable to play with her closest friend. I had no doubts that she played with plenty of other people.

She moved her hand a bit lower when she felt my body respond, but paused when she neared the waistband of my sweats. I didn't say anything, though my body tensed. I felt her posture weaken.

"You don't have to stop," I said, nudging her chin when she looked away. "I can't help how I respond sometimes, it's automatic. But it doesn't mean I want you to stop."

Her voice was tentative when she responded. "How will I know then?"

"I'll stop you when I want you to stop," I reassured her.

She nodded and kissed my chin, purring the whole time. "I like that you're talking now."

"I always talk." I looked at her oddly.

"Yeah, but not like this." She put her head back down on my shoulder.

Vanessa was right. So many things were changing lately, including my ability to express myself—at least to her. She let her fingertips sneak into my sweatpants and panties to lightly caress my scar. I shivered at the touch, trying to place the sensation. It didn't hurt, but it wasn't quite like Xany's tickles. When she felt my response, Vanessa stopped and stared at me with a risen brow.

"It tickles when you touch it lightly," I explained, uncertain how to express the fact it was different tickles.

"It's the only scar I couldn't heal because you kept it hidden so often. I couldn't get to it without being obvious." She peeked up at me.

"I think it would be very obvious." I couldn't help but laugh at the truthfulness in that statement. Imagine what my reaction would have been if one day I suddenly awoke to Vanessa between my legs and my decade-old scar gone. That would have been a sight.

She snickered and gave me an affectionate nip on the neck. "Mhmm," she said, then let her entire hand disappear into my pants. My heart began to race. She wasn't touching anything other than my scar, but my thoughts began to bubble again intrusively. I had to admit, even if it was just Vanessa, I was terrified of being touched any lower.

"What if it hurts?" I asked through bated breath. I tried to keep talking. Sometimes listening to my own voice was the only way to battle the echoes. I didn't have Mal here in my bedroom to help me.

"What if what hurts?" Vanessa stared down at me, apparently puzzled by my question.

"What if...when you touch me, it hurts?" I dug my fingers into her shoulder, holding on for dear life.

"Then you tell me and I stop. Does it hurt when you touch yourself?" she asked, suddenly concerned.

I shook my head and shrugged at the same time. "I dunno." Just talking about the potential for pain had me shaking. She removed her hand from my pants and wrapped her arms around me tightly.

"Shawnee, you've had sex before with men. Did you feel hurt then?"

"It didn't feel like anything. I can't remember," I said. "I'm scared it will hurt like when I wake up in the morning or when I have one of those blackouts."

"I know," she said. "I know you're scared. We don't have to do anything that makes you scared." She nuzzled me; her purring was soft and comforting.

"I hate it. Why can't I just want it like you do? You've had sex with men, too, and liked it, why not me?" I shifted position so that I was resting my head on her chest and listening to her purring.

"I wish I had all the answers for you." She ran her fingers through my hair.

"Please tell me you don't have to work today." I nuzzled her neck. The thought of separating from her was almost unbearable.

The smile on her face was sad. "I do. I can see if Caroline can cover the class if you want me to stay."

"No." I shook my head, sniffling a little bit. "You need to work. It's okay. I'll go for a walk by the lake while you're gone and try to sort out my thoughts."

"Are you sure?"

"Positive. We can't go calling out of work every time I have an issue with attachment." I smirked, trying to make light of my emotions.

"Hey, at least you're attached. That's a good thing." She snickered.

"Mhmm. Will you try something first?" A shy smile threatened to seep onto my lips. Bravery in these situations wasn't my strongest suit.

"Yeah, of course." She tapped her finger on the edge of my nose.

I moved so that I was lying flat again. I took her hand just as she had taken mine the night before and placed it on my stomach under my shirt. "I remember one time I liked something," I said and instead of guiding her hand downward, I guided her hand up toward my breasts. She smiled, and I watched her porcelain features flush a strawberry pink, which made me laugh.

"Are you being shy?"

She smiled but nodded, and we continued our playful exploring until Vanessa had to get ready for work.

While she got dressed, I laid in bed watching her. The blue velvet dress she'd taken from my dresser drawer melted over her torso as if it missed being there. The dress fit her perfectly and clung to her midriff without the slightest wrinkle. She usually kept a pair of work clothes or a leotard at my old apartment, but I didn't expect her to have it here as well. While she pulled up her black tights, my eyes lingered on her hands as she moved them over her endless legs.

"No leotard today?" My voice sounded huskier than usual. It surprised me.

"Not today. The children have a recital tonight. We have to look professional." She sat on the edge of the bed with her hard shoes in her lap. I preferred the hard Irish dancing shoes to the soft ones. To me the soft shoes looked just like ballet slippers and weren't anything special. The best part about Irish dancing was the pounding beats of the dancers as they clacked away to the Celtic rhythms. I imagined what Vanessa would look like dancing in her dress.

"I'll have to come watch you dance again sometime soon." I brushed my fingertips over the hem of her skirt. The velvet was soft and reminded me of the coat of a newborn wolf cub.

"I'd like that." She smiled at me while tying on her shoes, then leaned over and kissed my cheek.

"Good, because I wouldn't want you to hate it," I said, laughing and nuzzling her as she kissed me.

"That would defeat the whole purpose, Shawnee Twofeathers." She snickered and stood up. "See you tonight."

"Bye." I swatted at her playfully as she moved toward the window and disappeared into the inbetween.

I spent some time lying in bed for a while after Vanessa left. After sometime, I got up to go about my usual routine. The bathroom was empty when so I showered quickly and dressed. When I entered the kitchen, I expected to see at least one person around; however, all was quiet. I shrugged and decided to venture out to the lake.

Once outside the cabin, I could tell that Mal was somewhere close. A few yards in front of the cabin steps, the fire pit sat surrounded by big stones and some left over logs. The ashes in the center were damp. The air was brisk, but the sun was warm against my face. It was quiet out here, which I liked. The sounds of the morning birds singing and the rustling of the trees as the wind rushed through the branches was about as noisy as it got.

I walked around the east side of the cabin and followed the short trail toward the lake. The leaves on the ground were soggy under my boots. Salamanders scuttled away as I stepped. It was only about a five-minute walk to the lake. A huge rock was planted right by the shore. It was flat on one side and slanted on the other as if Gaia set this boulder down to serve as perfect, natural seating for a view of the lake. I helped myself to a seat on the rock and shivered when the coolness of its surface permeated my jeans. I sat cross-legged, tucking my feet under me, and gazed out over the water.

The lake was not very big, but I imagined it was probably a mile around. The water, now fully thawed, rippled lightly against the wind. The mountains in the backdrop looked farther away, and I listened to the water lap against the shoreline. I took a deep breath, inhaling nature's perfume, resting my elbows on my thighs and my chin on my hands. I closed my eyes and let my thoughts drift.

I didn't completely understand all the feelings that being in a pack again was bringing up. I may have remembered the culture and responsibilities from my childhood, but I certainly didn't remember the emotions. The physical stuff was the most surprising. Sometimes if Caden walked into the room, I could feel his power and protection inside me that instead of instilling fear, brought trust and safety. My brain was skeptical about trusting him, or anyone, my body couldn't fight it.

When Xany hugged me, my body was warm, and even though she could be enduringly annoying, my affection for her was growing. I couldn't help my responses to them, and I thought I was starting to like the feelings of connection and belonging.

The thing that I had the most difficult time

understanding was the way Mal made me feel. In all my life, I couldn't remember ever wanting to move closer to someone. Not even Vanessa. When his skin touched mine, it ignited a sort of fever inside me that warmed my heart, and sometimes it seemed like his fingers had threads that wove together the fragmented pieces of my soul.

The most baffling part about it was my attraction to him. I'd seen plenty of handsome men in my time, but Mal's beauty seemed to stand out among them. His sharp jaw line, crooked smirk, and luscious build. Sometimes I thought I could stare at him all day long, waiting for the moment when he'd flex his muscles or smile at me in the way that made my stomach do acrobatics.

And Vanessa. I couldn't even begin to process what was happening with her. I'd been avoiding the thoughts that could help me understand the nature of our relationship. I planned to talk to Xany about it. I thought she'd have the most insight.

Although spring was imminent, there was still a chill in the air. I pulled my jacket tighter around me. I had to admit that I liked living in Utah. Away from the city, tucked neatly into the folds of snowy mountains and bustling trees. The trickle of the stream emptying into the lake caught my attention briefly before a prickle on the back of my neck stole it away. Normally I'd get nervous, but I knew exactly who was approaching, because after all, I'd called him. Mal emerged from the trees, and my heart skipped a beat. He was wearing nothing but a pair of worn cargo shorts, which I knew meant that I'd grabbed him from the middle of something.

"I couldn't control my thoughts without you here. They keep messing things up and making me feel bad." I spoke to him before I even saw him.

"How did you know you could call my wolf?" he asked, both of us saying the first thing on our minds. He paused, then responded to me. "It will take some time to feel safe, even with the people you feel safest with."

"I just knew I could." I turned to look at him. His mere presence filled me with a sense of calm that I couldn't explain.

He sat next to me on the boulder, looking out over the lake. We were both quiet for a while, taking in what each other had said.

"My wolf likes you," he admitted in a soft voice.

"I know." My body had me leaning against him before I could even think about it. "I like your wolf too."

"What happened after I left?" He put his arm around me.

"Some stuff, but it was fine. This morning I got scared when she tried to touch me. I know it's illogical that I think I'm going to feel some sort of intolerable pain if someone touches me anywhere, not just in the bathing suit area." I let my eyes wander out over the lake. "I still flinch when Xany hugs me sometimes."

"What's different between me and Vanessa?"

"Vanessa I've known forever and she's never hurt me, and you..." I shrugged. "You don't scare me, and for some reason a part of me believes you'll never cause me pain."

"Maybe it's time you started challenging some of your belief systems, Nee, and your thoughts." He rubbed my arm right on top of my glyph.

It seemed like something I needed to do. How to go about doing it was another issue in itself. "I worry that Vanessa will take it as rejection when I get scared."

"Of course she will. In a way, you are rejecting her by giving into your fear and not trusting her. I know you've been through a lot of pain in your life and can understand the fear." He nuzzled me as he let me put the rest of it together mentally.

"I just have to keep telling myself that pain is only temporary, even if I do feel it." I looked at him to see if he agreed.

He nodded, and I experienced a jolt of pleasure. "Exactly. And pain isn't always a bad thing. It tells us there's a part of our body or our soul that needs help or attention."

I listened to him while resting my head on his shoulder. His free hand rubbed my forearm affectionately. I was pretty surprised that I allowed him this close to me, but I couldn't help it. Something just felt right about it, like I needed to be close to him. Our skin wasn't touching so it wasn't as intense as it had been previously. "I think I was supposed to come here."

"Here as in Utah or here as in sitting on this rock?"

"Well, both, but Utah specifically. I think I was supposed to meet you."

"I think I was supposed to meet you too..." He paused and then looked at me with a grin. "Calling my wolf, you're an audacious little one."

I laughed, then smiled my most innocent smile.

CHAPTER THIRTY

"What'd you want to talk about, Nee?" Xany asked the next morning as she bounced into the main room where I was sitting on the sofa. Mal and Caden had both gone to work at Hank's company.

"A few things, I guess." I set down the newspaper I'd picked up to scan for bizarre stories. It was a habit of mine to look for weird news that humans concocted in order to explain supernatural events.

"Is it about Vanessa? And Mal?" She asked in a singsong voice before hopping onto the couch beside me.

"Maybe." I slouched a bit, my confidence draining from me. "I don't feel like talking anymore."

"Hey! That's not fair. You can't be a tease about talking." Xany huffed as she glared at me. "And besides, I can tell you have something you want to talk about."

"Caden told me he thinks you're an empath. You lied to me." I shot her a playful glare. I wanted her to think I was a little mad at her, just for fun.

"I didn't know I was! I swear," she whined, then paused suddenly and thwapped my leg. "Stop being rude. You're only rude to me you know."

"Noted." I tried as hard as I could to prevent a smile

from appearing on my face.

"Stop it!" She lunged at me, knocking me backward onto the couch. "It's infuriating!"

I couldn't help but laugh. "Xany! Get off me."

"Nope. Not until you tell me why you're so rude to me."

"Because you always want more information and you're an empath!" I bopped her with a pillow. "You're not supposed to pry out my secrets."

"I wouldn't have to pry them out if you would just tell me the things I want to know," she said with a giggle.

"You're incorrigible." I sighed in an exaggerated fashion, turning my eyes to the ceiling.

"I know," she smiled, resting her chin on my chest.

"Your eyes remind me of Mal's sometimes." I brushed a bit of hair away from her face. With Mal and Caden off working for Hank, I couldn't feel the pack as closely as when we were all in the same house. Mal's absence was particularly noticeable.

"His are darker." She batted her lashes.

"Yeah... What does it feel like when you love someone?" The words rolled out of my mouth before I could even think about it.

"Like just love them or be in love with them?" Xany's expression brightened, and she tilted her head.

"Just love them." I shrugged, trying to play off the seriousness of my question.

"It's kind of a warm feeling, like..." She paused. "Like just talking to them or being near them makes you feel a little bit more whole," she said, a soft smile playing on her lips.

"And what about being in love, what does that feel like?" She had my full attention now. I wanted to understand everything she was telling me. One day I might love someone without realizing it.

"Instead of just feeling a little bit more whole, you feel a lot more whole. Your whole body feels that person and responds to them. It makes you smile, and cry, and laugh, and crave, and want all at the same time. And you miss them when they're gone, even if they were only gone for a little while." Xany had a dreamy expression on her face. I wondered if she was talking, or thinking, about Caden. "Think of one person you loved a long time ago. Even if it was a pet."

"My mom. I know I loved her, and I know she loved me too."

"Do you remember that feeling of loving and being loved?" She tucked a strand of hair behind my ear as she often did. This time I didn't swat her.

I closed my eyes for a moment, trying to remember. It came to me rather quickly as it often did when I thought about my mom. "I remember," I said, opening my eyes again.

"So see? You do know what it feels like, Nee. You just had to think about it." She smiled.

"I know I love Vanessa," I said after brief silence.

"I know you do too."

I tried to ignore the fact that her smile had turned smug. "I know she loves me as well."

"I know she does too." Xany giggled. When I didn't say anything else, Xany spoke. "What are you thinking, Nee?"

"Do you think it's possible to love more than one person at the same time?"

"You can love a hundred million people at the same time, Nee." She grinned, obviously entertained by my naiveté when it came to love.

Uncertain, I tried to rephrase my question. "I mean, can you be in love with more than one person at the same time?"

"Yes. I think you can." She tapped her lip, looking thoughtful.

Her answer only served to confuse me more. I needed to understand, needed to know that what I was feeling was not only acceptable, it was encouraged. "But how?" I tried to keep the desperation for a real, solid answer out of my voice.

"I think so because maybe you need both of them to fill you up and make you whole. Maybe sometimes there is so much to fill up that only two people can do it," she rationalized.

I mulled over her words for a few minutes. It seemed like it made sense. "I think I knew Mal before. In another life. He feels familiar to me. Like he holds half of me somehow. Does that make sense?"

"Mhmm. I think it does. And Vanessa?"

"Vanessa's just...always been. Always," I said and then lifted a brow at her. "If I love her, does that mean I'm a lesbian?"

Xany nearly cracked up. "Not if you like men too."

"I like men, but just one woman. What's that mean?" My stomach jittered with nerves as I awaited her answer. Being attracted to someone of the same gender was wrong, wasn't it? But then, why was it so right with her?

"It doesn't mean anything, Nee. You love who you love, why label it?" She shrugged, coupled with a grin.

"I like that idea."

"Four months here, Nee, and you've grown so much. Did you know Vanessa loved you before you came here?" she asked. I was pretty sure she was using this time to get some information out of me. Leave it to Xany to seek the opportunity.

"Not until that day that I remembered when she saved me, and we kissed." I looked away from Xany. It was still hard for me to grasp what was occurring between myself and Vanessa. We'd been friends for so long. Just friends. I was frightened of that relationship changing.

"You kissed? How come you didn't tell me!" Xany swatted my shoulder hard enough to leave a welt.

"Ouch! I didn't think much of it, and it was kind of private." Heat rushed my cheeks and I tried to cover it up by laughing.

"What's it like to have sex with a woman?" She grinned, trying very hard to stifle her giggling.

"We haven't. I mean, I haven't..." I stuttered. "I still get too scared when she touches me." This conversation was getting way too close for comfort. Part of me wanted to wiggle out from under her and run off into the woods.

"How can you bear to wait so long? Scared of what?" She groaned.

"That it'll hurt..." I trailed off. "And that things will change too quickly." I inhaled a deep, cleansing breath. It took a lot out of me to admit that.

"Hasn't your fear stopped you from doing enough? Just go for it, Nee. What's the worst that can happen?" Xany looked at me as if saying "duh."

"The worst is that..." I started to say but couldn't come up with anything.

"The only thing you have to worry about is that your two loves are opposite genders and opposite species..." She smiled sheepishly.

CHAPTER THIRTY-ONE

Xany and I cooked dinner together the night after our talk. It was bizarre, in a way, to feel like I was providing nourishment to other people the way family members would. It spoke to my readjustment to pack life. I remembered the times when my mother would be in the kitchen, cooking for me and my father.

While I stirred the rice noodles, I tried to distract myself from thinking too much. "Did you learn this recipe at your classes, Xee?"

Xany was searing salmon steaks and mixing some sort of special seasoning. "Yep! It was our first dinner recipe after learning to do sandwiches and heroes." She giggled. "The teacher said we should start with basics."

"I didn't think you cooked terribly before."

"That's because I only made you breakfast. You're lucky I never made you lunch or dinner." She grinned and pointed to the boiling potatoes. "Want to mash them?"

"Sure. How come you made mashed potatoes *and* rice noodles?" I drained the potatoes in the sink.

"Because mashed 'taters are your favorite. Vanessa told me so." She grinned over the fact she had garnered information without my knowing it.

"Remind me to thank her." I smiled, letting her have her moment, and began mashing the potatoes.

"You're welcome." Vanessa's voice chimed in as she snuck up from behind to give me a hug.

"Sneaky," I said, jumping slightly.

"Salmon is my favorite." She peeked over at Xany, lifting her chin in greeting.

Xany giggled a little bit at Vanessa before pouring some dark-colored sauce over the salmon steaks. "I made plenty for you too, Ness."

Both Vanessa and I stared at her for a moment, taken aback by her sudden warm demeanor.

"What?" Xany froze, blinking at us.

"Oh, nothing," I replied with a laugh. Vanessa snickered and nipped my shoulder. I finished the potatoes, then turned around to face her fully. "You still have your leo on." I glanced over her slender form clad in the tight black outfit, this time with a blue skirt.

"I came over right after work. Can I shower before dinner?"

"Of course." With only the slightest hesitation, I kissed her cheek.

She smiled, and her cheeks tinged pink. "I'll be right back."

"Okay." I watched her saunter off to the bathroom, then set the potatoes down on the table.

Xany grinned at me, her eyes dancing with merriment. "You made her feel self-conscious."

"She's affectionate with me in front of people, so why not return it. It must make her feel pretty awful when I pull away." I returned her grin. "And I like when she turns pink," I added.

"Naughty, Nee!" Xany snickered. "It's that way for wolves too. Has Vanessa been with women?"

"She's into men." I smirked. "Many, many men."

"I wonder when the guys will be back." Xany glanced at the clock and changed the subject.

"Soon," I said. "Mal is close. Maybe Caden is with him."

Xany shot me a surprised look. "You can sense Mal and not Caden?"

"Mal's easier." I shrugged. I wasn't really sure why it was easier to sense Mal. The Alpha usually had the strongest connection to his packmates and vice versa. I liked that I could sense Mal easily. It was comforting, in a way, and Caden still freaked me out at times.

"And you can call his wolf?" Xany put her hands on her hips.

"Why?" I asked, setting five places at the table. I didn't understand why she was grilling me so much about this. It didn't seem all that special to me.

"Just curious is all." With her lips pursed in thought, Xany turned back to the vegetables she was preparing.

I missed my chance to press her further because just then, Mal waltzed through the door. He brought a whiff of outdoors with him—the smell of fresh air and what I thought might be jasmine. "Evening," he said cheerily.

"Hey." My cheeks heated with a flush at the sight of him.

Xany began placing the food on the table. "Where's Caden?"

"Hank called him on the way home. He'll be back soon." He jumped right into helping Xany place dinner on the table.

Vanessa emerged from the bathroom wearing her usual dress with her hair brushed out long and wet. She sat down at the table, purring contently. I served everyone iced tea and Vanessa her typical glass of milk.

"Should we wait for Caden?" Xany asked Mal as she placed the salmon steaks onto the table.

"He'll be along shortly and probably wouldn't want us to wait, knowing him." Mal began serving everyone the salmon. Xany worked on dishing out potatoes and noodles. Vanessa was the first to begin eating once everyone was seated. She smiled at me. I imagined she was happy to be eating her favorite food. Mal shook his head, smiling as if he knew exactly what the cat was thinking.

After dinner, Vanessa sprawled out on the couch, nursing her full belly while Mal lit a fire. Xany and I cleaned up the kitchen as quickly as possible so that we could join the others by the warmth of the fireplace. Xany lingered to fix Caden a plate and set it aside for when he returned. Mal sat down at the edge of the sofa, and Vanessa pulled her feet back to allow room for him. I sat beside him, nudging Vanessa's legs into my lap. She purred and rubbed her foot along my inner thigh. I swatted her knee, then rubbed her long, soft legs. Mal watched and if it were possible, I could have sworn I felt fur cover his arm and bristle against me. Vanessa purred, and I moved my hand farther up her leg so that I was rubbing from her ankle to her thigh.

Can you call her like you call me? Mal popped into my head; this time I had to look at him to see if he was speaking aloud.

No. I had to focus for a moment to speak back to him in my thoughts. *I think it works differently. She can usually just sense if I'm in danger. Like, she shows up at the right moments. I can't call her though, unless I'm using a phone.* I smiled at him.

"What's funny?" Vanessa asked, looking between Mal and me.

Busted, Mal said in my head.

With a grin, I looked down at her. "Mal asked if I can call you like I call him."

"What's that mean?" Her brow furrowed at the new term.

"I can call his wolf. Like, if I'm far away and I want him to come to me, I can call him."

"I didn't hear him ask that." She frowned at us.

"I can initiate mind conversations, Red, remember?" Mal chimed in.

"Weird telepathic dog," she muttered.

"Weird devoted puss," Mal mumbled, his lips tugging into a smirk.

Vanessa hissed at him, then returned to her quiet purring, rubbing her foot against my thigh again to get me to go back to caressing her legs.

That was easier than I thought. Mal was back in my head.

I'm surprised she's sitting this close to you, but then again, I'm really not surprised at all.

She's clever, Shawnee. She's not going to deny you anything, even if it is a wolf...

I watched Vanessa, and she met my gaze with a smile. I leaned down and nipped her thigh before crawling up closer to lie beside her, our feet near Mal. She hugged me. I pulled the blanket down from the back of the sofa and tossed it over us while Mal clicked on the TV, turning to the news. I knew he was pretending that he wasn't paying attention. Xany scuttled about the kitchen in her anxiety over missing Caden and then brought a bag of marshmallows into the living room. She snatched up the fire poker and began jabbing marshmallows onto it to toast in the fireplace.

"Gross," Mal said as he wrinkled his nose in distaste.

Xany grinned and set the sweet treats ablaze on purpose. I laughed at their usual sibling antics. Watching Xany could be entertaining at times.

Vanessa watched the news along with Mal for a few minutes. Something must have sparked her memory because she spoke suddenly. "Have you done the stuff you need to get your Utah medical license?"

"Not yet. I have the paperwork, I just need to do it." I tore my gaze away from Xany to return it to Vanessa.

"Take your time." She grinned at me. "I like having you home a lot."

"I knew there was an ulterior motive to that question." I tried to tickle her.

Vanessa laughed and squirmed, then nipped my bottom lip. "Caught."

"Yes, you're caught." I smiled, giving her another kiss on the cheek.

Her hand fell to my stomach. She lifted up my shirt, then pulled the blankets up to keep us both hidden.

"Everyone's around," I whispered.

"No one's paying attention." She leaned in for a kiss. I let her lips meet mine until she sneakily slipped in her tongue. It surprised me at first. I pulled back, but she caught me again. I felt like a virgin who'd never used her tongue to kiss before. She broke the kiss to nibble my lip. A rush of warmth ran through me and lingered between my thighs.

"I think I like kissing like that," I told her.

"I think you do too." She snickered and leaned in to kiss me again, this time more delicately.

I broke the kiss to caress her neck and shoulder. My gaze wandered over her body, then back up to meet her gaze.

"What is it?"

"There's something I should tell you." I gnawed my lip. I had the sudden urge to tell her why I'd quit working at Mercy General. I wanted to tell her everything. The burden of keeping that from her seemed like too much to bear. I didn't know where it came from, but it was overwhelming.

"What is it?" she asked again, her voice gentler this time.

"It's about—"

I was cut off by Caden busting through the cabin door. Xany dropped the fire poker with a clang. "Caden—" Xany began, but he interrupted, his gaze falling on Vanessa first.

"Vanessa, you need to leave now. Hank's cubs popped at the same time, and he's having difficulty controlling them," he said, quickly filling everyone in on the situation.

Vanessa and I got up together as Mal rushed over to Caden.

"They're headed here?" I asked.

"Yes. When he told them to run, they disobeyed and headed this way. Mal, Hank is heading them off, will you..."

Mal nodded and disrobed quickly before leaping past him out the door, then down the steps to disappear in the woods.

"What do you mean they *popped*, Caden?" Xany asked.

"They came to their Firstings together. Hank has two sons, fourteen and thirteen, and a daughter who is twelve. The younger boy changed first, which set off the older boy. The sister has the fever. Vanessa, you need to go now," Caden urged.

"Shawnee too," she demanded as she growled.

"Shawnee is needed here. She'll be fine," Caden reassured her, then glanced to Xany who suddenly jumped when she caught his eye. She looked confused and stood completely still for a moment before nodding faintly to him.

"She'll be fine, Ness." Xany's voice shook. "You'll know if there's trouble." She glanced to me for support.

I caught on to the exchange that occurred between Xany and Caden. Vanessa looked to me when I spoke to her. "Ness, you need to go. They'll come after you, and in their frenzied state, they are harder to control."

"Why can't Hank control his own cubs?" She was gripping my waist so hard I thought she might knock me down.

"They're both dominant sons of a sept leader, and Hank's Beta has been injured," Caden answered. "They're his children, and he's worried that they won't survive the change if they can't get control of their beasts." Caden seemed like he was forcing his voice to sound calmer than his tensed body appeared. "How would you feel if they were your kits?"

There was a long, silent pause. "I'll go," she said and hugged me.

My heart raced while I imagined frenzied young

werewolves headed toward the cabin to tear up Vanessa. "I'll be okay," I assured her, caressing her cheek gently. "I'll call you when they're under control."

She leaned into my hand and let me go. Caden gave her a firm nod, and Vanessa disappeared into the windowpane. Caden seemed to let out his breath. I knew that cubs in the frenzy of their Firsting wouldn't hesitate to attack Vanessa. I also knew that Vanessa wouldn't hesitate to defend herself. That part scared me the most.

"What do we do, Caden?" Xany asked.

"We need to watch the Fevered one." I moved closer to Caden who nodded in approval.

"Mal will push the cubs toward the lake where we will have a better advantage. Hank's daughter, Arielle, is waiting outside." He opened the door.

"Cool." Xany giggled as she watched him. "Sleepover!" She grinned at me. I rolled my eyes.

The young girl stalked into the room with her arms crossed over her chest in annoyance. Caden chuckled at her attitude and glanced to Xany, giving her a light nod. "Arielle, you're to stay here with Shawnee and Xany." His voice was firm. The girl met his gaze with a defiant stare down, which of course she lost. Only a cub with the Fever would ever have the guts to try something like that with a wolf as dominant as Caden.

"Why should I stay with them?" She spat the words out like an angry cat. The girl was about the girth of Caden's left leg, and yet she was attempting to defy his orders.

"Because I'm going to help your father manage your brothers. You're to listen to Shawnee and Xany." He kept his gaze on Arielle, who again had her gaze broken by Caden's powerful dominance. She frowned at him, stomped over to a chair in the kitchen, and sat. Caden smirked and took off his shirt, tossing it on the floor.

"If she changes, guide her toward the mountains," he said, then disappeared out the door.

Arielle frowned at me first, then Xany. "I'll go where I

want," she demanded.

Xany, obviously stunned by the rudeness of the cub, stared openmouthed. I'd always wondered about Xany's pack experience, and this was proving that she had very little experience in handling Fevered cubs.

I put on my best, fake smile. "Of course you will," I said to Arielle, touching my hand to her forehead to feel for her temperature. She rolled her eyes at me and pulled away. "Xee, will you get the thermometer from the black bag in my room?" Giving Xany a task seemed to unfreeze her, and she trotted off to my room.

"You're not sticking anything in my ass." Arielle glared at me and stood up.

"It's an ear thermometer. You won't feel it. Now pipe down," I demanded, pressing her back down to sit in the chair. Arielle curled her lip at me but sat. Xany skipped back into the room and laughed at my sternness with the cub when she handed me the thermometer. I took Arielle's temperature quickly before she could push my hand away.

"One hundred and four," I told Xany who shrugged.

"Should we give her ice or something?" Xany asked.

I shook my head, knowing it would be useless. "No. That's prime temperature for an adolescent cub's Firsting."

"Oh. So...now what?" Xany looked at Arielle as if she were about to explode.

"You're both idiots." Arielle huffed as she crossed her arms over her chest. "I'm hungry."

"She's a brat, Nee. Can I smack her?" Xany frowned at the ornery cub.

Arielle stood up and growled a weak, human-sounding growl at Xany. I put my hand in front of Arielle to stop her forward movement.

"You're a bitch." She spat at Xany, "I want something to eat." Her human growl slowly turned into a deeper, guttural growl.

"So are you. I don't care if you're sick and going to turn into the big bad wolf, I'm not feeding you until you can be nice." Xany huffed and stomped away from Arielle.

One hundred and four degrees Fahrenheit...

The cells went through puberty...

Prime temperature for an adolescent cub's Firsting...

The voice of Doctor Reynolds, mingled with my own, suddenly echoed in my head. With wide eyes, I looked between Xany and Arielle. The pieces began to fall into place. Arielle moved in Xany's direction, but I blocked her and shoved her back toward her chair. My body reacted automatically to the situation playing, yet the only sounds I could hear were the echoes.

Create a serum to stop it...

"Oh God!" I said as dread raced through me.

I watched Arielle, who was seething when she was forced to sit. Her eyes locked onto Xany.

"What is it?" She glanced between me and the cub.

Arielle struggled against the grip I had on her shoulder. Then, as if she could sense my sudden distraction, she stood up and shoved me away from her. I fell backward and slid half way across the kitchen on my ass. She roared in victory and then blinked when she heard herself make the bestial sound. She looked at me, her expression a mix of fear and rage.

Xany hurried over to help me up. "What the hell is wrong with you?" she shouted at the young girl.

Arielle crouched on the floor. Her gaze fixed on mine and suddenly her angry expression turned into a fearful one. I got up with Xany's help and stalked over beside Arielle.

"Run to the mountains," I told her, my voice stern.

Xany fidgeted beside me, concern evident on her face. "She can't change in the house, Nee, she'll take out the wall."

"I know." I grabbed Arielle by her arm, dragging her out the front door of the cabin. She was in enough shock to not resist me.

Arielle's face contorted painfully, and she screamed as I

tugged her down the front steps. Her scream turned into a ferocious growl. I dropped her beside the fire pit. Xany leaped down the steps and stood beside me, her eyes wide with shock. She stood in front of me, her posture protective, though I could see her shaking.

The sun had set, and the full moon was rising over the mountains in the faint light of dusk. A Changer didn't need the pull of the full moon to change, nor did a cub need it for their Firsting. However, it surely didn't help the matter any. Wolves were more vulnerable to their instincts during the full moon, and I imagined that's what fueled the siblings to change on the same night.

"Run to the mountains, Arielle," I demanded, though my voice quivered some.

Arielle's small frame began to twist and contort, warping her little body into something grotesque. I grabbed Xany's arm, and she patted my hand automatically, staring in awe at the small girl distorting into a monster. I imagined she hadn't seen many Firstings in her lifetime. Arielle cried out in pain as nature took its course. Muscles began to bulge, tearing through her clothes, and hair started to sprout all over her body. Her slender fingers dug into the earth as claws sprouted from her fingertips. Arielle's bones popped and crunched loudly as her appendages grew into that of a gangly werewolf. Her soft, feminine facial features cracked and broke to reshape into a long, salivating snout filled with razor sharp teeth. Her ears and tail burst forth simultaneously. Her pained cries turned into a soft whimper as her body finished its first transformation. In the end, Arielle was a six-foot-tall beast with blazing yellow eyes that communicated confusion and hunger.

"Run!" Xany yelled to the new beast. "Run to the mountains, Arielle."

As if suddenly aware of our presence, Arielle turned and growled at us. She took a step closer, her foot thudding in the dirt, leaving a deep impression.

"Shit, Nee." Xany tugged my arm to move me away.

"We can't move. She'll chase us. She's a dominant." I spoke in breathless bursts as anxiety held my chest in a tight grip while I squeezed Xany's arm to hold her in place.

"Tell her to run too, Nee. Maybe she'll listen to us both."

I gulped but nodded. We both began shouting at Arielle to run for the mountains. Suddenly I was reminded of the two other new werewolves headed this way. I was afraid that they would burst through the woods and hurt Xany. I spoke firmly, desperately to Arielle, meeting her gaze and holding her in a stare. "Run, Arielle. You *will* run to the mountains, Arielle. Go!" I shouted and pointed toward the range in the distance.

Arielle broke the gaze easily and lifted a clawed paw as if ready to swing at us until I caught her gaze again. This time she paused and made a gruffing sound at me.

"Go," I demanded and pointed again.

She gruffed and with some hesitation, she turned slowly toward where I was pointing. She looked over her shoulder, but I kept on pointing. She began walking toward the mountains. Her new body made the task a clumsy effort at first. She ran on all fours before pushing herself standing upright on her hind legs and began to run strong. Her head was tucked low and her front paws grazed the ground when needed. Her harsh, thundering stomps shook the earth as she disappeared beyond the tree line and headed toward the mountains. When the earth was still and quiet, Arielle's roar echoed in the distance. A happy roar that spoke to the pleasure and freedom she felt as the beast took her over.

CHAPTER THIRTY-TWO

Xany kept her hand on my shoulder while she peered into the darkness in the direction Arielle had run. Adolescent cells. The serum. What had I done? Could that serum really have worked as a vaccine to werecreature transformation?

"Your serum is a success." I remembered reading in Doctor Reynolds's e-mail. Oh God. Adolescent cells. Had he? No. Oh, God...

"Shawnee? Shawnee!" The sound of Xany's voice brought me out of my own thoughts.

"Xany, the serum, I—"

She interrupted me by holding a hand up. "No, shhh...listen."

Thunder seemed to rumble in the distance though, instead of fading out, it got louder. "A storm?"

Xany dragged me toward the cabin. "I don't think that's thunder... Do you think she turned back around?"

"No," I whispered. "Once they run, they keep going until they find food to hunt."

Mal's presence got closer, and then unexpectedly I sensed Caden as well. It was like I wasn't alone in my body.

"They're close." I trembled at the intrusive feeling in my chest.

"No shit." Xany must have sensed the same thing.

"We need to hide. The cubs are running with them."

"You mean that..." She trailed off as if she were too frightened to finish the thought.

"That earthquake feeling? Yeah." We moved quickly around the side of the cabin to get out of the way.

"Nee," she whined. "I can't see from here."

"That's the point, Xany." I ran my fingers through my hair a bit violently.

Bright orange serum...

"Nee! Look!" Xany pointed to the trees when the earth beneath our feet trembled.

From the darkness at the base of the trees, out tumbled a full-grown werewolf in beast form. He was well over nine feet tall, covered in thick, chocolate-colored fur with bulging muscles. Xany shrieked as the beast landed gracefully on all fours.

"Shh! That's Caden." I frowned at her for not recognizing her own mate.

"How can you tell?" She glanced at me, her eyes wide and frightened.

"Be quiet and listen inside yourself."

Caden glanced in our direction. I knew he'd heard Xany's distracting chatter. His eyes were glowing yellow in the light of the reflected moon. He was probably the biggest werewolf I'd ever seen. His torso looked like a wall of fur. The most distinct thing about him was the fact that his entire coat was the same color. A roar drew his attention back to the tree line where a bundle of obsidian fur tangled around a smaller ball of tawny fur rolled out into the clearing. Mal was werewolf tangoing with a newly changed cub. The cub thrashed and tore at Mal, who quickly restrained, then subdued him, pinning him to the ground with snarling jaws clasped around the back of the struggling cub's neck.

Caden moved in afterward and lifted the cub effortlessly by the scruff of his neck. Like Arielle, her brother was about six feet tall and lanky. He growled and snapped rebelliously when Caden roared into his face. Caden locked eyes and stared him down while emitting a string of guttural yarps, gruffs, and grumbles before dropping him. Caden lifted his giant paw and pointed toward the thicket of woods that ran adjacent to the mountains. The cub tore his gaze away to look over at Xany and me. His nostrils flared, and his glowing yellow eyes flashed red. Just as he began to growl, Caden thwapped him in the back of the head. The cub snarled before lurching onto all fours and finally turned to run toward the woods. Mal and Caden remained still, watching the cub until his gait improved, and he ran freely into the trees. After a moment of silence, a howl was heard echoing through the forest, inevitably followed by three additional howls. Caden and Mal joined in the wolf song with Hank and his cubs before all was quiet again.

Caden shifted back into his usual thick, muscular human form while donning a pair of Valentine's Day boxers. "The young one popped, too, huh?"

"You took heart boxers with you?" Xany giggled.

"Hey, I was in a hurry." He laughed as he looked down at himself. Mal loped toward us like a giant black shadow, his eyes flashing when they caught the moonlight.

"Arielle had her change," I told Caden, but I couldn't draw my eyes away from Mal. "She was just as dominant as her brothers."

"She listened to us, Caden, and ran to the mountains." Xany bounced over to hug him.

"Did both cubs run?" I asked.

"All three cubs survived the Change and are under Hank's control. His bloodline is stronger than he realizes. Three dominants having Firstings under one full moon, damn." Caden glanced over his shoulder at Mal who crouched down near me.

"I wonder if any of his other kids will be submissives," Xany said thoughtfully.

Mal's hazel eyes lay tucked into the ebony fur on either side of the silver stripe that ran down his snout. My stomach lurched with excitement and fear when he came close and met my gaze. I didn't look away. He leaned his giant head toward me to sniff my hair and neck. I shivered. Xany gave him a warning glare though Caden calmly watched Mal's beast get a whiff of me.

Mal let out a puff of air from the sides of his muzzle, breaking up the sound into a heavy chuff. He lifted his hulking paw to nudge my stomach. His claws retracted naturally. I twitched my nose at him. He let out a long, hot breath near my face, which made me smile. Something behind my navel seemed to pull me toward him. I imagined it was some sort of buried instinctual thing. When he bumped my stomach again, I ran my fingers over his chest to feel his rippled muscles beneath the course fur. Despite his ferocious appearance, the feel of him soothed me, as if I was doing exactly what I should be doing. He chuffed at me again, which told me that he got what he wanted. Suddenly his paw swooped down and swept me off my feet, air rushing under me as if I were skydiving. I gasped and held tightly to him. He bent his arm across his torso so that I could sit on it. The laughter of the others rang out from below me.

"Easy there, bro, she's a little thing." Caden was monitoring Mal as any good Alpha would.

Mal chuffed, and I looked up at him. I was eye level with his massive jaws. His giant teeth were about three inches from my face, and I imagined the amount of damage he could do with them. On the side of his snout, there was a gash. I reached up to inspect his wound, but it was too late. His flesh had already melded back together, the only hint of an injury was the remnants of blood on his matted fur. Werewolves and other werecreatures healed faster than humans when the wounds were superficial. The bigger wounds required medical treatment or healing.

He nuzzled me as gently as he could with his big head. I had to grip him tight or risk falling off his arm. Smiling, I reached up carefully to stroke his ears. It was then that I remembered Bailey. And remembered the serum.

What have you done?

My thoughts began to race, and the comfort in Mal's bestial attention was stripped away. I remembered the e-mails. I had to do something. I had to stop Doctor Reynolds before he destroyed more werecreatures like the one that was holding me. I patted Mal's shoulder for him to let me down, and he placed me back on the ground as carefully as he could, which of course wasn't that careful at all. I stumbled, and Caden caught me with a chuckle. Mal crouched down and shifted back to his human form. His transformation took my breath away. Mal stood upright once he was back in his human form, as naked as he was the last time. He held his hand out to me, which choked me up.

You don't deserve him. You've caused so much pain.

My thoughts continued to attack me though I defiantly took his hand. Mal seemed to broaden when I accepted. I kept my eyes from wandering over his body. We followed the others back inside while I thought up a plan to stop Doctor Reynolds.

CHAPTER THIRTY-THREE

While the others made themselves comfortable in the main room to discuss the transformations of the cubs, I hurried off to my room. Leaving the others disappointed and confused by my abrupt disconnection from the group, I closed the door to my room and powered up my laptop to check my e-mail. I found about a dozen e-mails from Doctor Reynolds sitting in my in-box dating back from just a week after I left Wyoming.

"You've forgotten to e-mail me the formula, please do."

"Nice message. I get it. Tell me the formula, and we'll end it."

"I will find you."

"I've gotten some new subjects you may be interested in meeting."

"I will find you."

Each e-mail had the same theme, *give me the formula, I'll find you,* and *I've got some new test subjects*. As the e-mails grew, Reynolds's thoughts seemed to become more maniacal and threatening. I picked up my cell phone and dialed Vanessa.

"Shawnee..." Her voice was breathless, and I realized she could sense my anxiety even though I hadn't said a word yet. "I'm coming now."

"No. Wait."

"Wait? Why?" I could tell she was frowning.

"Come get me. You need to hurry, please. Take me back to Wyoming." I spoke as quietly as I could. I couldn't tell the pack what I'd done.

You'll hurt them. The Andrus will find them. Kill them.

"What? Shawnee, why—"

"No time. Please, Vanessa," I begged, tears welling in my eyes. I had to fix this.

"All right... All right..." She hung up.

Before I knew it, I was clutching Vanessa tightly and soaring through what felt like a swirling tunnel known as the *Inbetween.*

"Now are you going to tell me what this is about?" Vanessa asked as we arrived in her bedroom at her apartment in Wyoming. I let go of her once my feet were safely on the floor. She placed her hands on her hips and surveyed me. I wanted to melt into her arms, but instead I sat down on the bed.

"I can't tell you, Ness, you'll just have to trust me." I chewed the inside of my mouth. All I could think of was getting back to the hospital and stopping Doctor Reynolds. Though I had no idea how I was going to do that.

"Trust you? You nearly had me kidnap you away from your pack. You're being stupid if you think they won't come looking for you...and me."

"If they come, you'll be here to stall them." I picked up a sweat jacket off her bed and tossed it on. "I'll be back at some point."

"Where are you going?" she pressed, her pupils dilating as she tried to hide her fear. Her emotions were almost a tangible, living thing that dominated the room.

I watched her for a moment before leaning in to kiss her softly. "I love you. Don't follow me."

Vanessa's eyes welled up with tears. "I love you too, Shawnee..."

Reluctantly I let go of her and rushed toward the door. She dragged her hand across my midriff, and I could tell she was fighting the urge to grab and restrain me. I heard her phone ring just as I left her apartment. I knew that it was one of my packmates and that I had to get to the hospital before anyone could stop me.

CHAPTER THIRTY-FOUR

"Is Doctor Reynolds here?"

"Doctor Twofeathers," the unit secretary exclaimed. "I thought you left."

Without missing a beat, I replied, "I did. Is he in tonight?"

"Umm..." The woman hesitated as she flipped through a calendar. "He's not in the book, but I swear I saw him here around shift change."

"Thank you."

The gaze of the secretary burned into my back as I rushed away. I decided to take the stairs up to Reynolds's office rather than the elevator. I didn't think scanning my retinas into the system at this point was a good idea. I was panting for breath once I reached his floor. I had plenty of time to think about the dangers of what I was getting myself into.

I kept thinking about Mal. My only regret was leaving him in the dark. At least I got to say good-bye to Vanessa. But I had to keep telling myself that this was the only way to protect him. The Andrus couldn't know about the pack or Vanessa. If Doctor Reynolds was looking for me, my appearance would end his search. I put the others in

267

danger by living with them, and now I had to throw Reynolds off course. I had to protect them.

No matter what.

"Doctor T?" A voice assaulted me as soon as I entered the hallway.

"Kurt." I frowned and took a step away from him.

He grabbed me by the arm and dragged me into a corner behind a fake fern. "You shouldn't be here," he whispered.

"Neither should you." I jerked my arm away.

We shared an uncomfortably long gaze. "You know..." he said.

"You've always been clever, Kurt." I attempted to push past him.

Kurt thrust me back against the wall a bit harder than I think he intended to. "Wait. You don't understand. He wants you here. You need to go."

"You know I can't do that. Now move before I move you," I threatened.

"Shawnee..." he started.

"Fuck off, Kurt, you're the one helping him," I accused, grabbing Kurt by his scrub top and shoving him. He stumbled before slamming me against the wall again, pinning me and nearly knocking the wind out of me.

"Don't you get it? I'm trying to stop him...and you too," he whispered, beads of sweat forming on his forehead.

I surveyed him for a moment. "You! The failed experiments..."

"Yes. Now get out of here before—"

"Well, isn't this cozy," said a voice echoing from down the hall.

Kurt looked toward Dr. Reynolds before suddenly spinning me around and twisting my arm up my back. I cringed and shook off the uncomfortable memories that being jerked around brought up.

"I caught you a fish, boss." Kurt pushed me toward Reynolds.

"Most excellent. It's about time." He removed his hand from the pocket of his lab coat to show me the Taser he was holding. "I wouldn't run if I were you. Make sure she follows, Kurt." He clicked his heels before heading to the private elevator. Just the sight of him made my stomach churn with disgust.

I took a deep breath and followed him, glancing back to Kurt who simply nodded. My fingers twitched with nervousness as the three of us crammed into the small elevator.

***

"This could all end fast and painlessly. All you have to do is turn over the formula," Doctor Reynolds said.

"Noted." I pursed my lips.

Reynolds clenched his teeth and began to walk a slow circle around the lab with his hands clasped behind his back. "Oblivious suited you better, Doctor Twofeathers," he commented as he turned on one of the Bunsen burners. Kurt grabbed my elbow, firmly holding me in place. I jerked away from him.

"Failure suited you better," I retorted.

"Well," Reynolds said, "I imagine I owe my failures to you as well as my success."

"That's right." I glanced at Kurt as I admitted to his sins. He stopped his pacing long enough to stare at me.

"Except for the most difficult task. What changed your mind about causing this one to fail?" he asked. It was unnerving the way Reynolds spoke as if we were conversing leisurely. He slipped a large, double-edged dagger from its sheath at his waist and held the blade over the fire of the burner. The handle was etched in black with an insignia that I couldn't make out. When the blade was hot, he walked to me, and Kurt pressed me down to my knees.

"Tell me, Shawnee, how did you get the serum to be such an intense shade of orange?" He grinned and pressed the molten blade against the side of my neck. I screamed against the searing pain, and my stomach churned with disgust. With eyes watering, I forced myself to look at him. Flashes of faces grazed across my field of vision: Xany, Caden, Mal, Vanessa, the blue-eyed girl, the beast, Bailey.

"It must have been magic," I croaked and then snickered.

"You're a stupid bitch, Shawnee." He grabbed me by the hair and thrust me to the floor before commanding Kurt, "Take her to the cells. Maybe watching will change her mind." He then stormed out of the lab after tossing Kurt the Taser.

"Burning a human with a silver dagger... I must admire him for his symbolism at least." Kurt helped me up.

I swatted his hands away. "Don't touch me. Why haven't you stopped him yet? Who sent you here?"

"I'm working with the Alliance, and frankly, it was you who I was sent to watch." He nodded toward the door, indicating we should get moving.

"Me? Why me?" I frowned, ignoring my pain to gather as much information as possible. I tried to block out the thoughts of my pack, fearing that I might accidentally call them to me.

"We were watching Reynolds for a while. He's a meddlesome, arrogant man who thought he could attract the Andrus attention through his innovative sciences. But we soon realized he was an imbecile who failed at most of his experiments. Then suddenly he starts becoming successful. We learn of this and put him on watch again only to find that he had a genius young doctor doing all his dirty work. And that's where you came in." He spoke in a furtive whisper as we entered the private elevator to descend into the basement. "So they sent me in. I was in medical school anyway so they rushed me through it. After a few weeks on the team with you and Reynolds, I realized that you were completely unaware of who you were working for so I started messing things up and made all the replications fail. I'm sorry, I'm speaking to you like you know what I'm talking about."

"I *do* know what you're talking about," I said as the elevator came to a halt. "I know what the Alliance is too. How many does he have down here?"

"Just one. You knew?"

"Not at first. I quit when I finally realized it." I rushed toward the aisles of boxes, afraid for whatever werecreature he had captive in the cells. I hoped to Gaia that he hadn't found Bailey and brought him back.

"You know he'll do anything for that formula. Do you know what it—"

"Yes. I know what it does," I cut him off. Kurt opened the passage to the containment lair. "I found out today."

"What does it do?" He grabbed my arm, now pretending he was holding me captive again.

I raised an eyebrow at his question. "He didn't tell you?"

"No. All the glory for himself." He completed the retinal scan.

I kept my mouth shut. I didn't completely trust Kurt even though he seemed to know what he was talking about. He could be a *double*-double agent for all I knew. When we entered the containment area, I held my breath as the distinct odor of death and bleach wafted toward us. Kurt swallowed a gag while holding the Taser pointed at me.

Doctor Reynolds's voice echoed from somewhere beyond the containment cells. "Bring her down here."

We passed the cells, and I scanned each as we walked by. Two were empty, and two contained decomposing bodies, one of which was a human female whose stomach was torn open from the inside out. She was surrounded by a pool of dry blood. It looked like something had clawed its way out of her. The other cell had what looked like a decomposing dog on the floor. The last cell on the right, the one that Bailey had been in, contained a young girl of about twelve, who was huddled in the corner hugging her

271

knees. I tried hard not to look at her for too long. I didn't want Reynolds to notice my fear for her.

We turned past the containment cells and into a short hallway. The end of the hall was dark and reeked of blood, both old and new. The walls at the end of the hall were stone, much like a bomb shelter would be, and the floor had a drain in the middle of it. There were chains of all sizes bolted deep into the concrete floor, ceiling, and walls. This room was open to allow the captor full view of the captive.

Reynolds grabbed me by the hair and tossed me into the room. I stumbled into the back wall, catching myself, and felt my hands slam into some grimy residue. Reynolds dragged me to the center of the room and grabbed a set of chains that hung from the ceiling. The chains were heavy, and I could tell that they were crafted out of pure silver. He clasped the shackles around my wrists and pulled on the floor chains, causing my arms to jerk above my head.

"Now, that's better. Kurt, take the girl's temperature again and bring me a notepad and pencil. Doctor Twofeathers will be sharing some information with us shortly." He pulled a wooden stool over and sat down in front of me as if he were waiting for a show to begin.

I closed my eyes for a moment, deciding that no matter what he did to me, I wouldn't tell him what he wanted to know. I had to protect the werecreatures from having their only defense against the Tainted Ones taken away. I moved my hands around in the shackles to see if there was any chance of slipping out of them. Of course there wasn't.

Suddenly, I heard the whimpers of the little girl. She began to cry when I heard the glass lowering. I clenched my teeth and tried to block out the sounds of her terror.

"Don't like hearing that, do you?" Reynolds asked.

When I didn't respond, he stood and walked around the corner. After a short period of silence, I heard the little girl scream and the sound of shuffling feet. She shouted, "No!

Please stop!" followed by anguished cries.

"Please, Gaia, help her," I whispered, raising my eyes to the ceiling of my sarcophagus. My mind envisioned the horrors that Reynolds was inflicting on the girl. The hot stream of tears trickled down my face. A sudden haze washed over me, tangled with the sullenness of despair.

CHAPTER THIRTY-FIVE

The little girl screamed and begged for mercy. I couldn't see what was going on so my mind attempted to fill in the horrible images. I envisioned Reynolds torturing the girl, raping her, burning her with silver daggers. I pulled at the chains, lifting myself off the floor. I screamed in frustration at the same time as the little girl screamed. Then there was silence. Doctor Reynolds appeared in front of me again. He was sweating and had blood on the front of his lab coat. I heard the girl whimper from inside her cell. My heart leaped when I heard that she was still alive.

"Ready to tell yet?" He stepped closer to me, dagger in hand. He pressed the bloody tip of it against my chest, caught my shirt, and violently tore it open.

"Let her go, then I'll tell you."

Reynolds made a *tsk tsk* sound as he walked in a circle around me. "Now, Shawnee, that would be very stupid of me to do. You see, I need a test subject, and she is just perfect. If you tell me, and it works, I'll let you both leave together." He pressed the tip of the cold blade against my abdomen hard enough to pierce my skin. I flinched, and the hot trickle of blood ran down past my bellybutton.

"You'll have to do better than that. I'm used to pain." I

yanked myself up on the chains and used both feet to kick him in the gut, launching him backward over the stool.

Hearing the crash, Kurt came bolting around the corner.

Doctor Reynolds stood and rushed at me with the dagger. "You stupid bitch!"

I closed my eyes and hid my face against my arm, awaiting the impact and pain that I knew would follow his collision with my body.

"Don't!" I heard Kurt shout.

When I opened my eyes, I saw him restraining Reynolds. "We need the formula before you kill her. Don't be stupid." He released Reynolds, who calmed down immediately.

"Right," he said, straightening his coat. "Now where was I?" He went back toward the containment cells. Again the girl began to cry.

I glared at Kurt. I couldn't understand why he was letting this continue, why he wasn't putting a stop to that poor little girl's abuse. "Stop him, damn it."

Kurt looked sullen. I kicked at him as he disappeared around the corner after Reynolds. I cried out and struggled against the bindings that were digging into my flesh. There was no way for me to get free to help the little girl. Either I told him the formula and he used it on the girl, then killed us both, or he just killed us both. Either way, we died. I tried my hardest to block out thoughts of my packmates. My mind began to work in its usual manner, blocking out the screams of the girl and my own. I thought about Vanessa, and then just as my thoughts began to wander toward Mal, I heard his voice.

Shawnee, focus. Listen to me. Can you hear me?

I nodded, sobs catching in my throat.

I can feel you, answer me.

You're imagining it. He's not really here. You're alone, and you'll be responsible for the death of another girl. My thoughts began to batter me. I was suddenly weak and tired.

Shawnee, take me with you... Mal's voice pierced through my thoughts, and I gasped.

"I can't. I can't," I said aloud by accident. Doctor Reynolds shouted, and the girl screamed. The chaos inside me mirrored the chaos outside. There was little distinction between the screams, fear, and agony.

Think your words, Shawnee, focus. Mal's voice rang through my body. I felt him all over. His presence in my arms and legs, inside my chest and heart. I was full and complete. His command gripped me, sobered me. I was forced to answer.

He's hurting her. A little girl. He wants the formula.

We're all here, Nee. Caden, Xany, Vanessa, and me. He won't get away with this. Tell me where you are. Describe it like you do for Vanessa.

No, I can't. He'll hurt you, I can't, I pleaded with him in my head.

Doctor Reynolds appeared more frustrated with me than he had in the beginning. I imagine my sobbing had something to do with it. He stormed back over to me, dragging the bloodied girl by the hair. She had burn marks all over her body from the silver dagger he kept pressing against her skin. The girl was crying, but her brown eyes flashed yellow. Silently I wished she would change right at that moment. The cub would kill me, but she'd also kill Reynolds and Kurt. It was another way to end this.

"Shut up!" he demanded. "The formula or she dies! I can get myself another test subject." I shook my head no, and Reynolds seemed surprised. "I thought better of you, Shawnee, letting an innocent die for your cause." With blazing eyes, he backhanded me across the face. My head jerked to the side, and I cracked my jaw back into place, spitting blood out at him.

"Let her go, and I'll tell. Let Kurt take her away from here, then I'll tell you." I swallowed the metallic taste in my mouth.

The little girl stared at me with terrified yellow eyes,

growing closer to her change. Doctor Reynolds remained still, grinding his teeth. "Fine. Kurt, take the kid away. Leave her outside in the street alone, then return. She can have her change up there and die like the others did." He glared at me. "Shawnee would rather have the primed kid shift in the street and cause havoc."

Kurt hesitated and assessed Reynolds as if checking to see whether the doctor was serious.

"Do it! You blathering fool. We're running out of time," he ordered, thrusting the girl at him.

Kurt tossed her over his shoulder and disappeared around the corner toward the cells. I heard the girl's cries fade as the metal doors hissed and clicked shut. Then there was silence.

Mal? I swallowed. Even though I was thinking the words, it took a lot of effort.

I'm here, Shawnee. Describe it to me now, he ordered. It took every bit of strength I had to defy his order.

Wait. There's a cub. Kurt works for the Alliance. He's taking the cub to the street. She's primed for Firsting. Find her. Keep her safe.

Reynolds moved closer to me, staring at me with eyes filled with hatred and rage. Hatred for me and for the world, I imagined.

"Why are you doing this? Why are you hurting them?" I blinked a few times. It was getting hard to focus.

"Humans are quickly losing power over this world. If I can't stop it, I'm sure as hell going to benefit from it," he said. "Now, the formula, my dear. If it works, I'll let you choose the way you die." A cold grin spread across his cracked lips.

We see her, Shawnee. Caden has her. Tell me where you are. Guide us like you do Vanessa. Mal's voice burst into my head, his tone was softer and a little distracted.

Don't let Kurt back in.

We won't. Describe it.

"The way you're going about it was wrong," I croaked

to Doctor Reynolds. "Stopping it won't work."

"Go on."

"You...you have to prevent it." I swallowed my tears as I tried to buy some time. "Like a vaccine."

Reynolds paused to think about what I was saying. "Brilliant!" His voice was filled with excitement. "You're cleverer than I thought."

Underground. Containment cells. Six of them, I thought to Mal before answering Reynolds. I did *not* want them down here with me, and Mal knew it.

More, Shawnee. He's human, let us in. We'll handle it.

There are dangers here, Mal. All the walls are white. There's strong glass stuff used to contain the cells. There's a dead body. A woman. Something clawed its way out of her stomach. Blood. Her blood...and mine. Silver chains. Big refrigerator. A large gurney...

I wanted to be with my pack. I wanted to see them so badly.

You don't deserve them.

Part of me didn't want them here. There was too much silver and who knew what else Reynolds was hiding. As far as I could tell, he had no idea I was a Breeder, but the fact that he spoke to me so candidly led me to believe otherwise.

"A vaccine," Reynolds said, taking quick notes on a small pad of paper he pulled from his pocket. "How?"

Good, Shawnee, more. Mal persisted inside my head while Reynolds persisted outside.

The pressure was making me tremble. It was getting harder to hold myself up. My shoulders ached with the stress of my position, and my head throbbed in response to the dual demands.

"The gene..." I swallowed; my throat was parched. "The gene causes the fever. The fever is the catalyst. Prevent the fever, prevent the change in cell structure," I told Reynolds. His eyes gleamed with lust for more information.

The doors hiss, I told Mal. *There's a retinal scan to get in like a sci-fi movie. There's death here and silver. It smells like death and bleach. I won't let him hurt you. Make it stop.* My thoughts began to churn and bleed into what I was describing to Mal, leaving me feeling very disorganized.

It's okay, Shawnee, hold on. Don't let go. Mal's connection with me faded.

The shift in his presence sent a ripple of fear up my spine.

"You will show me how you created it. There are samples in the lab." He moved toward me, reaching for my shackled hands. With his face in front of mine, his breath was putrid, reeking of tooth decay. He held the dagger against my throat.

"Don't you dare kick me again. You're one brilliant bitch, Doctor Twofeathers. I'll never let you go," he whispered.

I shuddered in disgust. Suddenly there was a loud bang from somewhere near the containment cells. Silence followed. Reynolds froze. "Kurt, quiet is not your forte."

When no answer came, Reynolds' face was stone still. He put the blade of the dagger over my lips, warning me to keep quiet. The metallic scent of the blood filled my nose, causing me to gag. He went back toward the cells.

There was another bang from somewhere at the same time that a warm hand clasped my mouth. I struggled until Vanessa stepped in front of me. Her pupils were dilated into full, catlike slits surrounded by intense yellow irises. Tears slipped down my cheeks immediately, and I wanted to reach for her. She let go of my mouth and reached for the shackles. The color drained from her face when she realized my bindings were silver. I mouthed the word "silver" to her, and she nodded. She turned suddenly when Reynolds's shuffling footsteps scuttled back down the hall. In the blink of an eye, she was gone. I tried my hardest not to scream for her.

Reynolds reappeared, and judging from the look on his face, he was livid. "What did you do?"

"Fuck off," I spat, and as if rehearsed, Vanessa dropped from the ceiling with the silent grace of an acrobat. She landed on Reynolds, trapping him in a roll, and tumbled down the hall.

A loud crash announced the arrival of Mal in his beast form. He burst forth from the hall by the containment cells. Caden, in human form, along with Xany rushed behind him.

"Nee!" Xany shouted and ran over to me.

Mal's snarls and growls drowned out the screams of Reynolds and the hisses of Vanessa as the lights suddenly went out and a fire alarm sounded. Red and white strobe lights began flashing viciously, blinding not only Xany and I, but the Changers as well. The intensity of the light messed with their acute vision. A sudden, piercing tone screamed into the area. Xany and I flinched, but the Changers roared. Caden dropped to his knees and crawled toward us. He kept trying to cover his ears, which was slowing him down. The shadow of Mal's beast form flashing in the strobe light was roaring and thrashing at the ground beneath him, shaking his head painfully, tortured by the audio and visual violations. Xany and I both struggled against my bindings futility until Caden eventually made his way to us. He forced himself to stand. His eyes were closed when he reached up and grasped the silver chains around my wrists, crushing them in his hands.

Xany caught me as I slumped to the floor. My whole body trembled, and my shoulders screamed in flaring pain. With her help, I stood up and gathered my last bit of energy. When I attempted to race toward Mal and Vanessa, she grabbed me and kept me near. I struggled against her until I skidded to a halt as a gush of fresh, hot blood splashed across my torso. All I could see in the flashing light was Mal's frenzied form continuing to bash, lash, and tear at something on the floor.

Caden was on the floor again, struggling to transform, and Xany was shouting at me, though I could barely make out what she was saying. I was worried that the silver Caden had touched was interfering with this change. I'd never seen a wolf who could tolerate touching and crushing silver with their bare hands.

She pulled me close to her, her hot breath against my ear as she shouted. "We need to turn it off! It's hurting them!"

I nodded, grabbing her hand, and we ran toward the hall with the containment cells. Together we jumped over the bloody stump that was once a leg connected to Doctor Reynolds. I shrieked, but Xany kept pulling me forward. I looked back to see that Caden was half changed, and Mal was still thrashing, I couldn't see Vanessa. Xany jerked me forward, and we huddled together on the floor.

She leaned close to my ear again to shout. "Shawnee! Focus! Where is the shut off for the alarm system?"

I gripped her harder; the chaos of the sounds and lights made it hard to think.

"Shawnee!"

I blinked a few times and shouted back, suddenly remembering the panel that Bailey had showed me. "Panel! There's a panel in the wall somewhere here!" I shouted and pointed at the wall adjacent to the cells.

Xany and I began feeling our way down the wall. The wafting scent of bleach began leaking into the room. An additional phase of assault on the senses began. She grabbed me suddenly, banging her free hand on the wall.

"Here!"

We pried open the camouflaged panel and slammed on the buttons. The cells began opening and closing randomly, lights flickered faster, and my throat burned because of the bleach. Suddenly, Xany rammed her fist into the panel, and everything came to a dead halt.

Mal's growling ceased, and Xany looked around, dumbfounded while Caden stood up again in human form. Without looking at us, he bolted down the hall in the direction of Mal and Vanessa.

"Shawnee, hurry." His voice echoed in the now silent underground.

Xany and I rushed toward the others. Mal's oversized beast was blocking Caden and Vanessa from sight. He had scraps of Doctor Reynolds's lab coat tangled in his teeth, dripping with blood. He looked around with flared nostrils and dropped to all fours, letting out a long, drawn howl. Xany and I moved around him to where Caden was kneeling on the floor beside whatever was left of Reynolds. Lying in a pool of blood next to Caden was Vanessa, who had Doctor Reynolds's silver dagger protruding from her stomach.

CHAPTER THIRTY-SIX

Mal snapped his jaws at the dagger to try and grab it with his teeth, but kept howling at the repulsive silver. Caden lifted Vanessa off the floor and held her in his arms. I dropped down beside her and cupped her face. Xany stood above us with hands pressed over her mouth.

Vanessa met my gaze and tears streamed down her cheeks, washing away some of the blood on her face. Trembling, she reached for me. When her hand connected with my cheek, I could feel her weakening pulse against my skin. I gripped the hilt of the dagger, knowing full well that removing it could kill her, but the poison of the silver was acting faster. The dagger had been in her too long for her to shift and lick to heal herself. The silver's poison prevented her change.

"It's okay, Vanessa, I'm here," I whispered to her. She shivered when I spoke, as if she'd been waiting to hear my voice. *Oh God, please don't die. Please.*

"Shawnee, we have to—" Caden began, but I cut him off.

"I know! I know." I cleared my throat, and a burst of energy shot me into action. "Xany, go in the room back there and get the cart with the tools and paddles and as many towels as you can. Caden, hold her tight."

Both of them jumped into action. In my head, I spoke to Mal. *Be human, I need you.*

From above, I heard the snapping and popping of Mal's transformation. Slowly, I leaned in and pressed my lips to Vanessa's forehead, tasting her blood on my lips. *Please, Gaia, give me this, just this.*

Vanessa's lips trembled as she tried to speak to me. She wheezed out my name as her breath rattled. I kept my lips close to hers and spoke softly, gripping the dagger at the same time. "I'm here, stay with me, please stay with me."

I pressed my lips to hers at the same time that I ripped the dagger from her stomach. She cried out into my mouth as I tossed the dagger aside. I moved back and placed both hands over her gaping wound, pressing hard as blood gushed through my fingers.

Xany returned and tossed towels on top of my hands so that I could press them against her wound. Vanessa's emerald gaze caught mine. The life drained from her as the poison and blood loss took their toll. Her eyes became hazy, and I shouted. "Please! Vanessa, no, look at me. Look at me!"

She blinked slowly and tried to mouth something to me through shallow breaths, her blood seeping through the towels. Everyone was silent as they watched her die. Mal placed his hand on my shoulder. Caden held Vanessa, and Xany knelt beside me, helping me hold the towels to Vanessa's stomach. Her grip on my arm began to loosen.

"No! Gaia, please don't, please. You can't take her," I cried. "Mom, please help her. Please," I begged. For some reason, at that moment, I truly believed that calling for Gaia and my mother to somehow intervene would work.

Mal squeezed my shoulder. Vanessa's breathing grew erratic. I leaned down again and breathed her breath as she gasped for mine. I whispered to her, "I love you." Her lips mimicked mine. I closed my eyes, my hands still covering her wound. I didn't want to lose my best friend.

Please, Gaia, give me strength. I'll give anything. Anything! Please don't take her. Please don't take her from me. Take me instead, take me. She deserves life; she deserves happiness. I pleaded silently. I cried for Vanessa and thought about my mother, begging her again to somehow intercede.

Then suddenly, from somewhere inside me, I heard an unfamiliar voice say, *"So do you."*

My eyes shot open at the intrusion, and I gasped as an unexpected heat ignited in the middle of my chest. It rolled over my shoulders, down my arms, and settled in my hands. My gasp caught the attention of the others whose tearstained faces were hidden in lament. My hands began to burn as if I had just placed them in an open fire. Suddenly the image of my mother's face hovered in front of my eyes. She was smiling with hands outstretched and immediately the memory struck me...

"It's okay, Dodi,*" my mother's voice says. I lay on the ground beside a jagged rock, holding my scraped knee. My mother nudges my hands away and then cups my wound in her own hands. Warmth surrounds my knee and a blue-purple glow bursts from her palms, weaving and winding through the gash, mending it neatly. Her lips seal it with a kiss.*

Instinctively, I tossed the towels away from Vanessa's stomach and pressed my hands against her exposed flesh. I cried out when the palms of my hands burst as if they had caught fire. The others watched in confusion and awe. A soft, indigo glow radiated from the palms of my hands, wavering and weaving over Vanessa's torn flesh. My hands ached like they were about to char and fall off. Just as the pain grew intolerable, Vanessa gasped. The squishy wet flesh beneath my fingertips began to mend together and flatten into a perfectly intact abdomen.

When my hands cooled, Vanessa sat up and nearly knocked Caden over. She gaped at me, wide-eyed in obvious shock. I returned her stare and immediately began crying. She plucked me up off the ground in her usual effortless manner. Embracing her, I kissed every part of her that I could reach. She was trembling and obviously confused.

"What...the hell...just happened?" Xany asked, drawing the words out. Caden stared at me in a way that made me feel nervous, but Mal was beaming.

"Are you okay?" Vanessa whispered in my ear. I nodded, reached down, and touched her stomach to make sure her wound stayed gone. "What happened?" Her eyes searched my face as if awaiting some sort of explanation in my expression alone.

"Dude, you died... Kinda," Caden said in a shocked, juvenile manner. His usual calm, cool demeanor had turned into the essence of pure bewilderment.

"Shawnee healed you," Mal said.

"What?" She stared at me.

"She healed you." Mal reached forward and ran his fingers through my hair. "Apparently, our Shawnee is a healer."

I leaned into his touch and placed my hand on Vanessa's cheek. She kissed my wrist and smiled. "My hero."

"Just returning the favor, I guess." I was weak and happy at the same time. Suddenly everything felt like a dream. Vanessa laughed, and her purring returned. Xany giggled happily while both Mal and Caden tossed their heads back and howled out a wolven victory song.

CHAPTER THIRTY-SEVEN

"So let me get this straight," Caden began before stuffing a dip-covered chip into his mouth. "You accidentally created a vaccine to prevent a Changer from shifting while unknowingly working for an Andrus-infested hospital under the control of a corrupt human doctor who was using your genius to benefit himself and taking all the credit for your work, and his assistant was a double-agent working for the Alliance."

"Precisely." I smiled sheepishly.

Vanessa snickered into my shoulder while I sat in her lap. Xany giggled, and Mal grinned quietly as he listened to us.

"And then you accidentally found out that you have one of the rarest Breeder gifts on the planet when you're best friend, said weretiger, was nearly killed by a silver dagger wielded by the aforementioned evil human doctor," Caden continued in a mock-serious tone.

"Correct." I laughed at his antics.

"That all sounds logical to me." He shrugged. "Who's up for pizza?"

Vanessa laughed and playfully nipped my shoulder. I leaned into her and smiled.

"Only you, Nee, could come up with a story like that."
Xany giggled, reaching over to give my arm a squeeze. I
grinned.

"He wasn't exactly wielding the dagger though. I sort of
accidentally dived into it," Vanessa corrected.

Everyone laughed.

"I thought you were supposed to be a graceful cat,"
Xany said. "You barely make a sound when you move and
yet you manage to fall onto a dagger and nearly die?"

Vanessa hissed at her, but everyone else erupted with
laughter again. Mal seemed to be enjoying the jovialness
the most. I couldn't help myself from watching him.

Caden smiled at me with a sudden, radiating pride that
he made sure I felt. "Did you know you could heal?"

"No, my mom could though. I remembered as it was
happening. She could heal others but not herself. She
could heal all wounds and battle scars. Even wounds
caused by silver. Maybe I can too..." I trailed off, thinking
about the memory of when Mother healed my childhood
injury. "Healing Vanessa was the first time I've ever done
it. I think."

"You think?" Xany asked.

"Hey, you never know with me. I might have blocked it
out."

"I've never met someone with such a terrible and
incredible memory at the same time." Xany smiled. I
returned her smile and held out my arms to her, and she
hugged me. "What would we do without you, Nee?"

"Probably live a much quieter life," I said. Xany swatted
me, and I laughed. "The real question is, what would I do
without all of you?"

Vanessa squeezed me happily, and Mal gave me an
approving nod.

***

"You know I would have let him kill me if it wasn't for
you," I told Mal as he approached.

I had taken a short hike through the woods to help

clear my head and assemble the events of the night before. I followed the trail up the mountain. It stopped at a cliff that overlooked the river flowing between the mountains. The air was crisp and breezy. Mal followed without me having to call his wolf.

"I know." He moved up behind me, wrapping his arms around my shoulders and resting his chin on my head. "I guess we both have useful gifts."

I leaned into his embrace and breathed in his scent. "Yeah, we do." I smiled before growing quiet for a moment. "I tried not to think about any of you so that you couldn't sense me...so that I could protect you." I hugged his arms, the familiar fear bubbling up in my chest.

"I sensed you anyway. I knew when you left that something was wrong, that you needed us. I followed you." He closed his eyes when a breeze caressed our skin.

"I know." I turned around to face him, his hands falling naturally to my waist. "Xany says it's possible to love two people at the same time, especially if someone has a lot of emptiness to fill. Do you think that's true?" I looked up at him.

The cascade of the darkening sky dangling over the mountains reflected in his eyes. He looked to me after pondering the notion for a moment. "I think it can be true."

"Even if one of them is a cat and the other a dog?" I lifted a brow.

"If said cat and dog can play nicely." He grinned.

"I think they can... At least most of the time." I draped my arms over his shoulders.

"You know, only a mate can call the wolf."

"I know..."

"Does that mean you've accepted?" He tried not to sound too hopeful.

"If it means *you've* accepted. Not only me but my baggage too." I looked away from him. What about Vanessa? What if he couldn't tolerate being around a cat so much? It's not in the nature of a wolf to share.

He guided my gaze back to him with a finger under my chin. "I accept you and your duffle bag as well." He grinned. "And your cat."

"Then I accept you and your wolf."

"Good, because my wolf likes you." He moved closer to me. I bit my lip when he closed the distance between us, pressing his temperate, firm lips against mine. The truth was that I had no idea where things with Vanessa would lead. But I knew exactly where I was going with Mal.

Engaged in his kiss, I was warm and safe. Just as Mal slipped his tongue between my lips, the cry of an eagle echoed over the mountaintops. I broke the kiss abruptly and turned to look out over the canyon. An eagle soared with wings outstretched, diving low toward the water before changing course and climbing toward the clouds. Mal followed my distraction until our gazes met again.

"Now you remind *me* of eagles." He smiled.

I grinned and laced my fingers behind his neck, guiding him back into an undying kiss.

ABOUT THE AUTHOR

Max grew up just outside of New York City, spending most of her formative years outdoors creating wild ghost hunts with neighborhood kids, setting booby-traps to capture unwitting family members, and building clubhouses on top of ten-foot walls. Max wrote her first story at the age of twelve and titled it *Circles of Friendship*. Through the years, Max has written several short-stories and poems, all of which met the wrath of the "Not Good Enough" monster and ended in fiery demise.

Max regained her confidence when she began writing scholarly articles and research theses on her first trip through graduate school. It took several years for her to break the habit of the formal writing that marred her creativity. An additional Master of Fine Arts degree in Creative Writing was Max's biggest support in this. Max writes primarily sci-fi/fantasy, paranormal romance, and Young Adult stories

Printed in Great Britain
by Amazon

16184337R00169